Street Song

Sheena Wilkinson is one of Ireland's most acclaimed writers of fiction for young people. She has won four Children's Books Ireland awards including overall Book of the Year in 2013, a White Raven Award from the International Youth Library, an IBBY Honour Listing, and she has twice been shortlisted for the Reading Association of Ireland Awards. Sheena tutors for Arvon, runs a network for young writers in Belfast and is Royal Literary Fund Fellow at Queen's University, Belfast. When she's not writing or reading, she's usually walking in the forest or singing, sometimes both at once. She taught herself guitar especially for *Street Song*.

Street Song

SHEENA WILKINSON

INK ROAD

First published 2017 by Ink Road

INK ROAD is an imprint and trade mark
of Black and White Publishing Ltd.

Black & White Publishing Ltd
29 Ocean Drive, Edinburgh EH6 6JL

1 3 5 7 9 10 8 6 4 2 17 18 19 20

ISBN: 978 1 78530 089 9

A CIP catalogue record for this book is available from the British
Library.

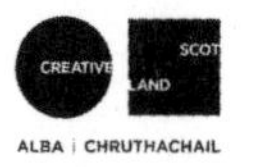

Typeset by Iolaire, Newtonmore
Printed and bound by Nørhaven, Denmark

For everyone I've sung and played music with over the years, but especially for Melanie Stone, who still remembers all the harmonies.

1

I woke early – it had been a weird night even by our standards; we'd passed out mid-fight – and there was Kelly, curled round my duvet with her back to me. Her hair, all smoke and hairspray, clogged my mouth, and through the thin sweaty cotton of her green top you could count each of her vertebra. I stretched out my finger and placed it between two of the green cotton bumps and shuddered. She whimpered and wriggled and turned round. Her eyelids cracked open the layers of mascara and eyeliner.

'Ryan?' she murmured. 'Iss not morning?'

I shook my head. I couldn't trust myself to speak because when she opened her mouth I caught a reek of last night's vomit, drink, smoke and, somewhere in the mix, the pizza we'd had on the walk between the pub and the club – she only ate when she was stoned. I half-turned my head away and focused on the far corner of my bedroom. The cold dawn light slanting through the slats of the wooden blind showed the dust on my guitar. If I looked above it I'd see the photo of me the night I won *PopIcon,* but I didn't look up.

Kelly smiled dopily and reached her hand out towards me.

I drew away. 'You have to go.'

Her face crumpled.

'I said last night – I can't do this any more.'

'Ry.' Her eyes widened. 'We were both out of it last night. We both said things we didn't mean.'

I had no idea what she'd said. She'd been talking all summer and I'd stopped listening about the start of August. I just knew that her cold thin fingers on my skin made me cringe.

And she'd called me Ry.

'You have to go *now.*'

If she stayed another minute I'd hurt her. I'd tell her she disgusted me, that I hated who I was with her. That if I didn't get rid of her I would lose myself. Again.

'Is it the drugs? Because I only—'

'It's not one thing.' I fell back on clichés. 'It's not you. We had a laugh, OK? But it's over.'

Clichés and lies. We'd never had a laugh. Kelly wasn't a laughy kind of girl. Maybe at the start, when she was a bit starry about me. I'd liked that – the flattery. And her friends were cool.

She cried and fussed and clawed at me and went out and locked herself in the loo for ages and came out all shiny-eyed and, God, it was boring. By the time I got her bundled out into the road, sobbing and yelling and calling me all kinds of names, I felt as knackered as I used to feel coming off stage, only without the buzz. I pushed the heavy front door to and took a second to lean against it, eyes closed in relief, breathing in the quiet, the glossy white paint cold against my bare arms.

'Ryan?'

I opened my eyes to see my mother. 'Hi, Louise.'

She frowned, then stopped as if remembering that Ricky always told her it made her look older. Dark roots showed in her long blonde hair. That wasn't like her. I suppose I hadn't seen her for a few days. I'd been staying out, different places, mates' floors, Kelly's bed; one night a few of us sat up all night on the beach, drinking and having a laugh. Kelly's mates. I'd have to make new ones now.

'What was all that row?'

I shrugged. 'Kelly just left.'

'Was that shouting I heard?'

'How do I know what you heard?'

'Ry.'

'*Don't* call me that.' I tried to push past her, but she blocked me with her arm. She was wearing a peachy satin dressing gown, and her bony wrist poking out reminded me of Kelly.

'Did you upset that poor girl?'

'We broke up.'

'Ah, Ryan. She was lovely.' Louise and Kelly had done a lot of girly bonding over hair extensions and calories. 'What did you do to her?'

'*Nothing*. She had issues. I can't stand girls like that.'

'Jesus, you're a little bastard.' She shook her head. 'Poor girl.'

'She was a bad influence, Mam.' She loved it when I called her Mam. 'I didn't want to worry you by telling you this but, she was using – stuff. I couldn't *trust* myself around her. You know I don't want to get back into all that.' I put a little crack in my voice, the kind of crack no mother could resist.

Right on cue, Louise's eyes softened. 'Ah, love. You've been doing so well.'

'It was too much temptation.'

Louise's eyes widened in alarm. 'But you didn't, did you?'

'I could have.' I made my eyes troubled and innocent, though actually I was telling the truth. 'If she'd stayed.'

Louise's bird-skeleton shoulders slumped with relief under the peach satin. 'Well, you did the right thing, son. And you'll easily find another girl.'

Now that she was in motherly mode, she started wittering about breakfast and keeping my strength up, so I followed her down the hall into the kitchen, where the marble tiles chilled my bare feet. The kitchen had been completely transformed since I'd been *in there,* and was now decorated in shades of grey and black. I sat on a stool at the breakfast bar and let Louise rummage in concealed cupboards for pans. She hummed one of my old songs while she cracked eggs into a white bowl. I tried not to hear it.

I'd reached the hungry stage of hangover and was

looking forward to getting stuck into the omelette Louise was whisking when Ricky slimed through the door, knotting his purple silk tie.

Louise spun round, flicking globules of egg over the marble worktop. Ricky broke off a frown, and then zoomed his attention straight on me. The attention I used to crave. The attention Louise still lived for.

'Haven't seen you for a few days.'

'I've been around.'

'The terms of your release require you to be at home for us to keep an eye on you.'

He made it sound like I'd been in *prison*.

'It's summer. I was only with my friends.'

'I've spent a lot of money on your recovery, Ryan. I'm not having you mess it up at this stage.'

Louise bent over the pan, swirling the eggs.

'And since you mention it, it is *not* summer, not now. It is the end of August and we have an appointment with Father O'Dwyer at midday.'

I sighed. 'I haven't decided—'

'There's nothing *to* decide. You messed up your exams. You're repeating the year.'

I didn't *mess up*: that implies I took my exams and failed. Whereas I did not take them because I spent most of what should have been my sixth year off my head and then learning to avoid getting off my head. At, as Ricky was so fond of reminding me, considerable cost. 'I don't know if I want—'

'It's not up for negotiation.' Ricky's voice was clipped, the way it was when he was telling some pop star wannabe *No*.

'I could go to a college in town. It'd be cheaper.'

'No. I – we need you where we can keep an eye on you.'

For someone who'd spent his life in the music business, Ricky could be ridiculously naïve. I didn't *want* to use any more, but if something sent me back down that road, Father O'Dwyer's school for posh boys would be as fertile a supply ground as anywhere else. Ricky thought that because it had a uniform and charged a fortune it would be some kind of monastery.

'Ricky, do you want breakfast?' Louise slid my omelette off the pan onto a square white plate. Regular round plates were too boring for Ricky.

Ricky frowned and looked at his watch. 'Just a coffee, Louise.' She busied herself with the cafetière. 'I've a meeting at nine. More problems with the Sweet Treat negotiations. Ideas above their station now, just because they had a number one in Lithuania. I need to remind them where they come from.'

I stabbed my omelette. It was runny in the middle.

Ricky sat down opposite me, all charcoal-grey suit, pointed shiny black shoes and spicy aftershave. He made me suddenly aware of my three days' stubble, grubby bare feet, and body that had been dancing, sweating and God knows what else since it was last in a shower. 'So,' he said in a conversational tone. 'Who are these *friends*?'

I shrugged. 'People.'

'People who use drugs?'

I stopped with my fork halfway to my mouth. A

bit of omelette shivered and fell off. 'Why do you—?'

'I found *this* in your bathroom.' He brandished the butt of a spliff.

Louise looked at me in alarm as she handed Ricky his coffee with a shaking hand.

'Must be Kelly's,' I said. Stupid cow. Why couldn't she tidy up after herself? And what was Ricky doing in *my* bathroom? No point in asking – the answer would come, as it always did, that on the contrary, like everything in the house, in our lives, it was *his* bathroom.

'I don't believe you,' Ricky said. Steam rose from his coffee, a dark bitter mist that wrinkled my nose.

'Ricky.' Louise's voice was a brave squeak. 'I'm sure it *is* Kelly's. Ryan's told me she has a – a problem. In fact, he felt it was better to finish with her, which *I* think was very strong of him. It was a very mature decision.'

'You still believe in the lying little shit, don't you?' Ricky shook his head pityingly. 'After all this time – all he's put us through – the lies – and the *money*. Christ, have you any idea how much that place cost *per day*?'

'It *was* Kelly's. I haven't used since I came out, I promise.'

'I don't believe you,' he repeated. He didn't raise his voice – he sounded as pleasant as if he was being interviewed on TV. 'You've told too many lies. So if you want to keep on living in this house you make a good impression on Father O'Dwyer – you're very lucky he'll even consider taking you. It just shows,

Louise' – he turned to her – 'that those hours on the golf course are worth it. O'Dwyer wasn't exactly keen but – well, I suppose he thinks of me as a friend.' Smug smile. He drained his cup. 'I'll be back at twelve. I expect you to be ready. If not…'

I escaped to my room. It smelt of Kelly and the sweaty bad breath of our fight so I crossed to the window and pushed up the heavy sash. Cool salty air rushed in, rattling the wooden blinds. The sea looked clean and blue. Seagulls screeched, out of tune. I leaned against the sill. I felt like a smoke – I even had a few grams stashed in the bottom of my guitar case – but I genuinely was trying to stay clean. I'd scared myself this year more than I'd admitted to anybody.

As usual the road was quiet: just a disdainful cat tiptoeing down the edge of the footpath as if she couldn't bear to dirty her snowy paws. I grew up on a normal noisy street with the smell of exhaust fumes, and dogs sniffing and bins spilling onto the footpath. But when Ricky married Louise he brought us to his white mansion beside Dublin Bay. *It's so private,* he loved saying, *I can just be anonymous*. Bollocks. He hated it if people didn't recognise him. And this area was full of celebrities – mostly real ones, not like Ricky. Or me.

Below me the front door slammed and the top of Ricky's head appeared. I smiled to see that his bald patch was expanding. As if he could sense me looking, he ran his hand over the back of his head and then zapped his keys at his silver BMW.

The crunch of its wheels swinging out of the

driveway depressed me, and I pulled away from the window. I didn't need reminding about what had happened to my own Audi A3, and yes, it was all my own fault and thank God I hadn't killed anybody, but the car was a write-off and it would be a long time before I'd be allowed behind the wheel again. You probably read about it – the Irish tabloids loved it. *RyLee In Crash Horror. Boy Racer's Drug Rampage.*

A soft knock on my door was followed immediately by Louise's anxious face. 'Ryan?' Her voice was pleading. 'Shall I come with you to see Father O'Dwyer? Would that make it easier for you? I could cancel my hair appointment.' But she ran her hands through her hair and I could see worry weighing down the corners of her mouth at the thought of another day of imperfect blondeness.

'No.'

It wasn't going to be *hard*. I just didn't want to do it. I was eighteen. There was hardly a town in Ireland I hadn't played in, or a local radio station I hadn't been interviewed for. I had turned the Christmas lights on in midland towns whose names I'd never bothered to find out. Two in one night once. I was not going to go back and sit in a classroom with a crowd of posh boys. They might recognise me, especially if they had kid sisters who'd been RyLeens. That would be mortifying.

Or they might not. Which would be worse. I wouldn't be Ryan Lee any more of course: I'd be Ryan Callaghan again, and hope nobody discovered my middle name and worked it out. Ryan Lee – RyLee –

had been Ricky's invention. I hated it. It sounded like someone else. 'Exactly,' Ricky had said. 'You're just a cheap Irish version of something else. Don't ever forget it.'

My phone, on the bedside table, glowed with a text. Just some abuse from Kelly. I deleted it, and her number. I pretended not to notice Louise watching me, chewing her bottom lip.

'He just wants you to get your life back on track, love. We both do. You've put us through a lot of—'

'I'm going to have a shower.' I started pulling off my T-shirt, but she didn't get the hint. 'Can you get out of my room?'

I stayed in the shower longer than it took to wash away the last few days, until the whole bathroom was steamy. Everything looked better in the damp haze, no sharp edges. I cleared a patch on the steamed-up mirror and thought about shaving. I was pretty sure Father O'Dwyer wouldn't tolerate stubble. But I didn't pick up my razor.

Back in my room, dressed as far as jeans and a clean, black long-sleeved T-shirt, I picked up my guitar and tried to blow the dust off. It had kept me sane when I was *in there*, but I hadn't played much since I got home. I bought it when I was sixteen, to replace the old cheap blue one I'd learned on, when people were already saying I was talentless and manufactured, even if I had won *PopIcon* with record viewer votes, mostly from the pre-teen female population. OK, they'd been saying it all along, only it took me a while to hear them. Ricky had me well protected in those days. So I bought the best acoustic guitar I could afford, a Taylor 320E, and spent hours strumming and picking and making up bits of songs. I told Ricky I wanted to play my own guitar, sing my own songs, but he said not to be ridiculous. I made him listen to my best song – 'Jenny', about this girl I was obsessed with at the time. After half a verse he had tousled my highlighted hair and said I should stick to what I did best, which was dancing and flirting onstage and belting out power ballads to a backing track and looking cute. I never got Jenny to go out with me and I never wrote another song.

Meanwhile, I discovered a new talent for sneaking into clubs underage – and getting photographed falling out of them under the influence of various substances. I stopped turning up for studio recording sessions, I forgot to turn up for gigs, or was too out of it to remember how to sing when I did. Pretty soon my label dropped me, everybody who had loved me hated me – or their mothers did – and I wasn't cute any more. My 'career' was over at seventeen.

I sat on the bed, bent over the guitar, and gave it a quick strum, wincing at how out of tune it was. I plucked at the strings in turn, turning the pegs until it was in tune. The thin B and E strings cut into my fingertips. I hadn't played for weeks. I heard Louise call something from downstairs and then the door slam. I wasn't thinking too much about anything, which was restful after all the fighting and fuss with Kelly, but my fingers found chords I hadn't played for a bit, and the chords grew into a melody. I played it through a couple of times. It was mournful and repetitive, but it made words batter at the side of my brain. *I kicked you out today; it was the only way ...*

OK. I'm not pretending they were *good* words. But it was the first song I'd made up since 'Jenny'. Words came to me all the time – sometimes my head was nearly exploding with them all bashing around in there – but I never did anything about getting them onto a page, or matching them up with chords. And I don't know why I did it that day – I mean, I wasn't *sad* about breaking up with Kelly. Maybe it was being alone in the quiet house for once, knowing nobody was listening; maybe it was just better than getting ready to suck up to Father O'Dwyer. My phone buzzed and I ignored it.

Minutes or hours later I looked up from the cool hard body of my guitar, fingers burning, eyes blinking, and I felt kind of fizzy. I'd *made* something. I sang the whole thing through.

We said goodbye today.
I couldn't let you stay.
Because you always wanted things
Your own destructive way.

It was nothing like the kind of song Ricky had ever given me to sing. It was rough but it meant something, though I wasn't sure what.

I pulled down one of my old school notebooks – Geography – from the shelf over my desk, and turned to the back page. I had to scribble it down before it disappeared. I scrabbled for a pen and all I could find was a red Sharpie which bled through the page. My hands, now used to the shape and feel of the strings, bent themselves reluctantly to writing, but at last the song was down. I wouldn't tell anyone about it. I didn't really have friends. Kelly's friends had been cool but they'd hate me now. People at school seemed to go off me when I got famous – OK, maybe I did become a bit of a dick. And the ones who'd started hanging round when I became infamous – well, they were a pretty good laugh but they melted away when things stopped being funny.

I set the guitar back on its stand.

I decided to celebrate my song with a quick nip from the bottle of whiskey Ricky kept in what he called his study, though all he studied there so far as I could tell from his browsing history was pretty pedestrian porn and the stock market. They'd taken to locking the actual drinks cabinet downstairs, but Ricky couldn't seem to give up his upstairs stash, and I couldn't seem to give up helping myself. Not every day, just when I had to. I could have *bought* drink but finding Ricky's pathetic, unimaginative hiding places was much more fun. Today was so easy that I almost felt sorry for him: behind the curtain. I saw the slight bulge the second I pushed open the door. It was unworthy of him.

From there everything went a bit hazy. Too much of the whiskey maybe. I shouldn't have taken it back to my bedroom.

Ricky came back. Straight to my room. Didn't even

knock. I was enjoying his whiskey and my song. He started shouting about Father O'Dwyer and disrespect and spoilt little bastards and wastes of space.

'You were nothing when I found you! Just another little wannabe.' Spit bloomed in the corners of his lips. 'And look at you now – you're still nothing. You'll ALWAYS be nothing!' I bent over my guitar to protect it.

I'm not saying he hit me that hard. I'm not saying I didn't deserve it. His punch made me reel. My punch made him fall. His head struck the bedpost. Blood. I remember the blood.

Even with everything that's happened since, I'll never forget the blood.

2

I was playing my guitar in this park on the north side when I met Toni. She was crying. I didn't know then how rare that was for Toni. And I didn't know it was the most important meeting of my life. Girls were the last thing on my mind.

It was dusk, the sky purply-grey like a bruise. My fingertips were zinging so I must have been playing for a while.

I'd dashed out of the house on a wave of panic, ramming my guitar into its case and slamming down the catches, throwing clothes, phone, wallet into a backpack while Ricky's body sprawled across my unmade bed, blood from his head seeping into the white sheet.

I must have still been drunk, running down the road – as well as you can run with a guitar case and a backpack. The sea sparkled in the corner of my right eye. I dashed up the main street, past cupcake cafés and gastro pubs, and across to the station, and there was a DART due in two minutes. I hesitated on the platform. I should go back. Anyone decent would go back. Then the little green train came round the corner, slowed, stopped, and I stepped forward and pressed the button to open the door.

The whole way into town the sun glittered too hard on the sea, and the rhythm of the train beat in my brain: *You've killed him, you've killed him, you've killed him*. At every stop I thought about getting off the train, crossing the platform and going back. But I didn't. Half an hour later I was walking across O'Connell Bridge, and nobody had paid me any attention at all.

I decided to empty out my bank account, so I'd have cash to take me wherever I decided to go, and I couldn't be traced so easily. I wasn't sure how much money I had – I hadn't earned as much as you might think from the RyLee days, and most of it had gone on the Audi. I checked my balance at an ATM. €1329, it said. Available balance today €500.

Shit. Thirteen hundred euro would have been grand if I'd been going to Father O'Dwyer's penitentiary and sitting in with my mammy every night revising for my exams, but it wasn't going to get me far in the big bad world.

How far did I want to go?

My fingers twitched as I waited for the cashpoint to release the five hundred euro. If Ricky was dead – *no, he couldn't be dead, he wasn't dead, he'd looked dead, oh God, he* had *looked dead and I'd gone out and left him lying there, I hadn't even called 999—*

'Son, your money.'

OK, I'd hit him in self-defence but just leaving him there—

'Here – d'you want your money or not?'

'Sorry, yeah.' I grabbed the wad of notes – ten fifties, it didn't look much – while the machine beeped. The man behind me in the queue – big, bald, and flicking his card impatiently with his thumb – shook his head.

'You're lucky I'm honest, son. I could have been away with that.'

Louise would be home by now. Had she found him?

The whiskey burnt its way back up my throat. I swallowed hard.

'You OK, son?'

I stuffed the notes in my wallet and dashed across the road, breathing hard through my mouth to stop myself being sick.

I was going to have to get a grip.

I bought some water, crossed the road and turned right along the quay, pushing past tourists with my guitar case.

I could go somewhere. Far away. Where nobody had heard of Ryan Lee or Ricky Nolan – that should be easy enough – and start a new life. Just me and my guitar. I could live in Brooklyn with hipsters. I could play my guitar in a bar at night and work in a diner by day. I could grow a beard.

But I hadn't enough money to get to New York. Brighton then. Brighton was meant to be really cool.

I looked in a travel agent's window. Lots of cheap last-minute deals to Ibiza and Magaluf. But I knew what would happen if I went somewhere like that. I'd fall in with a crowd of wasters, drink too much, take drugs, pass out on the beach, probably get arrested.

And I hadn't brought my passport.

So: I could stay home and get arrested instead.

Murder? Manslaughter? Even if he was OK, leaving him like that – not trying to help; that had to be a crime. Nothing he'd ever done to me had been in that league.

I had to do the deep breathing again and lean against a wall.

Something buzzed in my back pocket. My phone. I pulled it out. *Mum calling.*

I lurched across the road, cars beeping and swerving round me, and hurled the phone into the Liffey. Then I kept on walking along the north side of the river, until I didn't know where I was.

Which is how I found myself in that park. I must have walked for hours because my feet hurt, and my shoulders ached from the unfamiliar weight of the guitar case. I felt hollowed-out inside but not exactly hungry. And I didn't dare go into a shop, imagining the newspaper headlines: *Ricky Nolan Murdered; Stepson Flees. Nolan Murder – RyLee Suspect.*

No. It was too soon for that. But it could be on the Internet already or the radio. People might be talking about it. *Did you hear about that Ricky Nolan? He had it coming to him; he was an arrogant shite. Ah, but nobody deserves to die like that. And that RyLee – sure they all come to bad ends, those teen stars. Though you'd hardly call him a star …*

Thank God I'd got rid of my phone. I knew I wouldn't be able to stop myself checking to see what was going on.

I didn't even know what the park was called. I didn't know the north side at all. A black dog bounced over with a yellow ball in its mouth, and jumped up, its paws muddying my jeans. 'Sorry,' said its owner, puffing along behind. 'He's only young.'

I sat down on a bench. I was knackered. I made sure my wallet was safely squashed down to the bottom of my backpack – it looked a dodgy kind of park – and took my guitar out of its case and set the case beside me to deter anyone else from sitting down. Just holding it felt good. Its solid bulk between me and the world. I leant on it. I tried the strings. It was still in tune. I thought I'd try and remember the song I'd been making up earlier, but as soon as I started the words juddered to a halt in my throat. Because suddenly it wasn't about Kelly; it was about Ricky.

I couldn't let you stay.
Because you always wanted things
Your own destructive way.

Ricky always got his own way. But *I'd* been the destructive one.

My fingers kept on picking. It was a more complicated melody than I usually wrote; it took all my concentration and all the bad thoughts about Ricky just bled out to the edges. My arms goosepimpled a bit but I didn't mind.

The chink of metal on plastic made me jump.

I looked up. A red-haired girl was zipping up a small fabric purse. She gave me a wobbly grin, and I saw that her eyes were smudged with tear-stained mascara. They were great eyes, greeny-brown and shiny – I suppose that was the tears. She had a back-pack over her shoulder and a guitar case sitting beside her on the path. I looked at my own guitar case. A single euro coin gleamed.

'Oh, I wasn't—'

'Bit of a daft place to busk. I mean there's nobody around, is there?' She had a northern accent, and you could hear the tears in her voice.

'Yeah. I was more just – trying out something new.'

She sighed. 'I wish I could play like that.'

I gestured at her guitar case. 'So – what sort of stuff do you play?' I didn't really care but despite the tear stains she was pretty in a fierce kind of way. A diamond stud glittered in her nose, and she had a chunky, confident way of standing in her blue DMs and green leggings that made her feel very *present* somehow. The purpling sky lit her bright hair like the edges of a flame. She was wearing a short, swirly dress, and I suddenly felt uncool in a way I wasn't used to.

She wrinkled her forehead. 'Kind of indie. Ish. Acoustic. I'm in a band – me and my friend. We're called Polly's Tree.' Her northern accent made her sound a little American – like I was in Brooklyn already. It was cute. I wondered if she was a student at Trinity or somewhere. If I hadn't messed up my last couple of years at school that's what I could have been doing now. Meeting girls like this.

'D'you live round here?'

She shook her head, her short red hair bouncing around her cheeks. 'I came to stay with my dad in Marino. He was meant to be helping me sort out some better chord sequences for my new songs, but he's disappeared.' Her mouth wobbled, and she frowned hard, as if she hated to show any kind of weakness.

'*Disappeared?*'

'He's gone to play at some festival in Donegal. He forgot I was coming. He's a bit – unreliable.' She shrugged. 'His girlfriend wanted me to stay anyway but – nah. I'm just heading home.' She picked up her guitar case.

'Stay and play?' I suggested, my fingers automatically starting to pick out another melody. 'We could have a bit of a jam. You look like – well, like you need a bit of cheering up?'

'I'm fine,' she said. 'Should be used to him by now.' She narrowed her eyes and squinted down the path. In the dusk the trees had darkened into black looming shadows. 'And I don't want to be walking through here when it's getting dark.'

'Ah, sure, stay for a bit, and then I'll walk you home.' Girls loved all that protective stuff. And I didn't want to be on my own again.

'Well ...'

'You know you want to.' I did my classic irresistible RyLee pose – head cocked like a puppy, eyes as wide as I could make them. It was a bit dangerous – she was about my age; she could well have recognised me.

She clearly didn't. I'd never done anything in the north, and I suppose she was just a bit too old and, let's be honest, far too cool to have been a RyLeen.

'I've missed the last train home,' she said. She chewed her lip. 'There's a bus at ten. I don't want to be too late.'

'It's Friday night.'

She took out her phone and checked the time. 'I'll stay for twenty minutes,' she said, in the kind of tone that told me it wouldn't be twenty-one. 'And you have to promise to walk me the whole way to the bus.'

'Course I will.'

'OK.' She sat down beside me, shoving my guitar case out of her way. She took out her guitar, and I nearly gasped. It was a beautiful old Martin – from the seventies, I'd guess.

'Wow,' I said. 'That's—'

'I know it's old and scruffy,' she said. 'My dad gave it to me for Christmas. He restores them for people – I think this one just didn't get picked up and it meant he didn't have to pay for a present.'

'That's a *seriously* lovely guitar.' My fingers itched to play it, but the girl was already bent over it, and looking at me expectantly.

'Can you show me that chord you were doing? After the G? It sounded really nice.'

I played the bit I thought she meant. 'So watch my fingers,' I said. 'They go from there – to there.'

She bent over her guitar, frowning in concentration. She tried to copy me but she kept just missing it. 'You need to try to stretch your fingers more,' I said. 'It's easier for me because my hands are bigger.' I leant towards her and took hold of her right hand. She stiffened. 'Sorry.' I pulled my hand away. 'I was only going to show you—'

'No, it's fine.' She flexed her hand. It was smallish and square, her nails painted turquoise. 'OK, so show me.'

I placed my hand over hers and manoeuvred her fingers into the right position. 'Ow,' she said. 'That wrecks.'

'You just need to keep practising,' I said. 'I used to not be able to do it.'

'I need to get better by the end of September,' she said, looking at her fingers on the strings the whole time she was talking.

'Why?'

'We've entered this competition. Backlash. Have you heard of it?'

'No.' I guided one of her fingers that kept threatening to jump off the fretboard. 'There – keep doing it like that.'

'I'm a really good singer,' she said.

'Modest.'

'I don't believe in false modesty.' She didn't stop playing. 'I'm a good singer and we write awesome songs. But I *know* I'm a crap guitarist. I never really bothered until we started Polly's Tree.'

'You just need practice.' There was no way she

played well enough for a competition unless it was some kind of amateurish fun thing, but I wasn't going to say that. And she didn't strike me as the kind of girl who did things for fun. But I liked helping her. The panic inside me calmed. I'd never tried to teach anyone anything before, but I seemed to be OK at it.

'I promised Marysia I'd nail the guitar this weekend. Otherwise I wouldn't have come all this way. I'm going to *kill* Dad.'

I tried not to wince. 'You have a month.'

'He and Bernie – his girlfriend – are going to Spain for two weeks,' she said. 'It was now or never.'

'I could maybe help you,' I suggested. 'I've nothing on this weekend. I don't mind coming round to your house.' *And it's getting dark, and if I hook up with you I won't have to spend one of my precious fifty euro notes on a bed for the night. I could hide out at your house and keep my head down until I can sneak home and get my passport. Maybe when Mum's out at Ricky's funeral.*

My fingers skittered on the strings.

'You're not a bad teacher,' she said. 'For someone I just met in a random park.'

'Thanks.' I wondered how hard you'd have to work for actual praise from this girl.

'But you can't just *come round* to my house,' she said. 'It's too far.'

'I don't mind.' She must live in some crazy miles-away suburb outside the M50 – Blanchardstown or Ballymun or somewhere. Pity; I'd imagined a nice messy student bedsit in town.

'Look.' She chewed her lip as if she was nervous. 'I

have an empty house. My mum's in London on some work course. If you really mean it about coming to help, there's a spare room you can crash in.' Then she looked horrified and said, 'I mean – oh my God, *no.* That's a crazy idea. I don't know a thing about you. Sorry. Forget it.'

'It's not a crazy idea,' I said. It was. I could have been any kind of a pervert or weirdo or thief. But I wanted to go with her so much. Partly *because* she didn't know a thing about me.

'It's really not the kind of thing I would normally do. And – oh God!' – she glanced at her watch. 'We'll need to decide in the next thirty seconds because the bus is at ten, and it takes hours.'

'*Hours?* Where d'you live?'

'Belfast,' she said, as if I should have known.

Brighton – Ballymun – Belfast. What did it matter? I stood up and set my guitar carefully in its case. I took out her one euro coin. 'I'll take this for the guitar lesson,' I said, putting it in my back pocket. 'OK – so – Belfast.'

3

'I don't even know your name,' she said. 'Mine's Toni.'

I changed my guitar case to the other hand. Then I said, 'Cal.'

'Short for Callum? Or Cahal?'

'Neither.'

We didn't say much as we hurried to Busáras, the bus station. It was never Dublin's finest joint, but it was particularly grim that night. At the door a thin, dark-haired woman emerged from the shadows. She was dressed in a shiny tracksuit. She held her hand out. 'Have you a few euros towards a hostel?'

'Sorry.' I shrugged her off.

Beside me Toni stopped, and took out her little beaded purse. 'Here you go,' she said, her accent sounding very northern compared to the woman's Dublin whine. She handed her a coin. 'I hope things get better for you,' she said.

'God bless you, miss,' the woman said. They were always overly polite. I hated it when you walked past and ignored them and they shouted out *God bless you, have a good day* after you. They only did it to make you feel bad.

'She'll only spend it on drugs,' I said, as we went through the glass doors into the bus station.

Toni shrugged. 'It's up to her what she spends it on,' she said simply. 'But she's a person. She probably wouldn't have chosen for her life to turn out like that.'

She looked after the guitars and backpacks while I got myself a ticket from the machine. Belfast. *Single, €18.50. Return €28.50.*

My fingers dithered. I turned round and looked at Toni. She was so cute, the light shining on her short red hair, her boots the brightest thing in the grim bus station. I pressed *Single.*

'OK.' I stuffed my ticket into my back pocket and picked up my guitar case. 'Belfast here we come.'

'Cal,' Toni said. It sounded so weird. 'I don't want you to think I'm the kind of girl who normally—'

'It's fine. Look, the bus is in.' It was a blue-and-cream Ulsterbus; I'd never been in one before.

'I mean – there's a spare room.'

'I know. You said.' I gave her my most reassuring smile. 'It'll be grand.'

The bus was pretty empty so we could put our seats back and relax. It was weird sitting close to a girl that wasn't Kelly. Toni was much more solid than Kelly, much more *there.* As we headed along the quays and through the lit-up port tunnel, we settled into easy chat about music. I asked about her band.

'Polly's Tree's only just started,' she said. 'But we've written loads of songs. But this is my A level year so I can't give as much to the band as I'd like. I'll probably need straight A stars. And Marysia needs top grades too, for medicine.'

This was all foreign to me. I knew they had different exams up north, but even caring about exams seemed weird to me. She must be clever.

'I take it you've left school?' she asked.

I hesitated. 'Yeah.'

'So what do you ...?'

I hunched a shoulder. 'Gap year. I'm planning to travel.'

The bus came out of the tunnel and the motorway stretched ahead. 'You *are* travelling,' she said.

'Yeah.' I grinned the slow easy grin girls liked.

After the bus left the airport and started making proper speed we both lapsed into silence. The motorway lights sped by, mesmerising me into half-sleep. I slumped sideways, closed my eyes.

Think about Toni.

Think about the rhythm of the bus.

Don't think about Ricky.

Something cushioned my cheek. Soft. Nice.

I jerked awake, realising the bus had stopped. I smelt sweat and perfume. Rosy with something sharp underneath it. My mouth was open. I snapped it shut and swallowed quite a lot of spit.

I was lying against Toni's arm. My nose was practically in her boob. That damp patch on her sleeve – that wasn't sweat; that was my slobber. Was she asleep too? She *looked* asleep, her eyelashes dark on her cheeks, her mouth neatly closed, not slack and drooly like mine. Her lips were firm and pale with a couple of freckles on the top one. I shifted over to my own side of the seat, ran my fingers through my hair, looked out the window. We were somewhere. A bus station, lit up. A couple of people got off, and we had to wait while they collected their suitcases.

'Hey,' Toni said. She peered out the window. 'Newry,' she said, and yawned.

'Is this the north?' The wet patch on her T-shirt bloomed darkly. Her face was rumpled and pink.

'Just about,' she said. The bus left the station. I looked past her out of the window. The road signs were different. *Belfast 37 miles*. A siren wailed in the distance.

'I think I was asleep,' I said. 'Sorry. Long day.'

'Me too.'

We both slept again after that but I made sure to lean in the other direction, even though it wasn't as comfy. But oh, it had been lovely leaning against her like that. She must have thought so too – I mean, she'd *let* me lean. By the time the bus finally wheezed into the Europa Bus Centre in Belfast Toni's T-shirt sleeve was dry, no sign of my slobber at all.

4

'Hey.' Toni came into the kitchen dressed in jeans and a baggy jumper, her hair damp. 'I heard you playing.'

'I hope I didn't wake you.'

'No. It was kind of a lovely sound to wake up to.' She smiled.

'I made myself at home,' I said. 'I hope that was OK.'

She poured herself a coffee from the cafetière I'd set on the table. 'You been up long?'

I nodded. I'd been awake for hours in the small guest room, feeling how weird it was to be lying in a stranger's house in a strange city, trying not to think about Ricky, tempted and terrified to turn the radio on. In the end, playing the guitar was the only way to keep the fear at bay. And the guilt. A fat black cat had stalked into the kitchen and arranged itself beside me, and it blinked at Toni with its amber eyes. 'Traitor,' she said. 'You always hide when *I* play.'

I strummed a chord sequence. 'So when do you want to get started?' I asked.

'Let me get some brekkie first! Marysia's coming later, so we can have a proper practice.'

'So what's Marysia like?' I asked.

'Lovely,' Toni said. 'She's Polish, she's really clever, and she's brilliant on the bass.'

'That's unusual – a girl playing the bass.'

'Why shouldn't she?' Toni demanded. 'I haven't told her about you – just that I have a surprise. She's always nagging me about my bad guitar playing so she'll be thrilled.'

Marysia walked in about an hour later, tall, pale, slim, with thick light brown hair misted with rain and, when she spoke, a faint Polish accent overlaid with Belfast. She didn't look that thrilled to see me, her blue eyes narrowing with suspicion as she set her bass down.

'What's going on?' she said, pulling off her coat.

'This is Cal. The surprise. Can you not hear what he's playing?'

Marysia frowned, concentrating. '"Plastic Girls"?' she said, which was the name of the song Toni had been teaching me.

'Yep,' Toni said. 'He's a fast learner. I met Cal in Dublin – he's going to help us – well, me.' She grimaced. 'You know I'm pretty bad at playing. And when Dad let me down – well, Cal sort of stepped up.' She didn't say she'd picked me up in a park.

'Toni said you're brilliant on the bass,' I said. OK, I

was sucking up a bit. But I wasn't used to girls being so – well, hostile.

'Polly's Tree's a two-piece girls-only band,' Marysia said. 'That was our vision from the start.'

'He's not joining the band.'

I kept on strumming like I wasn't bothered at all. 'If you don't want me around, that's cool.'

'We do!' Toni said. 'Marysia – wait till you hear the difference he's made to me already.' She took up my guitar and nodded to me. '"You Think You Know Me",' she ordered, and I nodded and played the opening chords. Toni joined in, the two guitars sounding great together, and when it was time for the vocal she sang really confidently:

You think you know me but you really don't.
You think I'll love you but I know I won't.

She was right about being a good singer: she had a gorgeous voice – sometimes husky, sometimes high, always pitch perfect. It was an upbeat song about thinking someone fancies you when they don't. At least, I thought that was what it was about. By the third line, Marysia had plugged in her bass and was joining in, the bass keeping the whole thing grounded. By the second chorus, I was harmonising with their vocals.

'It'd be great with a harmonica in the chorus,' I suggested.

'No way,' Toni said. 'We don't want to sound folky.' She actually shuddered.

'It would suit the song.'

'Well, neither of us can play it.'

'I can,' Marysia said. 'It's the first instrument I ever learned – it was all I could afford when I was a kid. It's probably lying round somewhere, if Tomasz hasn't nicked it from me.'

'A harmonica's just a whiney drone that makes everything sound like Bob Dylan,' Toni said. 'Which is fine for actual Bob Dylan but nothing else.'

'OK, boss,' Marysia said. She pushed her heavy brown hair back and twisted it into a knot at the nape of her neck. I grinned at her, and for the first time, uncertainly at first, she smiled back.

After that it was all about the music. I wasn't used to making music with actual people, but I picked up all Polly's Tree's songs really fast – to be fair, they weren't the most complicated, musically, but also I concentrated like mad. Partly because I wanted to impress and partly because it helped keep my mind from thinking about what was happening back in Ricky's white seaside mansion. If Ricky was alive or dead.

Toni was singing even better. It was as if when she didn't have to worry about the guitar she could let go with her vocals. Marysia's deeper voice blended well with mine on backing vocals and let Toni's really soar when it needed to without the song getting shrill.

As the rain kept up outside, streaming down the windows so that we had to turn the lights on, the day wore on, full of music and occasional chat and, when we all realised we were starving, pizza.

It was magical. The living room became its own world, with the constant soundtrack of our songs.

'So d'you write your own stuff, Cal?' Marysia asked, when we'd reached the stage of lying around chatting, though I still had my guitar on my lap. My fingertips burned as they hadn't since I was first *in there,* when playing guitar most of the day had kept me sane.

'Not much.' I picked out the melody I'd been playing yesterday in the park – the one that had made Toni stop and give me a euro.

'Go on,' Toni said encouragingly.

'Nah, the lyrics are shite,' I said, suddenly mortified. 'Far too depressing.'

'You don't seem the kind of person to write depressing songs,' Toni said. What did that mean? She saw me as shallow? Carefree? And how did she know what kind of person I might be? But I was used to being judged quickly. ('Ten seconds,' Ricky used to say each week before *PopIcon*. 'That's how long it takes people to make up their minds about you.')

'I have a kind of love song,' I offered. 'I wrote it a few years ago.' I don't know why I thought of 'Jenny' after all this time. Maybe something about the effort to impress these girls – especially Toni – was bringing me back to that time. Jenny O'Neill had been an intern with the production company who made *PopIcon*. She had black corkscrew curls and she was nineteen. I made a fool of myself over her. The night she told me I was just a kid was the night I got stoned for the first time. And behaved in a way which no doubt proved her point, but which thankfully I couldn't remember.

I started playing a plaintive, simple chord sequence, and then, for the first time, I sang on my own in front of Toni and Marysia. I was strangely nervous. As soon as I started singing, I wished I hadn't. Their songs were clever and quirky and all the lyrics *meant* something – though I wasn't always sure what. 'Jenny' was just a standard pop song, and when I launched into the chorus, which, OK, went 'Jenny, Jenny, Jenny; oh Jenny, Jenny, Jenny', Marysia caught Toni's eye, and a snort of laughter escaped. They were trying not to giggle, but they weren't trying that hard. Even Ricky hadn't laughed at the song – just told me it was no good.

I stopped playing. 'Yeah,' I said. 'Told you I was shite.' I shrugged, like it didn't matter, and set my guitar down.

Toni looked stricken, though in fairness, ten minutes ago she'd put up with me telling her she played guitar like she had socks on her hands. 'Sorry,' she said. 'I think we're all played out.'

'Let's go out,' Marysia said. 'It's Saturday night.'

'Yes!' Toni turned to me. 'This is your first time in Belfast and all you've seen is my house.'

'I'm grand here.' I looked round the living room. It felt safe. 'You go,' I said. 'I don't mind staying here. I'm pretty tired. I can watch TV or whatever.' I wondered if they had boyfriends.

Toni hesitated. I saw the thought flit across her mind – *We don't actually know anything about this guy.*

What if we get home later to find all the computers gone or something?

'Well, it's still raining,' she said. 'And Mum's filled the fridge with food so we can have a feast.'

'Have you got any beers?' I asked.

'No beer. But there's loads of wine in the kitchen. Mum's pretty cool about drink; she won't have hidden it away or anything.'

'Actually the fact that we've been here all day playing music and nobody's even *mentioned* alcohol till now just proves how mature and sensible we are,' Marysia said.

Two hours later we were all smashed.

5

Marysia was sitting on the floor, leaning against Toni's legs, singing a Polish song and swearing in a mixture of English and Polish because she kept forgetting the words. Toni was playing with her hair, and the firelight turned the brown strands gold.

I couldn't believe I hadn't even come close to scoring with either of them.

I was sprawled on the other sofa, one arm slung round the neck of my guitar – I was too pissed to play but I didn't want to let go of it – the other hand caressing Billy, the cat, who'd done the rounds of our leftovers and was lying across my stomach, purring a deep bass note. I leaned down and lifted up a bottle of red wine, squinting at it. 'Not much left here.'

'*Not* my turn to go and get more,' Toni said. 'And I can't disturb Marysia.' Marysia kept singing, and swearing, leaning her slim shoulders against Toni's legs. It was like a picture: two hot girls. Only – I was starting to wonder if they were actually hot for *each other*? Was this just girls doing that girly affectionate drunk thing, or had I been missing something the whole time?

'No more for me,' Toni said. 'It's late.'

Marysia stopped singing. 'Oh no. Did I say I'd go to Mass tomorrow?' She groaned, and her shoulders slumped.

'So don't go,' Toni said.

'You know Mama and Tata'll be expecting me to be there,' Marysia said. 'It was the only condition on which I was allowed to stay at yours.'

She suddenly sounded very young.

'Oh,' she moaned. 'I am going to feel like shit in the morning, aren't I?'

'Not if we stop now and Cal goes and gets us lots and lots of water.' Toni smiled winningly at me. *Stop flirting,* I thought. *You can't have it both ways.*

'Ah, go on. I don't want to drink on my own,' I said.

'You could stop too,' Toni suggested. 'You've had way more than us anyway.'

'I'm a boy,' I said. 'I can take it.'

Toni threw a cushion at me, much to Billy's disgust, and I leapt up far too fast for someone who'd put away that much wine, and caught it. Then I groaned, fell back against the sofa, and closed my eyes.

'You'd better not puke,' Toni warned me.

I opened one eye. 'No. Give me a minute.'

Marysia wriggled and dragged herself up. 'Oh God,' she said. 'How did we get to be so drunk?' She looked at the mess of bottles and plates and discarded guitars. 'You're a bad influence, Cal.'

'It's been said before.' I opened both eyes, grinned, and said, 'OK. Three pints of water coming up.'

I stumbled off into the kitchen. When I got back Marysia's head was buried in Toni's lap, her hair spread like a veil. I set down two pint glasses of water on the coffee table. 'Get a room, ladies, will yez?' I wasn't going to *ask*, but I could *hint*. Show them I wasn't totally clueless.

'We intend to.' Toni downed her water, reached for Marysia's hand and led the way up the stairs.

I was too wired to sleep. Lying in the spare room, my shoulders ached, my fingers throbbed and my head buzzed with wine.

And now the fear was seeping back.

It had been OK when I was playing – then it was just about the music. And when the music had stopped the drinking started and that was always good for a bit of reality blurring. But now – I was on my own, sobering up, in a cold spare room with two hot girls next door who only wanted me for my guitar. What a waste. I put my head under the pillow to blot out their giggles and whispers.

It had been an unreal, magical day, tucked away from the rain in Toni's homely living room. No TV, no Facebook, no contact with the outside world at all. No way of knowing whether Ricky was dead or alive.

I couldn't hide for ever.

But for now – this was as good a place as any. Good company and plenty of distraction. From what I could see there wasn't likely to be anything stronger than alcohol on the agenda either, which was probably a good thing. I knew it couldn't last – I'd been invited for the weekend, and then I supposed I'd move on. Somewhere.

6

'No,' Toni said next morning. 'Staying in's not an option.' And she actually put her hands on her hips. 'You can't go home tonight and not have seen anything but the inside of my house.'

I tried not to process *go home tonight*. It was only 10 a.m.

Outside it felt colder than Dublin but maybe that was just because autumn was coming. Breathing in the cool, damp northern air chased away the hangover of wine and music. On Friday night I'd seen nothing except street lights, pub signs and the usual kind of city stuff. Now, walking down Toni's street, I could see that her area was middle-class and quiet – red-brick Victorian houses, small front gardens. We got to a main road, where the shops were mostly shut, but one or two cafés were open. The postboxes were red instead of green like at home, which looked weird.

Nobody gave me a second glance. It's not that I

was arrogant enough to think I only had to step into the street to be papped. But if there was anything about Ricky in the papers, and if I was mentioned as a suspect – well, it might bring me back into people's minds, that's all.

'You don't have to walk me all the way there,' Marysia said, when a large red-brick church loomed into view on the other side of the road. 'You could take Cal for a coffee, or go for a walk in the park or something.'

'Can you come back to mine after Mass?' Toni asked. 'We'll wait for you in Kopi.'

Marysia shook her head. 'Homework. Sunday lunch. No, you show Cal round Belfast.'

When Marysia had gone it felt a bit crackly between Toni and me, and I wasn't sure why.

'OK, you have to see Belfast,' she said. She put her hands in her jacket pockets. 'Let's see. We could get a bus—'

Before she could organise me into a guided tour with compulsory exam afterwards, I said, 'What's Kopi?'

'It's a café. It's the Indonesian word for coffee.'

'You have Indonesian cafés in Belfast?'

'Well – no,' she admitted. 'I think they just thought it was a cool name.'

'So can we start there?'

It was like a café anywhere – I don't know why I thought it wouldn't be, but that first day in the Belfast streets I expected everything to be different. It was crowded in the same way Dublin cafés were on

Sunday mornings – with families ignoring their kids, and couples looking at their phones and ignoring each other, and groups of people our age trying to make Saturday night last longer. The steamy air smelled of coffee and what I later learned was the Ulster fry. We got our coffees at the counter. I offered to pay but they didn't take euros, and I felt really stupid because of course I knew they used sterling up north, I'd just forgotten. Toni was OK about it, though; she said I'd earned a coffee with all my music tutoring. She squinted into the fug. 'There's a table in the corner,' she said.

Someone had left a Sunday paper behind. It must have been a Northern paper, because I didn't recognise it. The front page headline was about a sex scandal with a politician I'd never heard of, but who knew what might be inside? I swept it away, but Toni stopped me.

'Give it here. That paper's full of crap but it has good gig reviews.' She opened it and scanned it.

'Have you done many actual gigs?'

She shook her head. 'We did a showcase after the summer school we did in July. But that's it.' She frowned. 'I know we need more practice. But I don't know where to get it.'

'There must be open mic nights and stuff.' I took the paper from her and scanned it. 'OK – what about this?' I read out the details of an open mic night, but when she heard the name of the pub her eyes widened. 'No way, Dublin boy! Wrong part of town.'

'OK.' I kept looking. 'What about this? The Bluebell? That doesn't sound rough. *Open mic night, Wednesday. Solo acts and bands welcome.*'

'School night.'

'That's not very rock and roll!'

Toni laughed. 'I suppose we could go this week, when my mum's away.'

She stirred sugar into her coffee and when she looked up her hazel eyes were shining. 'I never really believed we had a chance. I only said I'd do Backlash because Marysia was so keen and because I wanted to show that two girls could be an awesome band. Only deep down I knew we weren't awesome enough. You need to be twice as good if you're a girl, to get taken seriously.' She frowned and fiddled with her spoon. 'But now – we sound so much better. It feels like it could really happen.'

She didn't say what *it* was. I didn't say *it* had already happened for me and it hadn't lasted long. But then Toni and Marysia weren't as stupid as me. Look how they'd known when to stop drinking last night. Even after being *in there*, I'd probably just have kept drinking until I passed out, left to my own devices.

'So – is it a TV thing? Like *X Factor* or something?' I carefully didn't mention *PopIcon*. Defunct after a season, though apparently the franchise was still going on some cable station in America.

'Oh my God. Did you not listen?' She actually shuddered. '*No*. That's the whole point. It's not about TV and image and getting famous quick and then being forgotten about. Deservedly.' She screwed up her face, her look of disgust making it very obvious I could *never* mention *PopIcon* or RyLee, not just because of Ricky. So I said, 'Um, yeah,' which probably ranked alongside 'Jenny' in my list of articulate moments.

'The clue's in the name – it's a backlash against all that shit. *Real music for real people*. So no – no TV; no autotuners; no deliberately staged televised auditions for the chronically deranged so we can all laugh at them—'

'Some of them are actually funny. Don't tell me you've never laughed.' At least I hadn't been chronically deranged.

'I've never laughed. Well, not since I was about ten.'

I believed her.

'It's for people who care about music,' she said. 'About writing songs and sharing them. Having something *real* to say.' Her eyes were suddenly serious. 'Not about being famous, or being on TV, or being rich.'

'But it's a competition? You want to win? So what's the difference?'

She sighed. 'Cal,' she said. I still felt weird every time she called me that. 'Do you really need me to spell it out?'

I kind of did, but at the same time I didn't want her to go over it all, and probably do me a diagram, so I said, 'No, I get it.'

She took out her phone and fiddled with it, then

handed it to me. 'Look,' she said. 'That's their website.'

I took it. A second later I was thinking, *I'm online. I could google Ricky and see if there's anything – well, anything. Toni wouldn't know.*

She was reading something about the Northern Irish Assembly with much comment, most of which I didn't understand. It occurred to me that Toni and Marysia, as well as being sensible and creative and hot, were probably quite a bit brighter than me.

I might as well know the worst.

If you've ever googled Ricky Nolan you'll know his website is all about how great he is. I mean, the guy's a promoter so obviously he starts with promoting himself. There's a lot of heart-warming crap about his rise from humble roadie to being one of the biggest managers in Irish pop. Quite a bit about him marrying Louise Callaghan, former member of a girl band you've definitely never heard of, whose 'career' took a tumble when she became a single mum (to me). Loads about his involvement as a judge on *PopIcon*; how he swore he only got together with my mum *after* I'd won the show; how he became my manager, and how he absolutely had not groomed me before I won the contest.

That's not what I was looking for.

I was looking for the story of how he'd been found dead in a pool of his own blood at his luxury south Dublin home on Friday afternoon, having sustained a blow to the head. I was looking for the story of how gardaí were searching for the only suspect, his stepson Ryan Lee Callaghan, also known as Ryan Lee, or RyLee. Former *PopIcon* winner. Former almost-star.

Former drug user, hell-raiser and general waster.

It wasn't there. The most up-to-date story was last month's claim (hotly denied by Ricky) that he'd been sleeping with one (or possibly all) of the members of girl-band pop-sensation Sweet Treat. I scrolled on to the next page and the next – but there was nothing.

I wasn't a murderer. I could go home.

'Oy,' Toni said. 'You're not just checking the Backlash website because it's only a page. So could you not use my phone to do whatever you're doing? There's no Wi-Fi in here. Use your own phone.'

'Sorry.' I went back to the Backlash page in case she checked, and handed her phone back. 'I haven't got one,' I said, remembering the dramatic gesture of throwing it into the Liffey. It seemed pointless now. But I'd been so scared. And I *had* left him unconscious and bleeding. So even though I most probably wasn't a murderer, and didn't really need to be a hundred miles away with an assumed identity and no phone, that didn't mean that I'd be welcomed with open arms.

'How can you not have a phone?'

I was about to say I'd lost it when I changed my mind. Might as well appear interesting and alternative. 'I don't need to be tied down like that,' I said. 'You know – possessions; plans. Sometimes it's good to just step off the path and look round you a bit.' I had no idea where that shit came from.

Toni shook her head. 'I thought my dad was an old hippie, but you – are you for real?'

'Yeah.'

Apart from the false identity.

But weirdly, even inside the web of lies and omissions, I felt more honest than I had for ages. And *free.*

'So you're a free-spirited troubadour?' I liked the sound of that. 'Are you against money and capitalism and everything?'

'Definitely not against money. In fact – can we go to a cashpoint?' It would be a quick way to get sterling. I couldn't sponge off Toni all day.

The cashpoint told me there was a problem with my card. *Please contact your branch.* I stared at it in disbelief. I pressed random buttons but the card wouldn't come back out of the slot. I punched the wall but all that got me was sore knuckles.

'What's wrong?' Toni said. She was behind me but not close enough to see the screen.

'Maybe I forgot my PIN,' I mumbled.

I knew I hadn't. It was my birthday – 2201. Which meant – what? A glitch with the machine? Trouble was, the machine had my card so I couldn't try it anywhere else. Had my account been hacked or something while I'd been camping out in a stranger's life? Or could this be something to do with Ricky?

Whatever it was, I couldn't do anything about it on a Sunday morning. Might as well just give myself up to the day.

Belfast on a September Sunday: smaller than I'd expected. And prettier, especially when you looked up above the shop fronts, which Toni kept ordering me to do. Lots of red brick and stone. The white marble City Hall was like a wedding cake. We passed a sign for the bus station. My steps slowed. 'You don't actually *have* to go home tonight,' Toni said, as if she could read my mind. 'My mum's not home until Friday. Unless you've got stuff to get back for?'

I shook my head. 'Nothing important.'

If I hung round, made myself useful musically and in any other way the girls wanted, it could fill up a week very nicely. Give the now-almost-certainly-not-dead Ricky a chance to calm down. Give me a chance to figure out what I was going to do next.

'I'll be at school all day. But you could – I dunno – hang out in the city. You should go and see the Titanic museum; it's brilliant. And—'

She rattled off an itinerary of worthy stuff that I knew I'd never visit, while I zoned out and tried to work out if the girls here looked any different from Dublin girls. Outside the university, a foreign woman thrust a *Big Issue* at us. I sidestepped automatically.

'—and of course the best thing about the Ulster Museum is it's totally free,' Toni was saying, pointing out something white on our left.

'Are you a cool indie rock chick or a hopeless geek?' I asked.

She play-punched me. 'I'm a devastatingly cool distillation of all that is best of both,' she said. 'And don't call me a *chick*. It's degrading.' But she grinned, and her little diamond nose stud glittered, and I hoped my week of camping in her life wouldn't go too quickly.

7

Apart from the nagging worry/guilt about Ricky, it was the best week ever: hanging out at Toni's, seeing her every day, playing music every night – *after* she'd done her homework; she was super focused on that. Her mum was at some conference in London – she was a teacher in a further education college – and not due back till Friday. I wasn't letting myself think about after Friday. In there we were supposed to focus on the here and now – let go of the past, and not fret about the future. So that's exactly what I was doing.

On Wednesday I found some lyrics lying on the coffee table, in Toni's neat, bold handwriting:

Thank you for giving me your secret self.
Don't worry that I'd ever tell someone else.
Thank you for showing the person you are.
I won't let anyone darken your star.

I didn't know exactly what it was about, but as soon as I read it I could hear the right melody in my head. By the time Toni got in from school I had it worked out. 'And I know you didn't write a chorus,' I said. 'But I thought, what about this?'

Alarm flickered across her face and I could see her remembering, 'Jenny, Jenny, Jenny.'

'It's not meant to have a chorus,' she said.

'It'd make it more catchy.'

'It's not meant to be *catchy*.'

I shrugged. 'Your song. You want to go to that open mic thing tonight?'

She shook her head. 'Marysia has a test tomorrow. And don't tell me that's not very rock and roll. She's coming to practise tomorrow night.' She looked round the room. There were books and papers and guitars and glasses and plates everywhere. 'We should really tidy up,' she said.

'Let's do it all in one big go on Friday,' I suggested. Tidying up would mean accepting that the week was going to end and I was going to have to go somewhere and do something.

On Thursday Marysia listened critically to the new song, her head on one side. 'Wow,' she said. 'I can't believe you made a song out of something so personal ... OK' – she became business-like – 'go back to the beginning so I can put in the bass line.'

Toni was singing, but she still needed to look at the words, and she had trouble doing that and playing guitar at the same time, so she kept making mistakes. 'Sorry,' she said, after she'd played an E instead of an A and Marysia winced.

'Just sing,' I said. 'Let Marysia hear how it's meant to be.'

It sounded OK with just the lead guitar and the bass underpinning her voice. Toni's strumming hadn't added much.

'It's – fine,' Marysia said, but she sounded unsure, twirling a long lock of hair round her finger. 'But I think it needs something. A chorus, maybe?'

'I've been trying to tell her that,' I said. 'I was thinking about something like this ...' I played her some rough chords, humming a melody.

'Yes!' Marysia said. 'That's *exactly* what it needs.' She looked at us approvingly. 'Nice collaborating.'

Toni groaned. 'But that's not what I—'

'So if we ever make an album we'll have to credit you as a co-writer,' Marysia said. She was all shiny. 'It'll be like Lennon and McCartney, only it'll be Flynn, Nowalczyk and – what's your surname, Cal? Cal?' She waved her hand in front of my face.

'Uh – Ryan,' I said. 'Cal Ryan.'

'Well, *this* song would just be Flynn and Ryan,' Toni pointed out. 'Which sounds – ugh – like an Irish folk duo.' She wrinkled her nose.

'Why does she hate folk so much?' I asked Marysia.

'Because of her dad,' Marysia said. 'That's his thing. And Anto – well, he's quite sweet, but he's a bit of an underachiever in the parenting department.'

'It is *not* because of him.' Toni looked pink and cross. 'And he is *not* sweet.' She looked round the untidy living room. 'It wouldn't have hurt you to do some clearing up today while I was at school,' she said.

'Sorry – I thought we agreed—'

And then we heard a key turn in the front door, and a voice call, 'Toni? I'm back.'

8

There must have been a taxi, but we didn't hear it because of the music.

Toni's mum was not still safely in London but standing in the living room doorway, looking with horror at the mess of plates, glasses, guitars, scribbled song sheets, DVD cases, bottles – oh yes, and one complete stranger (male).

The girls just sat there, gaping. She didn't look like Toni. She was tall, and dark, and very cross.

'Oh shit,' I said. 'I mean – hello.'

'Toni? What—?'

'Mum! You're not meant to be home yet! I was – we were going to tidy up. We were literally just about to …'

Marysia scrambled to her feet, setting her bass down carefully. 'Um – we're so sorry. We were just practising.'

Practising *what*? Toni's mum's face said.

I stood up and walked over to her, instinctively

going into RyLee charm offensive. I was usually pretty good with mums, especially the single ones. 'Hi,' I said. 'I'm Cal. I've been helping the girls with their music. We sort of got a bit involved. With the music, I mean. We'll tidy up this *moment*.' I held my hand out. I shook my hair out of my eyes, cocked my head slightly, smiled ruefully, eyes wide in a puppyish way that didn't often fail.

It failed. She looked me up and down and the look didn't say, *What a cute and charming young man*; it said, *Who is this scruffy waster?* She didn't shake my hand. She said, 'Toni – I'm going to unpack and have a bath. I'll be down in half an hour, and I expect this room – *every* room – to be pristine. OK? Then we need to have a chat.'

Marysia organised us both into stacking the dish-washer, filling the recycling – oh God, how could we have drunk so *much*? – hoovering, and then rubbing all the surfaces with a damp cloth. Toni opened the windows wide, and I felt suddenly sad, as if all the music was evaporating in the night air, along with the stale food smells and the alcohol fumes.

'Will she kill you?' I asked, when we'd finally reached the stage of surveying the living room.

'Yep. She's always going on about trusting me. And until now I've never given her any reason not to. God knows what she'll do now – ground me, not let me play in the band—'

She blabbed this all out incoherently while she scrubbed at a stain on the arm of the sofa.

'You haven't done anything *wrong*,' I said. 'We

weren't doing drugs, or having sex.' I sighed. 'You didn't have a party. You've gone to school every day. You've even done your homework! I mean, realistically, she hasn't much to complain about, has she?'

'We did drink nearly all her wine,' Marysia pointed out.

'I've let a total stranger stay in her house for—' Toni counted on her fingers, 'six nights.'

'Actually,' Marysia said. 'She doesn't *know* that.'

We all looked at each other.

'OK, so if we get rid of all your stuff from the spare room while she's in the bath she doesn't need to know you've been staying here. And then she'll only half-kill me.'

'So where am I meant to go? It's nearly ten o'clock at night.'

'Um – could he stay at yours, Marysia? Just for tonight?'

'No! There's no way my parents would let me bring a strange boy home to stay the night. And we don't have a spare room.'

'You have that big shed. If he sneaked in from the back entry and you smuggled him out a sleeping bag—'

'You're making me sound like the class hamster here.' I tried to hide the panic in my voice. 'And I'm not sleeping in a bloody *shed*.'

Water gurgled down the waste pipe outside the window.

'We haven't much time. If she goes into the spare room for any reason—'

'She won't. Why would she?'

'OK. I'm going up to grab your stuff. I have to, Cal. I'm sorry.'

'I'll get it,' I said.

'No – if she sees you upstairs—'

'I'll say I'm going to the loo. Christ's sake, Toni, lighten up. We haven't done anything wrong.' I was already starting out of the room, when a very sharp voice yelled down the stairs.

'Toni! Get up here right now!'

9

It was like *Goldilocks. Who's been sleeping in my bed?*

I hadn't been sleeping in anyone's bed. I'd been sleeping chastely and alone in the spare room. Which Toni tried to explain, not in that exact language, but it wasn't going well. Marysia and I were listening from the bottom of the stairs, and though the row had begun in hisses and whispers, Toni had started shouting and her ma had followed suit.

'You can't just open my house to anyone you feel like giving a bed to.' Never mind the class hamster; she made me sound like some kind of smelly tramp.

'He's my *friend,*' Toni said.

'Since when? I've never heard of him before.'

'I met him in Dublin.' Sulkily.

'When?'

Hesitation. 'Ages ago.' Six days probably was ages if you were a butterfly or something.

'Where?'

'Near Dad's.' Please let her not say she picked me up in a park.

'So he's someone you met through your *dad*?' She didn't sound impressed.

Another hesitation. Never mind guitar tuition; Toni needed coaching in how to lie. Then, 'Yeah. He's – he's one of Dad's musician friends.'

Marysia grimaced. 'That may not be the smartest thing Toni's ever said,' she whispered. 'Her mum *hates* her dad. Even more than Toni does.'

'So what's he doing in our spare room? Apart from drinking the place dry and – God, Toni – look at the mess in here!'

Please let her not go through my stuff. She so obviously wasn't the kind of mother who'd be cool about the tiny lump of weed she might find in the bottom of my backpack. I'd moved it from the guitar case because I didn't want the girls to see it. And the stupid thing was, I'd never felt less like taking anything in my life. OK, we'd hit the wine fairly hard, I suppose – I mean, it was just *there* – but other than that I was clean as a whistle.

'Look – he's just a nice boy on his gap year,' Toni said. Nice boy? Is that what she really thought? 'Dad let me down last week – you don't want to know – and Cal offered to help out. He plays the guitar like an angel. He's been so generous about helping me. You should hear the difference he's made to the band!'

'Well, it's time he went and made a difference somewhere else.'

'Mum – it's ten o'clock at night. We can't just throw him out on the street.'

Long silence. I held my breath. I had most of my five hundred euro left. I'd been to the bank about my swallowed-up card and they'd told me the card had been reported as stolen. I hadn't wanted to go into it in too much detail, obviously, but I took it as a sign from Ricky: he was alive and severely pissed off, and he could still control me from a distance by trying to starve me into coming back and taking what I deserved.

There were buses to Dublin all through the night. Was it time to go back?

But I couldn't *hide* in Dublin. Even though people didn't seem to recognise me – the stubble was coming on well, and the stupid highlights Ricky had always made me get to make me blonder and cuter (his words) were pretty much grown out and my hair was back to its natural brown – I didn't know how long it would be before I started seeking out old mates. Only they weren't really mates. Just people I knew. People who wouldn't be good for me. Or I could go home and face my mum's disgust and Ricky's rage. No way.

'Mum . . .' Toni sounded pleading. 'I'm sorry, OK? But don't take it out on Cal.'

'He's not my problem!'

'He's my friend.'

'*One* more night,' the ma said. 'And he goes in the morning – I mean it, Toni.' Even from the bottom of the stairs I could tell that she definitely did. 'And this is *not* over. Now let me get dressed and then I'm coming down to inspect your cleaning. And I'll have a glass of wine – if you've left me any.'

Toni came clattering back down the stairs, her red hair swinging as she shook her head. She blew out through her fringe.

'I'm sorry. She went into the spare room for – I don't know what. Just her dirty mind.'

'Should I go?' Marysia asked. 'Actually I sort of should anyway or *my* parents will be on my back. I was meant to be back at ten.'

'Oh God. I'm sorry.'

'It's OK.' Marysia hugged her and stroked her hair back into place. 'See you tomorrow. Cal' – she turned to me – 'will we see you again? I mean – you can't just *go*.' She gave me a sudden hug too, her long hair tickling me, her hands firm against my back. I hoped that Toni would join in the goodbye hug thing.

'I have to.' OK. Not Dublin. But there were other places.

'Cal,' Toni said, 'I know you want to go travelling, but would you not stay and be in the band? At least until the first heat? And see what happens?'

Oh God. This is what I didn't want them to ask. Going on stage again – the lights, the screaming from the dark audience, the high – and then the low. Always the low. I couldn't go back there. Sweat pricked my neck at the very thought. But I supposed it would be different. Just a low-key local competition in the upstairs room of a Belfast pub. And I could be the quiet guy playing guitar in the background.

But they'd have to know my name and everything. And there was no such person as Cal Ryan.

I couldn't say all that, so I just said, 'It's been – magical …' My voice cracked. Shit. I was always making friends – girls and boys – and just walking away. I'd been sleeping with Kelly all summer and I'd hardly given her a thought. 'Sorry.' My voice came out harsh and dismissive. 'I need to move on.'

10

The morning lightened to pale grey outside the window. I pushed my spare hoody further down in my backpack. I looked round the room that had been my home for nearly a week. It was your standard issue suburban guest room – odds and ends of furniture that didn't quite fit in anywhere else – but I'd got quite fond of it. I'd tidied it, stripped the bed and opened the window, so when Toni and her ma got up, it would be like I'd never been there.

It wasn't seven o'clock yet, but I'd decided to split. I'd been awake most of the night, and I didn't feel up to a long, drawn-out goodbye. And it would be easier not to have to face Toni's ma in the cold light of day. I hitched my backpack onto my shoulder, lifted my guitar case and left the house as quietly as I could.

I had planned to leave Toni a note – I didn't feel great about how we'd left things last night, but when

I tried I couldn't. I didn't know what to say and most of all, I couldn't sign it *Cal,* and I certainly couldn't write *Ryan*.

Lugging my backpack and guitar down the early-morning street, I shivered. I'd left Dublin with just a couple of hoodies, no actual coat, and a week had made a difference to the weather, especially at this time of the morning. To keep my mind off my greater existential problems, I focused on practicalities. I needed to change my euros into sterling – until I did that I couldn't even buy a cup of tea. Maybe it had been a bit stupid to walk out of Toni's before breakfast. I needed somewhere to stay that night too. Somewhere as cheap as possible. There must be a backpackers' hostel or something. I imagined myself sitting in a bright room with loads of guys from all over the world, and pretty Australian girls. I'd be popular because of the guitar. We'd have sing-songs and I'd go off with them, busking round Ireland. I'd keep on being Cal and it'd be brilliant.

But I couldn't do anything until I could get to a bank, and I was starving, with that hollowed-out chill that comes after a sleepless night. Wandering the streets, my guitar heavier with every step, watching people with normal lives rush to school and work, clutching takeaway coffee cups, talking into phones or to each other, made me feel lonely. By the time the banks opened and I was able to change my pitiful amount of euro, I was as shaky as I used to be coming down off the various substances that had kept RyLee going.

A café helped. And my first Ulster fry, which left me feeling I wouldn't need to eat again until Sunday. The café wasn't as nice as Kopi, but it was cheap, and cheap was going to have to be my number one priority.

Which is how, after one of the most frustrating mornings of my life, I checked into the Crossroads Hostel. The sort of place RyLee wouldn't have known existed. The sort of place that Ryan Callaghan wouldn't have known existed either. But by the time I was walking through its peeling front door, I was so tired, fed up and footsore that I didn't much care where I was. Not having a phone was a pain – I cursed myself for throwing it into the Liffey – because I couldn't look up hostels or even a map of the city. I trudged round for ages and finally found a tourist information centre, which gave me details of several hostels. Three perfectly decent, if basic, hostels where travellers from all over the world came to stay for the famous Belfast craic. And one really grotty-looking one, Crossroads, that I knew I wouldn't be seen dead in, in an area that even I had heard of. And when you've heard of an area in Belfast, it's not usually a good sign.

The first one, in a leafy suburban street not far from Toni's house, was fully booked for the next fortnight.

No worries. There were two more decent hostels on my list. Both of them had beds. Both of them refused to let anyone book in without ID. I tried all my RyLee charm, but it was no go.

'No ID, no stay,' they both said. 'We have to be careful.'

Careful of what? I wondered, but there was no point arguing.

Which is how I found myself at the Crossroads. A tall thin house with dirty barred windows in a short dead-end street about a mile from the centre. It overlooked a terrace of bricked-up industrial buildings, and a deserted play park with the swings thrown up over the bars and broken glass round the bottom of the slide. The street was dead-ended by a wall, covered in graffiti that meant nothing to me. The kerbstones opposite the hostel had been painted red, white and blue, but, like the peeling front door, not recently. I hesitated on the crumbling steps and looked down the empty street. Was I mad? A hundred miles away I had a lovely room in a comfortable, luxurious house. I hated Ricky but he wasn't going to abuse me or anything. He probably wouldn't turn me in to the police. And he couldn't actually *force* me to go and be a good boy for Father O'Dwyer.

So why was I even thinking about paying to stay in this dodgy-looking dosshouse in an area where I knew people would stare at me as soon as I opened my mouth and they heard my Dublin accent? Maybe more than stare?

The receptionist was an oldish guy whose belly pressed up against the wooden counter, straining against the confines of his red T-shirt. Both thick arms were tattooed with symbols I didn't recognise and didn't feel like analysing too closely. But he looked up in a friendly way when I walked in, scratched his woollen beany hat and said, 'All right, son?' His accent was so strong I had to concentrate to make him out.

I said I was a tourist, and needed a room for a few nights. I'd had my wallet stolen on the train – I was pretty good on details when I was lying – which is why I'd no ID.

Beany frowned. 'Not meant to let you in without ID.'

'Ah come on, sure it's only for a few nights,' I wheedled. 'I couldn't help getting my wallet nicked. I'll pay cash.' I pulled out a wad of twenty-pound notes.

He looked down at my guitar case. 'No drugs. No drink. Any trouble and you're out. I don't do second chances. No curfew, but there's a lockout ten till five. And, son – I wouldn't flash that cash round if I were you. Or that fancy watch. We can't take responsibility for anything lost or stolen. Single for fifteen pound a night, or a bed in a dorm for a tenner. Pay in advance. Breakfast and bed linen included. But not towels. I'll inspect your room personally before you leave and if there's any damage you pay for it.'

I couldn't stand the idea of a bed in a dorm, so I said I'd have a single and paid for three nights.

Beany shoved a dog-eared book across the counter. 'Sign here.'

I scribbled Cal Ryan for the first time, and felt like a criminal. The names above mine looked eastern European. I wondered if they were travellers, or new immigrants looking for work. I imagined befriending them, telling them about my talented Polish musician friend. Or maybe this wasn't the sort of place you made friends. I couldn't really imagine that international sing-song happening here. Beany took back the book and frowned so deeply at my name that I wondered if he'd somehow worked out that it was a fake, but then he looked at me quite kindly and said, 'Look, son, keep your head down, all right? I'm not saying this is a bad area, but – ach, you know what I'm saying. Mind yourself.'

He handed me a key and told me I could go and leave my stuff in the room – it was on the ground floor – but then I'd have to clear off and come back after five.

The room, down a long dark corridor that smelled of bleach – which was better than some of the things it could have smelled of – was tiny, with a single bed against the wall, a wooden chair, a few hooks for clothes and an incongruously pink sink in the corner. There was a bathroom next door, tiny, clean but damp. I'd have to go out and buy a cheap towel, which was just one of the many essentials I didn't have.

It wasn't even three o'clock. I'd been trudging the streets of Belfast all day and all I wanted to do was fling myself down on the empty bed and sleep. But Beany was waiting for me to hand my key back in and then I'd have to make myself scarce for another two hours.

I didn't want to leave anything behind, though my arms ached from carrying, so I hefted my backpack over one shoulder, grabbed my guitar case and set off again. I headed for the city centre. I'd seen enough of Belfast with Toni to know that parts of it were really nice so I didn't actually need to hang round the scuzzy bits. I'd find another café, relax until it was time to go back to the Crossroads and then—

Then what? I wasn't great with my own company. Last week would have been lonely if it hadn't been for Toni coming home every day. I could find a pub, and stay there until it was late and I wasn't sober enough to notice the surroundings of the Crossroads. But then I'd be even broker. And Cal Ryan wasn't meant to be that guy – the one who got off his head when things got tough.

In a café near the City Hall, I read the *Belfast Telegraph* and drank a cup of coffee as slowly as I could. They did free top-ups, but when a gaggle of women and prams crowded in, and then a group of girls in school uniforms, and all the tables but mine were full, the waitress gave me a meaningful look and told me I could pay at the till, so I sighed, picked up my stuff and left. It was still only four. Toni would be getting home from school soon. Why hadn't I said goodbye properly? She'd have given me her number, and even without a phone, I could have got in touch with her. There were still a few phone boxes around if you searched hard enough. In fact, there was a payphone in the hall back at the Crossroads beside Beany's desk.

Outside, a last-ditch afternoon sun had come out and the twang of a guitar, badly played, drifted from the next street. I walked past the busker, just to give myself a direction to head in. He was an old guy, bashing away on three chords. He was shite but he had a couple of coins in his guitar case.

This gave me an idea. I didn't know what the rules were for busking in this city, and I didn't care. I crossed a main road and found a street that was busy with people but away from traffic noise, set down my backpack, took out my guitar and started playing. I hammered out a few well-known songs. People don't want to be surprised: they want what they already know. For about twenty minutes nobody took any notice of me, though sometimes their steps bounced in time to the music as they walked past. It'd have been great if they'd paid me for making them feel bouncy but they never bothered. I kept thinking, I'll just do one more and then I'll go to the pub.

I strummed a few chords, not thinking about anything except the next song, looking down at my guitar because I felt weird about being so exposed.

'You're dead good.' I looked up to see two girls looking at me. What was it about playing the guitar in public and meeting girls? These were younger, though, and looked like sisters, both skinny and blonde and sort of fragile-looking, the younger-looking one in an untidy school uniform with a very short skirt, the other in jeans.

'My boyfriend plays the guitar,' the one in uniform said, and gave a little giggle. She had huge eyes, made bigger by false eyelashes, and eyebrows that looked painted on.

'Wise up, Shania, he's not your boyfriend,' said her sister. 'Come on.' She pulled at her arm.

Shania sighed. '*She* fancies him herself,' she said. She scrabbled in the pocket of her jacket, and placed a fifty pence coin in my guitar case.

'Thanks,' I said, and watched them teeter down the street in shoes that were too high for them. At the corner Shania turned round and gave me the thumbs up.

I smiled at her, and kept on playing.

11

Being in a pub on your own was shite. On Friday I took a shine to a couple of girls but their boyfriends turned up. On Saturday I found a bar with music, and it looked like the kind of place Toni might go to – kind of alternative – but it was a tenner to get in, and I didn't want to waste a tenner.

I paid for another week at the hostel. I told Beany I loved Belfast and wanted to get to know it properly. 'Fair play to you,' he said, leaning on his mop. He said I was no bother and he wished all his guests were as easy. He was cleaning up after a stag party. He put his hand into the small of his back the way Louise used to when she was tired. 'I'm getting too old for this,' he said. The stag party had been thrown out, even though they'd booked for another night. Beany's rules were simple: zero tolerance on drugs or what Beany called unacceptable drunkenness – which basically meant puking, fighting or trashing the place. He seemed to do all the work on his own, and I never saw any other staff the whole time I stayed there.

There was a so-called TV lounge with a shelf of crappy paperbacks and DVDs and two oversized sofas, but I only managed one evening of the old *Who are you? Where are you from? Where are travelling to? Isn't this a dive? Have you ever been to …?* After a day's busking I never felt like talking. Most of them were in groups anyway, chatting away in their own languages.

I still didn't feel that comfortable in the streets around the hostel, but I kept my head down and my wallet in a zipped pocket.

By Wednesday, I'd stopped feeling like I was on some kind of strange budget holiday. I turned right automatically out of the hostel, whereas on other mornings I'd had to stop and get my bearings. I was wearing my last half-clean T-shirt under a hoody that I'd managed to spill tomato ketchup on, so one of my tasks for the day was to find a laundrette. I'd washed some pants and socks in the bathroom at the hostel, in shower gel, and hung them round my bedroom to dry but they were wrinkly and itchy so I can't have done a great job. I had my dirty clothes in my back-pack, so I was a bit more laden-down than usual, but I no longer even noticed the weight of my guitar case.

I could busk all morning now without getting tired, though my fingertips were permanently hot and I had to keep drinking water because my throat got rusty. I'd bought a bottle in a supermarket, and stocked up from the tap in the Crossroads kitchen every morning. You didn't get much money in the mornings, so sometimes I gave up early if I'd earned enough for a coffee, and then went back to catch the lunchtime trade. I made a commitment to myself only to use busking money for day-to-day expenses. It became a kind of pride thing. When I was RyLee, Ricky used to negotiate my contracts and yeah, I earned enough for that Audi. But it felt much more like I'd earned the coins that plinked into my guitar case every day, like I *owned* them.

I had about five places I liked, in various parts of the city centre, and so far nobody had come up and told me to piss off. There wasn't as much going on in the streets as there was in Dublin. Fewer buskers and beggars, hardly anyone selling flowers or tatty tourist souvenirs – in Dublin you couldn't move for them. And far fewer addicts. I wasn't naïve enough to think there weren't drugs around, but the kind of people who roared at each other in the centre of Dublin, all cheekbones and bad teeth and tracksuits – they just weren't here. Or at least not in the streets where I was. And that was another thing that made me stay. I felt safe.

It was a good morning. An American tourist gave me a fiver, which had never happened before, and which paid for getting my clothes washed. The laundrette was warm, and someone had left a paper behind which distracted me while my clothes were swirling round. It was last weekend's, which was bad from a news point of view, but good because there was an Arts section with listings of films and bands and clubs. There looked to be plenty going on, but the names of the pubs and venues meant nothing to me. I didn't know much about Belfast, but I knew how easy it would be to walk into the wrong pub in the wrong area. There was a pub round the corner from the Crossroads, with wire mesh across the window, and I knew by instinct that it wasn't somewhere you'd want to open your mouth with a Dublin accent.

It was the same paper I'd looked at with Toni in Kopi the Sunday before last. When we'd talked about gigs and I'd said she should go to that open mic night – where was it? Something to do with a flower. The Daffodil? No. But suddenly there it was – the same listing as before. The Bluebell. Open mic every Wednesday; all welcome.

Not on a school night, she'd said, but surely there was a *chance* she'd go? With the competition so soon?

It was worth a try.

It rained all afternoon, that cold, northern rain that lashes sideways and settles in the backs of your knees. My hair dripped down the back of my hoody and made me shiver. The spot in the arcade was already taken by the time I finished at the laundrette, so I put my guitar back in its case and went to sit in a café even though my wet jeans were sticking to my legs. I knew from experience there was no point in going back to the Crossroads a minute before five. Even though Beany liked me, he liked his rules more.

I had to break my own rules. I'd spent all I'd earned on the laundrette, so I had to dig into my dwindling stash to pay for a cup of tea and some chips. I could skip tea that night since I'd have to spend some money in the Bluebell. But maybe Toni would be there, and her mum would have calmed down, and even though I knew she wouldn't want me staying there again, it would give me somewhere to go that wasn't the streets, or a café, or the Crossroads.

I wasn't used to this much of my own company and I found me pretty boring. Maybe that's why things worked out the way they did at the Bluebell. Or maybe I'd just been too good for too long, and I was ready to break out.

12

By ten I knew they weren't coming. But I stayed.

I stayed because it was more fun than lying on my bed at the Crossroads. I stayed because the Bluebell, grubby round the edges but full of gig posters and cheerful bar staff, and with old 1970s album covers pasted to the ceiling, was my kind of place; and because I liked watching the succession of musicians getting set up and guessing which ones would be good and which would be shit. At the moment, it was about half and half. Nobody was as original as Toni and Marysia, even though some of the musicians were technically better. The four lads on stage now – The Maloners – were enthusiastic and loud, but not overly burdened with talent. They had their fans, though – a gaggle of girls about my age, all taking photos on their phones and cheering when the lead singer introduced a song.

I leaned over the bar and ordered another beer.

'They're class, aren't they?' said the girl beside me, placing her elbows on the counter. She had red hair like Toni's but hers was long and dyed; you could see the brown roots. I thought, very briefly, of Louise. She had a strappy top which showed a tattoo on her shoulder, and she was thin and pretty and tall, but when I looked down she was wearing stilettos. The heels reminded me of that kid Shania who'd given me my first Belfast busking money.

'Yeah,' I lied. She was probably one of their groupies.

'We're all doing performing arts at college,' she said, indicating the table full of girls.

'Are you in a band yourself?' I asked.

'I do musical theatre,' she said importantly. 'I sometimes get up and do a song but it's not really the right crowd for it here. They like you to do your own stuff. But Liam – see Liam, on bass?' She leaned closer and whispered in my ear, 'I'm trying to get into his pants. So – have to show him I'm keen.' She smiled, showing small white teeth.

'Ah, no,' I said. 'Act like you're not keen. That's the way to get him interested.' I gave her a RyLee smile and she giggled, but I felt suddenly depressed. A rush of what-the-hell-am-I-doing-here rolled over me. I downed my beer and ordered another one.

'So where d'you come from?' the girl asked. 'You look dead familiar.'

I stiffened. 'Tipperary,' I said. I didn't think I'd ever been to Tipperary. I hoped she hadn't either.

'And did you ever work in Starbucks on the Lisburn Road?'

I shook my head. 'No.'

'Because there's a guy there is the spit of you.'

I relaxed. She asked me what I was doing in Belfast and I said just passing through. She said she shared a flat with Nicky and Vanessa. Nicky and Vanessa turned round and waved at us. Her name was Olivia and she was from Derry and she was twenty. She'd fancied Liam for ages and she didn't *think* he was gay – she had excellent gaydar, because, like, musical theatre? – but he'd never shown the slightest interest. So maybe he just didn't fancy her?

'Ah, he'd need to be mad if he doesn't,' I said. Flirting with her cheered me up. It wasn't hard. She was pretty and friendly and we were both fairly pissed. I stopped caring about the money I was wasting. I forgot that I'd come here looking for Toni and Marysia. I even stopped listening to the music, though the band on now had a girl with a great bluesy voice. Liam, a short guy with a large head, sat down with Nicky and Vanessa and downed a pint of Guinness that someone had left for him. He didn't seem gay. But then, I did *not* have excellent gaydar.

'Is he looking over?' Olivia asked.

'Who cares?' I touched her ponytail.

'If you want to kiss me, you can,' she said. It wasn't the most romantic offer I'd ever had. But I leaned over and kissed her small mouth. She responded enthusiastically and it was good, because kissing is good, and for nearly a week I'd hardly talked to anyone, let alone kissed someone. Her exploring hands suggested that she was up for more than just kissing. She whispered, 'D'you want to go outside? There's a place – round the back. Private.' She pulled me to my feet. My head swam with beer and surprise, but I lurched after her down the stairs and out through the back door.

She'd done it before. I don't mean sex. Obviously she'd done that quite a few times. I mean sex in an alleyway behind a pub, with a stranger. She had a condom ready. It was rushed. She didn't look at me. She kept hold of her handbag in one hand the whole time. Afterwards I zipped up my jeans. She wrote her number on a scrap of paper. (*I can't believe you haven't got a phone! That's so weird!*) I shoved it into my pocket and knew I'd never call her, and I knew she wouldn't care.

I got lost on the way back to the Crossroads. Maybe just as well, even though I wandered into an area that would have been scary if I hadn't been so pissed, because by the time I was dragging myself up the front steps I felt very sober. No danger of getting thrown out for unacceptable drunkenness.

Lying in my bed, with the room spinning if I opened my eyes – maybe not as sober as I thought – I let myself think of Louise. She used to hate me coming home drunk or stoned. Or not coming home at all. She must be worried. I shouldn't have just disappeared. Maybe I should get in touch. Tell her I was travelling, and I was fine, but I wouldn't be home for a bit.

Was I fine? I had somewhere to stay and something to do, and being a free-spirited troubadour had been enough for a while, but now it wasn't. I thought of the lump of weed stuffed into the bottom of my backpack, and if I'd had matches I'd have skinned up and to hell with Beany finding me and chucking me out.

The trouble was I was crap at being alone. I didn't like picking people up in bars and I didn't seem to know how to make friends in a normal way. Toni and Marysia weren't just the only people I knew in this city; they were the most interesting girls I'd ever known, and they made me feel I could do something right. When I was with them I didn't feel like the kind of person who shagged strangers in alleyways and then tore up their phone numbers. RyLee had been that kind of guy. I'd hoped Cal Ryan wasn't.

And the music. I could put up with a lot just to be part of the music.

I thought I could remember Toni's address. I wouldn't just turn up because of her fearsome mother, and I couldn't phone her or email her or look her up on Facebook. But I could write an old-fashioned letter. I could ask if the offer to join the band was still open.

And if not, maybe it was time to move on.

13

Dear Toni and Marysia,

Hope things are going well. I'm still in Belfast. I'm sorry I didn't say goodbye properly. If you'd still like me to join the band, or help with your guitar playing, or even just listen, then let me know. I don't have a lot on, and it would be great to see you again. I ended up getting a phone so you can call me on 07987701239.

Cheers

Cal

14

Marysia's shed, at the end of a long, slightly overgrown garden behind a small terraced house, was dusty and cold, and full of broken garden furniture, pots of paint and old bikes.

'It's not brilliant,' Marysia admitted, 'but you can't hear us from the house.'

'I thought we'd be at your house, Toni,' I said, trying not to sound disappointed. I set my guitar down but didn't take off my hoody.

'Well – you're still not my mum's favourite person.'

'Fair enough.' I shrugged and opened my guitar case.

'We've thought about your role,' Marysia said. 'You can do all the lead guitar and help me with backing vocals.'

'Cool. And I get – what – a third of what we make?'

'Um. We've never actually made anything yet.' Marysia looked at Toni a bit helplessly. We were all slightly shy.

'OK. Let's start,' Toni said. We tuned up. It was so cold that the best thing to do was to play as hard as possible.

By the third bar of 'Plastic Girls' I relaxed. It was pretty crowded, and hard to play without bumping elbows and tripping over each other, but Toni kept turning and grinning at me, her eyes sparkling. And the music sounded better than ever. Busking had made me sharper, and it was lovely just to play and not worry about singing, except for backing vocals.

We went through all seven songs, including 'Secret Self' (plus chorus), and then we flopped down on the only furniture in the shed, Marysia and Toni sharing a saggy sunlounger and I on a deckchair.

Toni high-fived me. 'Sounding good,' she said.

I smiled. 'It's nice to have someone to play with. I've been busking on my own all week.'

'Is *that* what you've doing? I assumed you'd moved on.' Did this mean she'd been thinking about me?

'I thought I should see a bit of Belfast. And I started busking and that's been going really well. So I thought, if I can make enough to keep myself going I might as well. And then – well, it was stupid to be in town and not get in touch with you.' I made it sound like it wasn't a big deal. I made it sound like I hadn't written about ten drafts of the letter I'd sent them.

'You've been busking for a living? That's impressive,' Marysia said. 'We should busk some time, Toni.'

'I wouldn't call it a *living*. But it's enough to get by. I made enough for a phone yesterday.' I couldn't keep the pride out of my voice.

'No way. It took me months to save for my iPhone.' Toni sounded impressed. 'Have you been busking for millionaires?'

I slipped my hand into my back pocket and brought out my phone.

'Oh my God. That's the most tragic thing I've ever seen. That's even worse than my dad's.'

I laughed. 'Fifteen quid. Fiver for a SIM. Pay as you go.'

'Don't let anybody see that when you're with us,' Toni warned. 'Though I suppose they might think it is ironic.'

'So where are you staying?' Marysia asked.

'A hostel.' I didn't say exactly where.

'And you'll definitely stay till Backlash?' Toni asked. 'We don't want to get used to you and then have you walk out on us. Again.'

'Of course I won't.' I was about to remind her that it was her ma that had thrown me out, but I knew what she meant so I held my tongue.

'A flat'd be cheaper than a hostel, wouldn't it?' Marysia asked.

'I suppose. But then you need to have people to share with, and references, and sign contracts and – ah, you know, all that shit.'

'We have a gig on Friday night,' Toni interrupted.

'Hopefully,' Marysia corrected. 'We have to audition on Monday. It's for the school charity concert, in aid of Malawi.'

'We have to *audition* to be in the school charity concert?'

'It might only be a school concert, but we need the practice.'

'OK. So I get to see all your friends? Cool. Are they all as hot as you two?' I waited to see them blush and look shy and pleased at being called hot. They didn't. Which made me burble on stupidly, 'Actually – they're not, are they? I saw some girls from your school in town – recognised the uniform – and they were mingers.'

'Hey! You're going to have to work on your attitude to women if you're going to be in this band,' Toni said. 'You're not using words like minger. And we don't care whether or not you think we're hot.' She said 'hot' like it was something ridiculous.

'God, I love bossy girls,' I said with a grin. 'Boss me some more.'

She looked me up and down. Not in a good way. I looked me up and down too, and saw what she meant. I was a lot scruffier than the boy she'd picked up in Dublin. My clothes were clean but rumpled.

'Cal,' she said. 'Our image – I mean Polly's Tree's image – is quite – you know – well, clean cut.'

'Is it?' Marysia said. 'I didn't think we had an image.'

'Of course we have an image. Look, Cal, don't take offence but would you mind shaving?'

'Shaving?'

'Yeah. It's just – that hairy hipster look? It's not really *us*.'

I stroked my chin. 'I haven't been growing a beard on purpose. I just left home in a hurry and a razor was one of the things I didn't pack.'

'That was totally my fault,' Toni said quickly.

'Huh?'

'Spiriting you away from the park?'

'Oh, right. I don't mind shaving. I've sort of got used to the beard but it's not a fashion statement.'

'Not like your phone, then?'

I threw my capo at her and she caught it and laughed, and I had this sudden rush of joy.

'I'm going to get us a drink,' Marysia said. 'Won't be long. Don't come up to the house – they'll all get far too excited at seeing an actual *boy*. And I bet you're a Catholic, aren't you?'

'I suppose so,' I said. 'God, you northerners are obsessed with religion. Even the Polish ones.'

Marysia laughed.

'Why Polly's Tree?' I asked, when she'd gone and Toni and I were just messing about with the guitars. She'd obviously been practising since I'd left. Maybe now we'd be able to practise together. If only I could get round her mum.

'It's the name of a Sylvia Plath poem.'

I grinned. 'Course it is.'

'Stop it.'

'At least it isn't one of those girl band names with pussy or doll or kitten or something in it.' I wondered if she had heard of Sweet Treat, but I didn't ask.

'Ew. Hardly. And I suppose now it's not a girl band at all.'

'Does that matter?'

'Well – no. It's just that we kind of started the band after this songwriting workshop we did in the summer and it was nearly all boys. And that annoyed us. So we just saw it as a girl thing, I suppose.'

'I don't mind being in the background. You can think of me as your session guitarist.'

She looked at me closely. 'Is that really enough for you?'

'Totally.'

Marysia came back with a bottle of Coke and a packet of Polish biscuits, and we sat round and had a sort of picnic, chatting about what to play at the audition. The electric light in the shed was harsh, and we all had our coats on, but even so, it felt cosy. I was in no rush to get back to the Crossroads.

When a knock came to the door we all jumped, and Marysia swore in Polish. The door opened and a fattish girl, younger than us, came in. She ignored Toni, gawped at me, and said to Marysia in a whiney voice, 'Have you taken my hockey skirt?'

'Piss off, Krystyna. Toni and I could *both* fit into your hockey skirt. Why would I have it?'

Krystyna's eyes filled with tears. 'Yeah, you'd probably like that, you big lez!' she cried.

I waited for Marysia to hit back with another insult, but she didn't. She blushed and bit her lip. Toni flung her arm round Marysia and gave Krystyna a hard stare. Then she stuck her tongue out at her, waggled it suggestively and said, 'Oh, you'd better watch out, Kryssie, in case I just can't resist—'

'I'm telling Mama!' Krystyna yelled, and blundered back out of the shed.

Marysia shook Toni's arm off. 'You shouldn't tease

her,' she said. She still looked flustered. 'You only make her worse.'

'She asks for it,' Toni said.

'My lovely little sister,' Marysia explained to me. 'She just wanted to come and nosy because she knew there was a boy here. She's an idiot. Gets all her ideas from reality TV.'

But is she right? I wanted to ask. *Are* you and Toni more than friends? Is Polly's Tree *a girl thing* in more ways than I know? And if so, why not just say? It's not like it's a big deal these days. But I didn't ask.

15

Beany put down the *Daily Mirror* and whistled. 'Didn't recognise you there, big man.'

I fingered my smooth jaw. 'Fed up with the shaggy look.' I wasn't going to admit I'd done it to please a girl. Especially not a girl who was so resistant to my charms.

'Away busking again?'

I shook my head. 'My band has an audition.' I didn't say it was for an insignificant school concert. It felt good to have an appointment – somewhere to be, someone waiting for me.

'So you're sticking around a while?'

I nodded. 'Is that OK? I mean – the room?'

Beany pursed his lips. 'I'm not meant to let people stay long term. It's registered as a tourist hostel, not a dosshouse.'

'Ah, Mervyn.' I gave him a RyLee smile. His name was Mervyn, and I always remembered to use it, but I still thought of him as Beany.

He looked at the computer screen. 'But we're not too busy.' He scratched the side of his nose. 'And you're no bother. At least you don't come home shouting and boking. You should have seen that bathroom this morning after them rugby players.' He shook his head. 'Dirty hallions. Aye, you can stay.'

'Any discount?' I asked hopefully.

'Get away! You'll not get a bed this cheap outside Maghaberry.' I had no idea what he was talking about, which must have shown on my face because he said, 'That's the jail, son. So I'll put you down for – what? Till the end of October?'

I nodded. The end of October was ages away. I had just about enough to pay for the room until Backlash. After that – well, I'd worry about it when the time came.

I was getting used to walking everywhere, so I didn't mind the hour it took to get to Toni and Marysia's school, following the map Toni had drawn for me since my phone wasn't up to that kind of thing. Whatever else happened as a result of my Belfast adventures, I was going to end up fitter. Especially since I'd pretty much stopped going to the pub. I'd made eleven quid yesterday and I still had most of it because we'd rehearsed again in the evening and Toni had cooked a big curry for us for afterwards. Her mum was out. She hadn't actually *said* that was why it was OK for me to come over, but I sort of knew. It would take more than RyLee's charm and puppy dog eyes to get round that one.

It was weird being in a school. I hadn't been in

one since Ricky pulled me out of school and into rehab in the middle of last year. I was about to be thrown out anyway. Toni's school smelt of polish. I had to wait in Reception under a line of portraits of headmistresses, each one more disapproving than the last, with a hatchet-faced biddy watching me from behind her glass partition. I began to see why Toni'd vetoed the beard. Then a bell rang, making me jump, and suddenly there were girls in maroon blazers spilling out of doors all along the corridor. Every single one of them stared when they saw me and my guitar case. I recognised Krystyna, stomping along behind a group, who all giggled and gawked. But they weren't RyLeens. It was finally sinking in that Northern Ireland was one of the many places in the world where RyLee's brief and modest success hadn't penetrated.

'Hey.' Toni was standing in front of me. I'd forgotten how much her maroon blazer didn't go with her red hair, and she looked different in some way I couldn't put my finger on. 'You found it. Don't look so scared! The audition's in the drama studio. Marysia's meeting us there.'

Lots more girls stared on the way to the drama studio. I did spy a couple of hotties, but when I was with Toni they seemed a bit boring. Though I decided, turning round to look after an Asian girl with a long dark plait and even longer legs, that I could quite go for the short skirt, black tights look.

Toni hit me with the back of her hand. 'Behave,' she said. 'She's way out of your league. And you're here to help us get the gig, not drool over girls.'

Suddenly I realised what was different about her.

'Where's your diamond stud?' I asked.

Embarrassment flickered across her face. 'Oh. Not allowed it in school.'

I grinned. 'Must be awful to have to live by all those petty rules.'

'Come on, Troubadour.'

The drama studio was small and dark, and surrounded by the lunchtime roar that was exactly like my old school, only less raucous because it was all girls. Two girls with clipboards and a woman who looked like she'd rather be eating a sandwich in the stafroom were sitting on chairs like TV judges. A few random girls hung round. It all felt eerily familiar, and it was stupid that I was suddenly more nervous than I had been at any of the *PopIcon* auditions. The room was filled with the screeching of strings being tuned. Marysia, with her bass slung round her neck, stood slightly apart from four girls who were obviously the string quartet.

The woman clapped her hands and raised her voice. 'Girls!' She didn't seem to notice that I wasn't a girl, or maybe she'd just been clapping her hands and shouting 'Girls!' for so many decades that she couldn't stop now. 'We'll have Serendipitous Strings first, and then Polly's – er – Tree.'

Marysia came and stood with me and Toni, grimacing. 'Don't be nervous,' Toni whispered. 'We're *not* being beaten by a group called Serendipitous Strings.'

Serendipitous Strings were probably brilliant if you wanted music to accompany a coffin being lowered into the ground, but even the old woman, whose face had collapsed lower and lower into her chins as the four bows scraped slower and slower, couldn't hide her smile when Toni struck a bright G chord, grinned out at the audience and said in a confident voice that sounded like she'd been performing all her life, 'We're Polly's Tree and this is "Plastic Girls".' She turned back to me and Marysia, nodded, and the song burst into life. It was better than we'd ever rehearsed it. Even an audience of ten made a difference to our spark. Being on a stage with Toni and Marysia was a million times better than singing in the street.

We got the gig no bother. 'Headlining,' Toni said smugly when we were packing up the instruments. 'I insisted.'

Marysia raised her eyebrows at me and sighed. 'She gets like this,' she said. 'She'll be unbearable if we ever have groupies.'

'So how many people will be at the concert?' I asked.

'It's always well attended,' Marysia said. 'Two hundred. Maybe even two fifty.'

'Is that OK, Cal?' Toni asked. 'You won't get stage fright, will you?'

The last gig RyLee had played had been to two thousand, and it had been televised. OK, on an obscure cable channel that clearly nobody in this country watched, but still.

'I think I'll be OK,' I said, grabbing my guitar case.

'So, you little schoolgirls have to go back to class now, don't you?'

* * *

It was sunny for the first time in days, and instead of going back into the city centre I busked on the main road near the school. It was very like where I lived in Dublin only without the sea – cafés and smart shops and lots of yummy mummies hauling buggies out of shiny Range Rovers – and people looked surprised to see a busker.

'Are you collecting for charity, dear?' asked an old lady in a blue coat, fumbling with the clasp of her handbag. 'Which one?'

'Distressed musicians.'

'Oh,' she said, and walked on.

But other people were more generous, and I ended the afternoon with nearly twenty quid. I stopped at Lidl on the way back and stocked up on cheap food. There was officially a kitchen at the Crossroads. It wasn't up to much but you could manage pasta, toast, that kind of thing. Cheaper than going to Burger King every night like I'd done last week. And healthier – I'd been mortified to find a rash of spots lurking under my beard. RyLee had never had spots and Cal Ryan wasn't going to get them either, not with his first real gig on Friday night. I bought some apples to make sure.

'You look cheerful,' Beany said, when I bounced up the steps as he was bending to unlock the bottom bolt of the front door. He stood up gingerly, pressing his fists into the small of his back, his belly straining against his tracksuit top.

'Is your back bad?'

'Ach, I'm tortured.'

'You need somebody to do the heavy work,' I said. 'A man of your age should be taking it easy.'

'Here, less of the cheek.' He shuffled back to his desk and picked up his paper. Then put it down again. 'Would you want a few hours' work?' he asked. 'Cleaning, like.'

That wasn't what I'd meant. I was only being nice. I couldn't think of anything worse than cleaning the Crossroads, especially after a stag party or a crowd of football supporters. But I *was* worried about money – not every day would be as good as today, and it didn't look like Polly's Tree was actually going to earn anything. 'Maybe.'

'Fiver an hour. Cash in hand.'

'That's *way* below the minimum wage.' I thought about the day I'd gone out and bought my Audi.

Beany looked sly. 'Son – you've no ID. I don't know what you're doing here and you're no bother to me, so I don't care. But it's a fiver an hour, cash in hand, no questions asked. Take it or leave it.'

'I'll take it.'

'Good man. There's a big match on Thursday night. The place'll be heaving.'

16

I was heaving myself on Friday morning when I faced the upstairs toilets and the two eight-bed dorms with my mop and bucket. I tied a bandana round my mouth and nose and tried not to breathe in at all. It made busking, even in the rain – it was pouring today – seem like easy money. But when Beany came out to the yard where I was sluicing out the bucket and handed me a tenner, it felt worth it, even though I'd soon be handing it back to him.

'Fair play to you,' he said, grimacing into the drain. 'There's tea made in the kitchen. Come on in out of that.' He looked up at the overflowing gutters splashing into the yard.

I shook the rain from my hair and followed him into the kitchen where two steaming mugs of tea sat on the scratched Formica table. Beany handed me a Penguin. 'Go on,' he said. 'Bonus.'

'Thanks.' I sat down at the table and unwrapped it.

I hadn't had a Penguin for years, and the chocolate was still as thick and delicious as I remembered. Beany sat down opposite me like we were old pals and took a long draw on his own tea.

'You did a good job, son,' he said. 'It's not always that bad. But them dirty beasts is banned now.'

I blew on my tea. And because he was being so friendly, I said, 'B— Mervyn, you're always banning people. But you don't really get much repeat business, do you? And most people only stay one night anyway. So what's the point?'

Beany didn't answer for a while. He twisted his Penguin paper and tied it into a knot. Then he said, 'Look, son, I've been in this city all my life. And I don't mind telling you I've been in the odd wee bit of trouble. I was in and out of jail for most of my twenties. Too fond of the drink. Too fond of a fight.' He sniffed. 'But in there – it wasn't the drink. The drink's nothing. It's them drugs.'

I looked into my cup.

'See in the old days? There was no drugs in this city – well, there was, but the paramilitaries had it under control. See now? Free for all. I've seen what they do to people. I've been running this hostel for seven years and I've never had no bother. 'Cause I have a Zero. Tolerance. Approach.' He unwrapped another Penguin. 'It's the only way, son. I know this isn't the fucking Europa Hotel, and I don't mind a bit of noise and a bit of craic and the odd bit of a mess. But the one thing I won't have is drugs. So I show people I mean business if they overdo it with the drink. And the word gets out: no point trying it on at the Crossroads.'

He drained his cup and pushed back from the table. 'I'll give you a few hours when I can. The oul' back's not getting any better. And since you're an employee now, you don't have to stay out all day. Special perk. Seeing what the weather's like.'

My room at the Crossroads wasn't luxurious but it was dry and private and fairly warm, though the eccentric radiator never kicked into life until halfway through the evening, and with nobody else around until five, I could go into the lounge and see if there was anything on TV. After days busking in the street, this felt like a big treat.

I wondered how my life got so small and simple, and why it somehow felt better than it ever had. But before I settled down to daytime TV, I pulled out the wrapped-up lump of weed from the bottom of my backpack. I wasn't about to get rid of it – I mean, you never knew – but I thought I'd find it a better hiding place. Maybe keep it on me in future. Just to be safe.

17

'Are you sure it's not just nerves?' Toni sounded more rattled than I'd ever known her.

Marysia shook her head, clutching her stomach. 'You know what my periods are like.'

'Um – I should probably start carrying the gear in,' I said.

'If you're going to be in Polly's Tree you'll have to learn not to freak out at the P-word,' Toni snapped. 'Do you want some ibuprofen?' she asked Marysia.

'I took some already. I'll be fine.' She didn't look fine. Her face was the colour of cottage cheese and even her floaty short blue dress looked like it was weighing her down.

'When you get on stage, the adrenalin will kick in,' I said.

'What would you know? Have you ever had crippling period pains?' Toni demanded.

'I've played with a hangover.'

'That's hardly the same.'

'Guys, can we not fight?' Marysia begged. 'Cal's right – the adrenalin will kick in.'

We had to do a soundcheck with one of the music teachers. It was funny being surrounded by leads and mics again, sort of homely, and part of me felt meanly glad that Toni clearly hadn't much of a clue.

'The hall looks huge from here, doesn't it?' she said, giving a little shiver.

I'd been thinking that it looked kind of small, but I said, 'It'll be grand.'

Toni looked down at her denim shorts, black tights and DMs. 'Maybe I should have worn a dress like Marysia,' she said. She chewed her lip, rubbing off half her lipstick. I felt suddenly desperate to say something reassuring but the only words in my head were, *You look beautiful. Those black tights make your legs look amazing and it's all I can do not to touch you.* I fiddled with a lead I'd already checked. 'Don't be nervous,' I said. 'It'll be brilliant.'

Waiting backstage – a music classroom – was the opposite of brilliant. A folk group diddly-deed for hours on stage, which Toni clearly hated. She kept asking Marysia if she felt OK, and Marysia got so fed up that she went outside.

Small dancing girls shrieked and drank Coke and dashed around. Two plain girls bustled about with clipboards. A group of girls in short metallic dresses and stilettos kept looking over at me. One of them, with a huge mane of brownish-gold hair and endless tanned legs, smiled in a way that no girl had smiled at me since Kelly. I'd have given anything for Toni to look at me like that.

'Who are they?' I asked Toni.

'They do really crappy covers to a backing track,' she said. 'Hey – you'd better be focused on our music, and not on Jess's legs.'

'Relax. It's fine.' The truth was, those girls were like loads of girls I'd known in the RyLee days. Cal Ryan had no more than a healthy male interest in them. I took a swig of water from a bottle of Ballygowan and leaned back in one of the too-small chairs, and looked over to where Jess and her clones were practising dance moves.

'Should I go and check on Marysia?' Toni said.

'She said she was going out for some air. You just wind her up.'

'I suppose.' She chewed her lip, smudging her lipstick even more. 'I'm just nervous. And – well, I'm pretty hopeless with sick people.'

'Remind me never to get sick, then.'

The clipboard girls bounced up to tell us we were on after the year nine dancers.

'Oh my God,' Toni said.

'It's going to be brilliant.'

'I wish you'd stop saying that.'

But I was right.

Even though it was only a school concert, it felt *real*. I hadn't expected the lights to be so bright and hot, or the hall beyond the stage to be so dark. Marysia's family were all out there somewhere, and

Toni's mum and some of her friends. I had a sudden feeling of emptiness that there was nobody in the audience for *me*. Beside me, Marysia looked pale in the spotlight but her hair shone, and the light played on the black gloss of her bass. On my other side Toni, plugging in her guitar, looked small and determined and wonderful.

She stepped up to her mic. 'We're Polly's Tree, and this is "Plastic Girls". One, two, three …'

And then it was just us and the music. When Toni realised how good the mic made her voice sound, she started really playing with it. She could stand close and almost whisper and she sounded amazing and echoey. I tried not to look too much at her lips against the mic. Marysia's bass underpinned the song and even when Toni was slow on a few chord changes my lead guitar was there to cover it up. We all helped each other. I'd never had that on stage before. I'd always been alone.

The applause was intoxicating: clapping, a few cheers. I turned to both Marysia and Toni and grinned and they grinned back. Toni stood beaming in the spotlight, and forgot that she was meant to be announcing the next song, so I stepped up to my mic and said, 'Thanks. This is called "You Think You Know Me",' and Toni caught my eye and smiled a gorgeous slow smile and the stage was the world and we were all the people in it.

It seemed to last for ages and yet be over in seconds, and then we were in the wings, with a little girl dressed as Dorothy, clapping and telling us we were great and she wished she didn't have to follow us.

'Ah, our first groupie!' I said, pulling one of her dark plaits. 'I love your ruby slippers.'

'Hey.' Toni was beside me. 'No flirting now. Shelby doesn't just look twelve because of the plaits and the gingham, she actually is twelve,' she said, but she was smiling. 'You were fantastic.'

'No, *you* were fantastic.'

'*You* were.'

'Was *I* not fantastic?' Marysia asked in a plaintive voice.

'Yes!' Toni pulled us all into a sweaty group hug.

From the stage we could hear Shelby singing 'Somewhere Over The Rainbow' in a sweet high voice.

We were all hyper, hugging and laughing, but when we went back into the classroom to get our guitar cases, Marysia sat down heavily on one of the desks and groaned. 'Owww. I think the adrenalin just wore off.'

'But we're going out for a drink.' Panic stabbed me at the thought of the evening ending. I wanted to sit in a bar, reliving every note, every word of the performance, prolonging this wonderful high.

Marysia shook her head. 'I need a hot water bottle and my bed. I'm going to catch Mama and Tata for a lift. I'll give you a call tomorrow.'

Toni looked at me. 'I don't want to go home yet. Do you?'

'No way. Going straight home on your own after a gig – especially your first gig – that's not allowed.'

'There's a post-concert party but—'

'It'll be crap. So take me somewhere amazing.'

The South Tavern wasn't exactly amazing; it was a quiet suburban pub with a middle-aged crowd, but it was nearby, and easy to walk to, our guitar cases bumping together. Toni could have given hers to her mum to take home, but somehow I knew she loved walking with it, being seen with it, looking like a musician.

'It's a shame Marysia had to miss out,' she said, once we were settled in a corner, the guitar cases under the table, and two pints of cider on it. I didn't disagree out loud; and I didn't ask, *Look, what's the story with you two?* because I didn't want anything to risk this fragile high. We clinked glasses, and I downed about a quarter of mine in one go. Toni sipped more cautiously.

'That's better,' I said, wiping my mouth. 'Must have sweated out about a pint of liquid.'

'Nice.'

I leaned back in the chair. 'I'm glad you came out,' I said. 'I couldn't have stood just going back to the hostel on my own. You know – you feel so high; you don't want to come down.'

'Is your hostel not full of fit Australian girl backpackers? You mean to say you haven't been having loads of really meaningful, spiritual experiences?'

'Hardly. You should have seen what I had to clean up this morning!' I started telling her, hoping to impress her with my hard work.

'Stop it!' Toni said. 'I don't want to hear about – ugh!' She wriggled her fingers in disgust. 'I don't know how Marysia can want to do medicine.'

'Sorry.'

'So what's *your* ambition? I mean – what will you do after your gap year? Uni?'

I shook my head quickly. 'Haven't got the qualifications.'

She wrinkled her forehead. 'But you've left school. You're older than me.'

'Didn't finish sixth year.'

'How come?'

I wrinkled my nose. 'Boring story.'

'I have a high boredom threshold.'

'Well, I sort of dropped out.'

She was silent for a few seconds. 'Why?' she asked.

I took a long draw on my pint. I really didn't want to tell her this. But something about being on my own with her, having shared that magic time on stage, something about not having been able to talk to anyone for ages, made me want to be truthful. Or at least semi-truthful. 'I had a few – um, issues.'

'What sort of issues?'

'Substance issues.'

'Ah. Like what?' I could tell she was trying hard to sound cool, but that she was a bit freaked.

I sighed. 'This and that. Pills mostly. I wasn't really *addicted,*' I added quickly, because her expression had graduated from a bit freaked to properly shocked. 'Not the hard stuff. I just partied too hard and it all got a bit out of control, so they packed me off to this place for a few months, and now it's fine.' I drained my pint.

'You sure?'

'Yeah.' I looked at the empty glass. 'OK, I like the odd drink. But I haven't touched anything illegal for – well, ages. And since I've been up here I'm not even tempted. Last year things were so – complicated.' I wished I could tell her how complicated, but I couldn't. Apart from anything else, I didn't want to sound all, *Poor me, I couldn't take the pressure*. 'And now life's simple,' I went on. 'I play my music, earn enough to stay at the hostel. It's grand.' It sounded pretty aimless even as I said it, and Toni might not have meant to look disapproving, but she did. 'Not everybody's a high achiever like you, Toni.'

She twisted her glass. 'Who's *they*? You said *they* packed you off to rehab.'

I didn't answer for a bit. 'My mum and stepdad. He's a bit of a control freak and one of the things he liked controlling was me. That's another reason to stay up here. He wanted me to go back and finish school but – I don't know; I feel too old now.'

'But you can't just give up your education. You don't imagine,' she added, as if I were about ten, 'that Polly's Tree is suddenly going to be *discovered* or anything, do you? I mean, we're great, and we're even better since you joined, but Marysia and I – well, we're not naïve. We don't have dreams of stardom or anything.'

I laughed. 'No, Toni, I have absolutely no dreams of stardom. Now, it's definitely your round.'

While she was away at the bar, the two yummy mummies at the next table, all blonde bobs and Boden, started chatting to me, and I used the old RyLee charm just to see if I still had it. Their lip-glossed mouths drooped when Toni showed up.

'You're in there,' she said, when they turned away. 'If you like older women.'

'They're meant to be more grateful. But I like them young and fresh.'

'We're seriously going to have to work on your attitude to women,' she warned.

'Maybe at the same time as we work on your sense of humour?'

She smirked.

'So what do *you* want?' I asked. 'If it's not rock stardom?'

'Well – uni, obviously.' Yes, of course it was obvious for someone like Toni, who was clever and focused. 'I want to be a lawyer. Oxford, maybe.'

'That sounds like harder work than cleaning the Crossroads, even after a stag night.'

'I know.' She sighed. 'It's serious pressure.'

'You sound like you don't really want it?'

She looked into her glass. 'I think it's more my mum's dream. She had a place to do a PhD in Oxford. And then she met my dad, and fell madly in love, and got married, and had me, and stayed here instead because he wouldn't move to England. Only Dad ran off with a fiddle player from Galway.'

'When?'

'Oh – I was eightish. Old enough to know what was going on.' She took a long sip. 'And it's not like the Galway fiddler was even the love of his life – there's been I don't know how many since then. It's like – he always just went for what he wanted. And Mum – well, she went for *him*, but she lost out on other stuff.'

'And she blames you?'

'No, not blames. She wants me to have more options than she did. I mean – mums always do, don't they? I bet yours didn't want you to be a druggie drifter.'

'Not exactly how I'd describe myself.' My lips tightened.

'Oh God, Cal – I'm sorry.' She grabbed my arm, but only for a few seconds. 'It's not how I'd describe you either. What I mean is – does she mind you being up here?'

'She hasn't said anything about it,' I said truthfully. I sipped my pint, more slowly than the previous ones. I felt self-conscious now she knew more about my past. Now that she saw me as a *druggie drifter*. 'My mum was in a band in the nineties. Just covers in pubs, but she always loved music. Always wished she'd gone further with it. But she had me and that kind of stopped her. My dad was around for a lot less time than yours – like about eight years less. But she was glad when I got into music. And my stepdad – well, he was kind of into music too. But he's a bastard.' And that was all I wanted to say about Ricky. I twirled my fingertip round the top of my glass and the silence felt heavy around us.

'Well, my dad's a cheater and a liar,' Toni said.

'Sounds like a country song,' I said, trying to lighten the mood.

'Maybe we should be better at having our *own* dreams,' Toni said. 'So what's yours?' She smiled at me, her eyes big and starry, her cheeks pink, a little drunk; and I was a little drunk too, and very aware that the night had to end soon, and the only dream I could think of was the one where she felt about me like I felt about her. I stretched out my hand towards hers on the table.

Before I could touch her, she said, 'I should go,' and pushed her glass away.

'I'll walk you home.'

We were silent on the short walk to her house. It was in darkness, the street silent. I couldn't help looking up at the window of the room I'd stayed in and thinking how much cosier it would be to be snuggling down there, with Toni next door, than walking another two miles to the Crossroads.

'See you Sunday.' We had a rehearsal in Marysia's shed. I wanted to hug her – two hours ago all three of us had been tangled together in a sweaty band hug – but the high was over now, and she was looking up at me with tired, gritty eyes and swinging her guitar case like she couldn't wait to get inside.

One of the things about being *in there* was learning to be more mindful of what they called your triggers. And most of the time I didn't think about it because, like I'd told Toni, I didn't have any issues now. But I recognised the sour icy feeling that was creeping from my core and making me irritated with stupid things like a drunk man reeling down the street opposite me singing 'My Way', which an hour ago I'd have found funny, and maybe even harmonised with. It was my old enemy, the post-gig low. Which often followed the post-gig high.

RyLee used to do all sorts of daft stuff to keep it at bay, even when he was being driven home by a smug/raging/critical (depending on how the gig had gone) Ricky. Cal Ryan had more sense. OK, he was slightly pissed, and he had a lump of weed tucked away, but he never thought about using it – and he certainly wasn't shagging some random girl outside a bar.

Because he was falling harder and harder for the girl he'd just walked home.

18

The Internet café was dark and smelled of sweat. I seemed to spend a lot of this new life being grateful for places I wouldn't have been seen dead in before. If you'd asked me a month ago if Internet cafés even still existed, I'd have said no, not in the developed world. The Crossroads had Wi-Fi but that was no good for someone whose proper phone was at the bottom of the Liffey. I hadn't been online since the day I'd borrowed Toni's phone and checked that Ricky was alive. I hesitated before logging on to my email.

You have 79 unread emails.

I deleted all the ones telling me I hadn't been on Facebook lately, and the ones trying to sell me Viagra, and that left 26. A message from Kelly – I had a moment of thinking, *Who?* – telling me I was a shit and she never wanted to see me again. I don't know why I bothered to read it. Three from Ricky that I deleted unread, and the rest from Mum.

I'd been trying not to let myself think about Mum. But my talk with Toni had made me feel terrible about leaving her without a word. The cumulative effect of her emails made me feel worse. It started with *Please come home, son. Ricky's very angry but he'll let bygones be bygones.*

Went through *I don't where you've gone, Ry. Ricky won't let me report you missing because he knows there'll be bad publicity. That's the last thing you need.* (By which she meant, the last thing Ricky needs.)

And then, *We know you're OK because of the activity on your bank account. Ricky's reported your card stolen. We know you'll be home when you run out of cash.*

And then *Ricky hasn't spoken to your friends because we don't want to run the risk of them talking to the press. This is for your protection! You're lucky Ricky didn't press charges for you assaulting him.*

Ricky, Ricky, Ricky. Yeah, she cared about me, and even missed me, but it was obvious what mattered most. I gave up after that. Clicked *Delete All*. Then I composed this.

Hi Mum. Sorry about the silence. I lost my phone and it's not easy to get online. And I'm sorry about the way I left. I panicked. I didn't say I was sorry for hitting Ricky. *But I'm fine. I have friends and a place to stay. Don't ask me to come home. Ricky wants to control me too much. I know I've put you through a bad time. Again. Please don't worry about me. I promise I'm fine.* I read it over and then added: *AND I'M NOT TAKING ANYTHING. NOT EVEN TEMPTED. xxx*

I pressed *Send* before I could change my mind, then

logged off. I didn't want to be tempted to Google Ricky and see what he was up to, or go on Facebook. There was nobody I missed or cared about except Mum. And not enough to go back. I didn't think of it as *home*. Home was – well, I wasn't sure. But it wasn't Ricky's house.

* * *

The low seemed to have affected the girls too. Or maybe it was nerves about the competition which was now a few days away.

On Sunday in Marysia's shed – which was even colder than last week – we huddled in coats, and argued about the set list. We had to play two songs.

'"Plastic Girls", definitely.' Toni wrote it down. She was wearing a really brightly striped rainbow scarf that clashed gorgeously with her red hair 'And "Secret Self"?'

'"Secret Self" isn't your best song,' I said.

They both turned on me. '"Secret Self" is really important to us,' Toni said. Marysia smiled, and I had this sense of something going on that I wasn't part of and wasn't meant to know about.

I looked away. 'The chord sequences are practically the same as for "Plastic Girls". "You Think You Know Me" shows your range better.'

They looked at each other, and then at me, as if in disbelief. Even I didn't know why I was being so insistent. The songs weren't *that* different.

Toni strummed an A, aggressively. 'No offence,

busker boy, but you're getting a bit up yourself – you've no more experience than us.'

I bent over my guitar, noticing, in the harsh light from the bare light bulb, that it was scratched and had a patch of something sticky just under the bridge. *Busker boy.* I frowned, licked my finger and rubbed it over the stain. I wondered what they would say if I told them how much experience I did have – that I knew my way round a recording studio, that the TV studio where they'd filmed *PopIcon* was probably ten times the size of the pub function room where Backlash was happening—

But it was crap, that experience. Glorified karaoke. RyLee sang to a backing track, the songs Ricky or the production company told him to sing. He had an autotuner to correct any wonky vocals. The dancing, the clothes, the blond highlights – they were more important than the music. I could hardly even remember any of the songs. *Busker boy* was meant as an insult but I'd learned more about music in two weeks of busking than RyLee had ever known, so I made myself look up and smile at both girls, and say, 'I know. I don't know why you let me play with you.'

'Right.' Toni unwound her scarf. 'Let's get started.'

We decided to play the two contenders with 'Plastic Girls' in the middle to see which sounded better with it. Even though we were only in Marysia's shed, and my fingers cramped with cold for the first few bars, we sounded great. That one live gig had made all the difference. Toni was far more confident, letting her voice soar for the:

You think you know me but you really don't.
You think I'll love you but I know I won't.

and then going really quiet and cracked and heart-breaking on:

My heart's too wise to be fooled like that again.

And Marysia, always proficient and reliable, hit the bass with a verve that lifted her playing into another realm. As for me – well, I stepped up to the mark too, especially for 'You Think You Know Me', picking out the guitar solo with the precision of a classical guitarist, showing off. *Busker boy* indeed. Mind you, I played 'Secret Self' really well too, to show how professional I could be, even though I didn't want us to play it at Backlash.

When we were done we flumped onto the damp-cushioned garden chairs. Toni pushed her short red hair back behind her ears and blew out through her fringe. 'OK,' she said. 'It does sound better.' She grinned. 'I was wrong.'

'Wow. *World exclusive: Toni Flynn admits she was wrong*. Can I have that in writing?' I asked.

She threw her rainbow scarf at me. I wound it round my neck, trying not to let myself breathe in its scent – perfume, wool, and something rosy and sharp that was just Toni, and that I'd have recognised anywhere. *Rainbow – wasn't that a gay thing? Why couldn't I just ask them?*

'What are you wearing on Saturday?' she asked.

'Um – jeans? T-shirt?'

'That's a bit ordinary.'

'I'm only the guitarist. Nobody'll be looking at me,' I argued. My clothes were starting to get pretty shabby, but what with paying for food and a place to stay, they weren't a priority. 'And the more ordinary I look, the better you girls'll look in comparison.'

'Hmm,' Toni said. 'Well, you need to get new strings too. Yours sound really dull.'

She forgot to ask for her scarf back, so I kept it. It looked like it was all I was going to get from her.

19

Frets, the guitar shop, was one of my favourite places in Belfast. Even though I was only ever in there for strings and picks, they never minded you looking at the walls of guitars. Sometimes you'd get into casual conversation with someone trying one out. Mostly guys. For the first time I saw what Toni meant about girls and music. There were days when those were the only conversations I had, apart from passing the time of day with Beany.

So I didn't rush after I'd picked up a couple of packets of strings. It was another wet day and business was crap. There was a poster for Backlash behind the counter, and I had an idea of telling the friendly shop assistant with the ponytail that I was going to be playing at it, but I didn't. Safer to talk about guitars. There was a beautiful Gibson hanging up. I stroked its cool body.

'Gorgeous, isn't it?' Ponytail said. 'That's redwood and spruce. New in this week.'

I turned over the price ticket – £3,200 – and sighed.

'Not today then?' he asked.

'Maybe tomorrow.' After paying for the strings I had less than a fiver left.

'Oh my God.' It was a girl's voice. 'I *thought* that was you.'

My chest tightened. No. *Please* not a RyLeen. Not after all this time of anonymity and self-respect. I turned round, my hand still on the price ticket, ready to act bemused, but I did half-recognise the thin blonde girl with the huge eyes. Someone from Toni's school? The Bluebell? No, of course not – it was Shania, the girl I'd met on my first day busking.

'Hey,' I said, and relief probably made me over-enthusiastic. 'How are you? That's crazy, seeing you again.'

'I know! It must be fate.' Her eyes shone in her thin face; you could see spots pebble-dashing her skin under her thick make-up.

'Fate?'

'I came in here to buy Joe – my boyfriend' – she said the word *boyfriend* like she wanted the whole shop to hear her – 'a birthday present. He's really into his guitar. But I haven't a clue what to get him. You could help me?'

'Course. How much do you want to spend?'

'Fifteen quid. I've been saving.' She sounded very proud of herself, and I imagined Joe, spotty, bum-fluffy, writing songs for her in his sweaty bedroom.

If he was the same age as her he could only be about fifteen.

'Strings? Always useful.'

She shook her head. 'It has to be something special.'

All my suggestions – and let's face it, there wasn't much you could buy in Frets for fifteen quid – she dismissed as boring. 'It needs to be *romantic,*' she complained. She frowned at the boxes of picks and the hanging straps. She picked up an engraved leather strap and then let it flop sadly back down when she saw it was £49.99.

'What music is he into?' I asked. 'Does he write his own stuff?' I remembered myself at that age, earnestly penning 'Jenny'.

She shook her head. 'I could get him a music book,' she said.

There was a box full of song and chord books – Beatles, Dylan, Coldplay, Ed Sheeran – everything. She pounced on one with a rose and a heart on the cover.

'*Favourite Love Songs*!' She clasped it to her chest. 'Oh my God, that's perfect.'

She turned it over to look at the price and her pink-lipsticked mouth drooped. 'Oh.'

It was £17.99. I thought she was going to cry. When her eyes went all big like that, and her lips wobbled, she looked weirdly like Louise. Maybe that's why I dug into my jeans pocket and held out three pound coins. 'Go on,' I said.

'Really?' She flung herself at me and hugged me with her thin arms.

Ponytail turned round from tidying the guitars and

laughed. 'Never saw this place as a pick-up joint,' he said.

She's about fourteen, I wanted to say, discomfort pricking all over me. I didn't hug her back.

But I did say, 'My band's playing at that on Saturday night.' I indicated the Backlash poster. 'You and Joe should come along.'

'Yeah,' she said. 'Maybe we will.'

I knew they wouldn't really. I paid for my strings and went out into the cold drizzle, looking for a place to play.

20

The pub for the Belfast heat of Backlash was reassuringly small and shabby. We queued with the other bands to give in our details. Nerves had nibbled me all day – I hadn't been able to eat a thing. Toni and Marysia, in short patterned dresses that weren't identical, but sort of similar, were clearly nervous too. But not about the same thing as me. I didn't worry about fluffing a chord or missing a high note. I wasn't looking round at everyone else with their instrument cases and wondering if they were better than us. I worried that someone would recognise me. The atmosphere of anticipation, and people running around with lists and phones, of the silent checking out of each other, was so reminiscent of the early stages of *PopIcon* that I'd lapsed into silence.

'There were loads of tweets this afternoon, from the venue and the organisers,' Marysia said. 'I feel like I'm going to make a show of myself in front of the whole of Belfast.'

'You won't,' I said. 'Is Toni OK? That's the third time she's gone to the loo.'

'Anto said he'd try to come,' Marysia said. 'So she's extra wound-up.'

'I thought she didn't like her dad?'

'She doesn't exactly *like* him – but she's desperate for him to take her seriously, musically. She wants his approval, but she's annoyed with herself for wanting it.'

I sensed, as I often did, how much these two girls knew about each other.

'Yeah,' I said. 'I know exactly what you mean.'

Toni was walking back towards us, a little pale.

'Don't tell her I told you,' Marysia whispered.

'Hey,' Toni said. 'What's the hold up here? The queue hasn't even moved.'

'Yeah,' said a loud voice ahead of us, and a guy I hadn't noticed before, with a shaved head and an electric guitar case, leaned over the guys in front of him, to shout at the girl at the desk about their van being on a double-yellow and if they got a parking ticket they'd expect the venue to pay. She kept apologising and saying she'd be with them in a minute, and turning back to the duo with acoustic guitar cases and straggly beards, whose names she couldn't seem to find on her list. She was pretty and worried-looking, with short blue hair.

'Frigging shambles, this is,' said electric guitar guy. His gaze swept over Toni and Marysia without interest and then focused on me. 'They can't expect people to leave their kit in the frigging street. Them drums cost three thousand. More than the frigging van. They need *men* out here helping, not a couple of brainless girls.'

'Do you mind?' I asked.

'He clearly *doesn't* mind,' Toni said. 'Ass.'

Luckily, the beardy guys got sorted and shuffled off down the corridor with the blue-haired girl. The electric guitar guy and his mates swaggered up to the desk and shouted more, even though there was nobody there to shout at. I noticed for the first time that they all had the same thing embroidered on their denim jackets: NASTEEZ. Was it a play on nasty or Nazi? Either way, they weren't the kind of band I'd imagined in Backlash.

'God, I hate those bastards,' said a voice behind me. I turned to see a tall thin girl with dyed red hair in a long ponytail, carrying a bass guitar case. 'They're always like that. Throwing their weight around. They nearly got a recording contract once – or so they say. They think they're too good for everything.'

Marysia's eyes lit up for a moment. 'You play bass?' she asked.

The girl giggled. 'No! I'm carrying it for my boyfriend. He's parking the car. He plays bass for The Maloners.'

I should have recognised her. I should at least have recognised the name of the band, but I didn't.

'They're dead good,' she said. 'Me and my friends have been following them for ages. And now me and

Liam's together.' She gave the bass case a stroke. 'Are you in a band?'

Toni nodded. 'Polly's Tree.'

She frowned. 'I don't think I've—'

'We're pretty new,' Toni said crisply. 'This is Marysia and Cal.'

'Oh!' The girl's cheeks reddened slightly as she checked me out. 'Cal from Tipperary!'

Uh? I thought. That's when I recognised her. 'Oh. Um – Olivia?'

'Hi,' she said.

A stocky guy in a check shirt came in and pulled her ponytail. 'Hey, babes,' he said, and her face lit up. Three other guys piled in after him. 'Chatting up the opposition, Olivia?' one of them asked. I wondered what he'd have said if she'd told him she'd done way more than chat me up, but she just laughed.

When it was our turn the blue-haired girl, Gillian, showed us down the corridor to the room where we'd be waiting – basically a scruffy back bar with a pool table and doors leading to the toilets. A few other bands – mostly boys – were hanging round the bar, or grouped round tables, talking in low voices and tuning up.

Toni took off her coat and put it over the back of a chair. She fluffed up her hair. 'So what's the story with you and that girl?' she asked.

'Met her in the Bluebell.'

'*Met?*'

'Maybe more than met.' It wouldn't hurt for her to know *someone* fancied me.

'She has a boyfriend.' I tried to kid myself Toni sounded jealous, but it was more like disapproval.

'Not that night.'

Gillian brought us on stage for a soundcheck and to meet Paddy Cann, the local radio DJ who was MCing. I'd never heard of him. 'You're number five,' she said, 'so you won't have that long to wait.'

She explained that, unlike TV talent shows, the judges wouldn't be sitting at a special table, and there'd be no gimmicks. They'd just be in the audience, sitting at tables like everyone else. Bands were allowed to stay in the audience after they'd played, but not before, she said, because they wanted to bring all the bands on from backstage to make it more of an occasion.

'It's quite enough of an occasion for me,' Marysia muttered and Gillian said, 'Och, you're adorable,' as if we were about twelve.

Waiting to go on, it wasn't that unlike *PopIcon*, only scruffier and smaller. Lots of soundchecking. Paddy Cann chatted nonsense to us which I think was meant to make us relax. Then the same endless hanging around backstage eyeing up the opposition. The first band went on, but you couldn't hear much from where we were – just noise and occasional applause.

Toni's phone bleeped. She looked at it and shrugged, but she couldn't hide the look in her eyes. It was one of the things I was getting to know about her – her eyes were very expressive. And what they expressed now was hurt.

She passed the phone to Marysia. 'Says his car's broken down,' she said shortly. 'Typical.'

'Oh, babe,' Marysia said, and gave her a hug. Someone gave a wolf whistle and I wanted to go and tell them to fuck off, but instead I got us all pints of cider. As I queued at the bar I remembered my first meeting with Toni in the park, how upset she'd been at her dad letting her down. I understood why she wanted his approval even if she didn't like him much. Part of me, even though I never really wanted to see Ricky again, and even though I knew he'd dismiss Backlash as an amateur thing, wished he was out there to hear us, and be impressed.

Marysia's teeth chattered on her glass. 'Remind me why we're doing this,' she said.

'To show all these boys what two girls can do,' Toni replied.

'Hey,' I reminded them. 'Two girls and a guy.'

21

'And now give a big Backlash welcome to – Polly's Tree!'

We ran on and got plugged in. Toni took hold of her mic stand, blinked out into the darkness and turned round to see that we were ready.

'Hi, how're you all doing?' she called out to the crowd. She sounded like she'd been doing this all her life. She looked the part too: on stage those little dresses looked really cool. The audience gave a friendly roar in response.

'Brilliant!' she said. 'We're Polly's Tree and this is "Plastic Girls".'

I played the single G chord that introduced the song and then we were away.

Like the school concert, it went far too fast. Toni's voice soared and then broke and whispered, flirting with the mic. My fingers flew up and down the neck of my guitar. Then Toni grabbed the mic again, ready for her last chorus:

Don't try to make us into plastic girls
Cos that's not our world
No, that's not our world
Don't try to make us into plastic girls
Cos we're flesh and bone
And we know how to hurt

I think we could all have cried as the last chord died away.

There was a tiny silence, then a thunder of applause. I looked at my bandmates and grinned. I loved them both. We were so inside the music that it wasn't like we were three separate people, three separate egos, at all. We were a band. And we had another song to sing.

* * *

'You were brilliant!' Toni's mum said. 'I mean, I always knew you could *sing*, but you had that audience eating out of your hand. I've got some lovely photos of you.'

There was a brief hiatus while Nasteez were setting up – there was some sort of issue with the sound desk, surprise, surprise – and we took advantage of it to get settled at her table.

'Mu-um!' Toni said. She looked round the room. 'Oh, look,' she said. 'There's a whole crowd from school!'

Some girls waved over, and I recognised Jess from the school concert. Her hair seemed to have got even longer and shinier, to match her legs maybe.

Nasteez started up then, with a clash of cymbals, so all we could do was wave back and slide into the seats Toni's mum had kept for us.

I don't think Nasteez could really have almost got a recording deal. The lead singer spat when he sang – not in a 1976 punk way; just in a lack of salivary control way.

'Well, you were much better than these guys anyway,' Toni's mum said.

'I should hope so!'

'We could make out every word you were singing. This is just noise!'

The Nasteez lead singer gyrated and banged his mic stand up and down. I felt sorry for whoever had to sing into it next, with all that spit on it.

Toni's mum went to the bar and came back with halves for the girls and a pint for me.

'Mum!' Toni protested.

I grinned. 'Cheers, Mrs Flynn,' I said. Maybe I was forgiven.

'It's Dr Carey,' she said. So I guess she did do that PhD even if she didn't go to Oxford for it. 'But I suppose you can call me Jane.'

I raised my glass to her. 'I could call you "Queen Jane Approximately",' I said, trying to woo her. 'That's a Bob Dylan song. Or' – I saw her face – 'maybe not.'

There was a delay before the next band – probably to repair whatever damage Nasteez had done to the equipment – and Jess and a few others came over.

There was a lot of *Omigod, you were amazing!* Jess

threw her arms round the girls, and then she did the same for me, leaning into me with one foot off the ground so I had to steady her and hold her properly. Which I didn't mind. She smelled gorgeous and I was happy when she squeezed in beside me at our table, but to be honest, I was more focused on Toni and Marysia, and that lingering feeling of having performed together. We weren't saying much, just grinning from time to time. I wished we were still on stage.

'And now – give a warm welcome to – The Maloners!' called Paddy Cann.

'Oooh, Olivia's friends,' Jess said. 'They're meant to be amazing.'

She kept up a commentary as The Maloners set up. 'That must be Liam there on bass – oh yeah, I suppose he is quite cute – not really my type – she's been obsessed with him for months – the drummer's got nice arms, hasn't he? – what did she say his name was? – Stuart – or Steve?'

I guessed it was Olivia who'd assessed The Maloners as amazing. Compared to Nasteez they were: they could all play their instruments, and the lead singer had a strong voice. But their two songs sounded identical – not only to each other, but also to about ten things in the charts. I exchanged glances with Toni and Marysia as they went off stage, and Olivia ran to meet and snog Liam.

'We're better.' I answered Toni's unvoiced question in a low voice.

'Thank God you made us do "You Think You Know

Me",' Marysia said. 'You were right about the songs needing to contrast.'

'You should listen to me more often.'

Jess was smiling and looking from one to the other of us, aware, I suppose, that she wasn't part of it. I took her hand, just to be friendly, just to stop her feeling left out.

OK, I took her hand because there was still a tiny stupid part of me that hoped it might make Toni jealous. Jess's hand was slim and manicured, with long pink nails. I kept looking at Toni's nails, painted black tonight and short on the left hand, like mine, like all guitarists', and I wanted to touch that hand so much I squeezed Jess's without thinking about it and she squeezed back and smiled up at me.

The next two bands were really good, and one of them, Clio, was four girls in what Toni said were vintage dresses who did amazing harmonies and whose lyrics were quirky and clever. The lead singer was gorgeous too. Jess said she'd talked to one of them in the toilets. 'They've been together for five years,' she said, as Clio left the stage to huge applause, and Paddy Cann said there'd be a break for the judges to deliberate. 'Apparently they have a huge online presence.'

Polly's Tree had no online presence, which was exactly how I wanted it to stay.

Suddenly Toni gave a yelp. 'They're coming back!'

We all exchanged glances. Marysia held her thumbs. 'That's what we do in Poland,' she muttered, so I held mine too, even though I suddenly knew that

I dreaded winning. Dreaded anything that was going to bring us attention. 'Good luck,' Jane whispered across from her table, and showed us her crossed fingers.

There was a lot of talk from the chief judge, some bald guy whose band had got to number seven in the charts in 1992. He was skinny and small, with a strong Belfast accent, but when he started to speak you could feel his passion for music, and though the audience was wired and impatient to know who'd won, there was total silence as he spoke. He said, to be honest, the standard was very mixed, and that too many people were content with sounding like people on MTV, and that there was no substitute for practice, practice, practice and keeping it simple and honest. It was a million miles away from the way they used to go on in *PopIcon*, all that rubbish about stars being born and TV history being made.

The winning band, he said, stood out for their lack of gimmickry and their energy and pure love of what they were doing.

'That's what this competition is all about,' he said. 'Not TV. Not image. Just kids playing their own truth. And so,' he went on, 'the moment you've been waiting for. The runner-up tonight is ... Clio.'

Whistles and claps and cheers. OK, so Clio were only second. That meant that one of the first four bands, the ones we hadn't heard, must have been totally amazing to have beaten them. Which was perfect. As long as Polly's Tree kept on playing. As long as I still got to be friends with Toni and Marysia.

I smiled and clapped really hard as the Clio girls went on stage to get their prize, which was a piece of glass shaped like a guitar and a cheque to be spent on equipment or recording.

'And the winner of Backlash Belfast 2016, representing Belfast in the Ulster Final in the Ulster Hall next month is … Polly's Tree.'

22

The girls screamed and pulled me into a jumping hug. When we pulled away there were mascara-streaked tears running down Toni's cheeks. I reached out and blotted them with my fingers. I felt her cheeks soft and wet under my rough guitarist's fingertips.

'This is what you get for being in a band with soppy girls,' I said, and then we all fell back into our hug.

That was the picture they printed in the *Belfast Telegraph* next day: you couldn't see our faces, just Marysia's hair flying free and our arms all wrapped round each other.

If I could go back to one moment, and stay there for ever, it'd be that one: Marysia's hair in my mouth; Toni's arm across my back; her happy tears on my fingertips.

Moments before I blew it all apart.

23

It was surreal. The girls kept looking at each other and shrieking, 'We won!' Queen Jane sploshed champagne into our glasses and we all laughed when the bubbles went up our noses.

A skinny blonde girl pushed through the crowd, dragging a stocky, dark-haired, bearded guy. I hadn't really expected Shania to show up so it took me a second or two to recognise her. 'Oh my God!' she shrieked. 'Yous were brilliant!' She turned round to the guy. 'Joe, didn't I tell you?' Her big eyes shone, and I realised she was on something.

That was Joe? Up close he looked older than me – mid-twenties, I'd have said, unless his beard made him look older than he was? Or maybe Shania wasn't as young as I'd imagined.

'Yous were brill,' Joe said. 'I knew yous'd win.'

'Thanks.'

'We go to McGroarty's all the time,' he went on. 'You should come and play there; the bands they have are crap.'

Toni was looking quizzical, and I was suddenly glad that I had *someone* who was there to see me. I introduced them as friends of mine: it seemed a bit sad to say Shania was a random girl I'd met in the street, and Joe a complete stranger. Then Paddy Cann and the judges and the organisers congratulated us. Nasteez walked past with their gear, and gave us dirty looks, and we laughed more.

It was all grand, until this guy in designer glasses came up and said, 'Hey, well done. I'm Matt, from *LiveScene BT*. Can I do a quick interview?'

'Back in a sec,' I muttered.

'I'll get you a pint,' Joe said.

I stayed in the gents' as long as I could. On the way out I saw Jess with her coat on.

'Hey,' she said. 'Where've you been?' She shook back her hair. 'They're talking to some journalist. Toni told him she picked you up in a park, completely randomly. Is that right?'

I kissed her, mainly to shut her up. She gave a tiny giggle of surprise and then leaned into me, opening her mouth to deepen the kiss.

It was only a kiss. She pulled away, moistened her lips and said, 'Hmm. Get my number off Toni. My taxi's here, unfortunately.' She waited as if she wanted me to tell her not to get the taxi or something, but I just said, 'Oh, you'd better go then,' and she did, with a great swishing of hair.

'Cal! Where've you been?'

It was Toni.

'What was that all about?' she said, breathless.

I shrugged, feeling my cheeks burn. 'Toni – we won! Jess and I just had a bit of a celebratory kiss. It's not a big deal.'

'Do you do that a lot?'

'What?'

'Randomly shag girls.'

'It was a *kiss*!'

'But you shagged that Olivia, didn't you? I had a *really* interesting chat with her in the loos just now.'

For a second I had to think who she meant. 'Well, yeah. Once. It was nothing.'

'But sex should be – well, special.' She sounded wistful and then seemed to recover herself. 'You shouldn't treat girls like that. It's degrading.'

'It was Olivia's idea. She had a condom in her pocket.'

'Too much information.' Her eyes flashed with something I couldn't read. I wished I could have told myself it was jealousy but it wasn't. It was more like disgust.

'Look,' I said. 'I was drunk. I probably wouldn't even have remembered her name if we hadn't met her tonight.'

'Do you not see how offensive that is?'

'I don't know what you're so worked up about. We're both consenting adults. And it was weeks ago!'

'And what about that wee girl? Don't tell me *she's* a consenting adult? She's jailbait.'

'Shania? Now *you're* being offensive! I've never touched her. I hardly know her.'

'I didn't think that mattered to you. And what about your mate Joe? Don't tell me *he* hasn't touched her?'

She stood in front of me in the corridor which smelt of that chemical dirty-clean smell from the loos, all glowing with indignation. Her eyes sparked and her hair was damp with sweat from being onstage, her cheeks still smeared with mascara. She was fierce and lovely and we were arguing about *sex*.

I bent down and kissed her.

For few seconds she was kissing me back – or I thought she was, hands entwined in my hair. For a few seconds I registered that her lips were firmer than Jess's, without the sweetness of lipstick – hers had worn off – but with a salty tang under the taste of champagne.

My hands tightened round her waist, and her rosy, spicy smell was stronger than ever, and then I wasn't thinking about Jess, or about anything, and something stirred inside me that I'd never felt before, something disturbing and delicious that I almost couldn't bear—

And then she yanked herself away, eyes wide and staring as if she couldn't believe what she'd done.

'I am *not* one of those girls,' she said. 'And that – that did *not* happen.'

And she stalked off.

24

I rushed back into the bar, but the table where we'd been sitting was empty. There was no sign of Joe and Shania either. My guitar case sat across two stools, looking very abandoned, and a barman was collecting glasses. 'They're away, mate,' he said.

I grabbed my guitar and dashed outside. It was a long straight street, mostly bars and a few offices, and right at the end I could see them – Toni's mum and aunt walking together, and Toni and Marysia beside them. They walked arm in arm, each of them carrying a guitar case in her outside hand.

I could have run after them. If I'd been drunker, I might have. And God knows what kind of scene we'd have had in the street.

The post-high low was hovering just over my head, and I knew when it fell it would smother me in its black cloud. But I knew how to keep it at bay. The pubs were still open. In fact I was standing right in front of one, the street littered with cigarette butts, and a pulse of rock music coming from inside. I pushed open the heavy door and lost myself in the noise and the heat and the drink.

* * *

Some instinct got me back to the Crossroads. I had no conscious thoughts about where I was, it was all a jumble of streets and closed-down factories and walls and gates and graffiti, and some of the kerbstones were painted and some weren't, and then I turned a corner and recognised it. The crooked Crossroads sign winked under a streetlight. But the steps looked higher and steeper than usual. I stood at the bottom of them, frowning up at the faraway wavering door. It was hard bloody work hauling myself up those steps. I had to stop a couple of times. The rail was cold and hard under my hand. Inside me hot and swimmy and sour. All the drink sloshing around. I burped.

I couldn't find my key! Shit. But Beany would let me in. Beany loved me. I bladdered at the door.

And there was Beany, pulling the door open, in a dressing gown. He looked like an angry dad. His legs were bare and hairy and so skinny for such a fat man that I found myself transfixed by them. I started shouting, 'Hey Beany, we won, we bloody won,' because I suddenly remembered that we had. But not Beany. That was wrong. No wonder he looked so cross. What was his name? Something beginning with M. I stumbled through the door. 'Mervyn!' I tried to hug him.

'What the fuck?' he said. He took a step back from me. 'What kind of state—?'

'We won!' I said. My guitar felt heavy. I set it down and leaned against the counter because the room was swaying.

The solid feel of the counter must have sobered me up a bit because everything shifted into sharp focus and I knew exactly where I was and why Beany was so annoyed. The clock on the wall said quarter to three.

I also knew, with a lurch of horror and nausea, that I was about three seconds away from puking.

I looked round for something – a bin, anything. Nothing. Spun round – maybe get back outside in time, yanked at the door handle, bloody thing wouldn't budge.

Too late. It spurted out, all over the door, all over the doormat, and all over my feet.

And as I stood there, sobering up, the glass of the door icy against my forehead, I knew I'd puked all over my future at the Crossroads Hostel.

25

Sunday morning. Too early. Beany frowned into the tea I'd just made him.

'I don't do second chances,' he said. 'If anybody knows the rules it's you.'

'I've cleaned it all up. I'm not used to champagne, Mervyn. I must be allergic to it.' I made myself sound very young and innocent.

Beany humphed. 'I'm allergic to people waking me up at three in the morning and boking all over my hostel.'

I made my most irresistible RyLee face, even though I despised myself for it. 'It was just such a big night for us. It went to my head. I'm so sorry.'

'So you should be,' he said. He shook his head. 'If anybody knew I'd bent the rules for you … I swear, son, see if you do that again – no excuses. No more chances. You'll be out on your ear. I don't care if it's three o'clock in the morning. I mean it.'

'I know,' I said quietly. 'I promise I won't.'

I meant it, too.

So that was Beany sorted out. Phase one of Mission: Damage Limitation. I didn't think phase two – Toni – would be so easy.

I'd reached the stage of hangover where all I wanted was to lie on my bed and feel sorry for myself, but that wasn't an option. One, because, though Beany sometimes bent his daytime lockout rule for me, I couldn't expect it today; and two, I had to go and face Toni while I was brave enough. I felt disgusting after three hours' fitful sleep in my clothes, and my early-morning cleaning exertions, which included washing my Converse in the pink sink in my room, so I had as long a shower as the Crossroads facilities would allow. It was still early, so there wasn't a queue for the bathroom, and when I emerged, wrapped in a towel, I felt clean on the outside, though still pretty dodgy inside.

I dried myself in the room I'd so nearly lost, looking at it with new affection. My clothes flung in a heap over the chair; my guitar case in the gap between bed and wall, where it fitted so perfectly; my phone charging on the bedside locker, my favourite red hoody hanging on the door, with Toni's rainbow striped scarf over it – it was all homely and familiar now. I pulled the duvet up neatly, opened the window to let out the smell of alcohol and sweaty clothes and, leaving my guitar behind for once, grabbed my hoody and my phone and let myself out into the street.

This part of Belfast on a Sunday morning was silent

and grubby. There was a shortcut through the gate in the wall, which led to a long, traffic-choked road I usually avoided, even though it got me to Toni's end of town more quickly than walking though the city centre, but today I took it. It was quieter than usual and its long uphill drag tired me out enough to give me something to focus on apart from what I was about to do. It also warmed me up – which was good, because it was the kind of day when you really needed a coat, and I didn't have one. Well, I did. I had coats and dry shoes and a laptop and a bed I could lie in all day if I wanted, and an en suite bathroom and everything. Three hours away. And today, crushed by my first real hangover in months, I had a moment's wobble when I walked past the bus station.

I didn't want to be the boy with the hangover. The boy who woke up worrying about what he'd done the night before. RyLee had had a lot of mornings like that. And despite how rough I felt right now, I knew my chances of not being that boy were a lot better up here.

About a mile away from Toni's I realised it was only half nine, which was too early to call on someone on a Sunday morning. I went into the nearest café – it was Kopi, where I'd been on my very first day in Belfast, and even though it was more expensive than the cafés I usually went to these days, I hoped it might be a good omen. Maybe Marysia had stayed over – maybe, just like that other day, she'd have to go to Mass, and Toni might walk her there and come in here …

But probably not. I ordered a tea, and had a nasty

twist of nausea when a waitress walked past me with a steaming plate of eggs.

My memory of last night was in shifting fragments, but up to and including the kiss, I remembered everything. So what exactly had I done? I'd kissed a girl who hadn't wanted me to. Who thought I was just a player. A girl I was in love with but who was never going to feel the same way, and who was in fact possibly in love with her best friend. A girl who'd given me the chance to play the best music ever. A girl who had made me feel like Cal Ryan was a decent, talented human being. A girl I'd do anything not to lose.

26

Queen Jane looked surprised and not that delighted to see me on her doorstep.

'Toni has a lot of work to do,' she said.

'I just need to talk to her for five minutes,' I said. I tried out RyLee's lopsided, apologetic smile, but I might as well not have bothered. Louise always fell for that smile – even after everything I'd put her through – but Jane was made of sterner stuff. Like her daughter.

'Five minutes,' she said.

She showed me into the kitchen, and called, 'Toni!' I sat at the kitchen table and remembered the first morning I'd been here. The room smelt of coffee and bacon, and Billy was crouched over his dish, lapping water with a delicate tongue.

Toni appeared in leggings and a big jumper, her hair damp.

'Oh,' she said.

'I've explained to Cal that you have to work today, that you can't be giving all your time to this band,' Queen Jane said. She poured coffee from the cafetière and set a mug down in front of me. I spooned three sugars in.

'He's not staying,' Toni said.

'We had an argument last night,' I said to Queen Jane. 'My fault. I just wanted to apologise.' I didn't even try to access RyLee's smile repertoire.

'I'll leave you to it.' Queen Jane took her coffee and headed for the door. 'Tell Marysia I'll give her a lift home after *The Archers*.'

'I'm sorry,' I said the moment the kitchen door closed behind her. 'I shouldn't have ...' I looked down at the table. But *what* should I not have done? What would happen if I told her the truth – that I kissed her because I was in love with her?

Toni blew into her mug and sat down opposite me, cupping her hands round her coffee mug.

'We don't need – complications – in the band,' Toni said.

'Is there someone else?' I asked, which I thought was a subtle way to let her tell me if she and Marysia were more than friends.

She made an exasperated noise. 'Why do boys always assume that? If I don't want you it has to be because I have somebody else? Well, I don't. I just don't – I don't feel that way about you.'

'You did kiss me back. From what I remember.'

'I did not,' she snapped. 'And like you said – sometimes it's just nothing.'

OK, now I really wasn't going to admit I was in love with her – I had some pride – but I didn't want her thinking that the kiss had been nothing to me.

'The music last night was brilliant,' I said. 'You felt it too, didn't you?'

She nodded.

'I suppose it went to my head. I felt so – so close to you.'

For a moment her lips relaxed into a smile, but then she said, 'And where were you when we were talking to Matt? We're meant to be a band. Do things together. Things like talking to journalists, I mean. Oh yes, I remember: you were getting off with *Jess*. Did you feel close to her too?'

I put my hands up like a captured prisoner. 'Look, I'm sorry about the journalist. I guess I'm – well, I'm not that comfortable with talking about myself. I just want to play the music. You and Marysia are the main men – I mean, women. Can we just pretend last night didn't happen? And carry on the way we were? It's not that long till the final.'

'Five weeks,' she said. 'So can you keep your hands and your lips and – well, everything else to yourself for five weeks?'

I gripped my mug tighter. 'Yeah,' I said. 'Christ, you're not *that* irresistible.'

I wished that was true.

27

A bright, chilly October Saturday. I pulled Toni's rainbow scarf tighter round my neck and shoved my free hand into my hoody pocket as I ran down the hostel steps into the street. I'd need to invest in some winter gear. Even my feet were starting to feel cold in my battered Converse. I thought of my clothes at home, sheepskin-lined boots and padded coats all waiting in my wardrobe. If I could spirit myself back there, grab all I needed and magic them back to my room at the Crossroads, I'd be totally sorted. But I was scared if I walked back into that house I'd never be able to walk back out again. And even if Toni was never going to feel the way I did, at least I could prove to her I wasn't going to let her down.

Anyway, Cal Ryan didn't care about designer coats: there were such things as charity shops.

The coat choices in Oxfam on Botanic Avenue weren't extensive – I could go down the old-man's tweed overcoat route (which had a kind of indie rock star retro chic but also smelt like the old man might actually have died in it, or at least experienced some loss of bodily control), or the puffy anorak in a fetching sludge-green. I held one coat in each hand, frowning, and in the end I paid £5.50 for the green monstrosity and left the tweed one (an inflated £8.00) for some hipster who could afford dry cleaning.

I can't pretend I cut a fine figure in the anorak but I was warm and anonymous as I wandered up towards the university. I'd busked in the Botanic Gardens a few times at weekends and it had been a change from the streets, with families coming out of the museum and couples walking through the park.

'Don't you get fed up busking all day and then rehearsing with us?' Toni had asked me once when I'd turned up to rehearse with my fingers almost bleeding.

'I don't mind. It's good practice.'

'But people mostly busk for the craic,' she had persisted. 'It's not a *job*.'

'I need to earn money and this is the easiest way.' I had sucked the sorest fingertip.

'But it's so – so hand to mouth,' she'd said. 'What happens if nobody gives you anything?'

I'd shrugged, because that was one of my deepest fears, and deepest fears, whatever they tried to tell us in there, are best left unspoken. 'It'll be grand,' I'd said, and it became a kind of Polly's Tree catchphrase. 'It'll be grand,' Marysia would say when Toni fretted that the new song she was working on wouldn't come right. 'It'll be grand,' Toni said in a poor imitation of my accent when her mum refused to let her go to the Bluebell for more gig practice. 'We'll find a weekend gig instead.'

And amazingly, we did – one of the teachers at their school, who'd liked us at the Malawi concert, asked Polly's Tree to play at her daughter's wedding when the real band all went down with salmonella. It was a tough gig, and they hadn't wanted our original songs – though we shoved a few in when they were all too drunk to notice. But my busking experience came into its own – for the first time I had to do most of the lead vocals – and best of all we were paid £400 between us. It was the first time I'd had proper money for ages, and so that I wouldn't be tempted to spend it on rubbish I'd given most of it to Beany to pay for the next few weeks' B&B. I was booked in until the day after the Backlash final. After that – well, I wasn't thinking about it. He hadn't asked me to do any cleaning since my lapse – mainly because he wasn't busy, but also I sensed that he regretted giving me special treatment. Once you were out of Beany's good books it was hard to get back in.

Today in the Botanic Gardens was rubbish. After an hour of my hands freezing – fingerless gloves were next on my winter-proofing shopping list –with 57p and a Lithuanian coin to show for it, I gave up and started on the long walk back to Crossroads.

Beany was squinting at his computer screen, checking in a group of giggling girls with ironed hair cascading from pink Stetsons, and cheap bright pink bomber jackets with *PAULA'S HEN WEEKEND* embroidered on the backs. They all turned when I walked in, showing bright orange faces.

'Ah, brilliant. Is the entertainment laid on?' one of them shrieked in an English accent.

'Never mind your guitar, you can play me anytime,' said another one and they all cackled.

'See you later, big boy,' they shouted after me, as I went past down the corridor that led to the safety of my room. I guessed the place would be rowdy later. They'd be hogging the bathrooms for the next couple of hours, then they'd head out on the town in five-inch stilettos with half-bottles of vodka shoved inside their handbags. I'd wait until the place was quiet then go and watch TV in the lounge.

So eight o'clock saw me heading for the lounge with a bowl of pasta and pesto – I was getting good at that – and a bottle of cheap beer, and expecting to have it to myself. I didn't think there was anyone staying apart from Paula's Hen Party, so I was surprised to push open the door and hear, above the roar of a TV talent show – for a moment I thought it was *PopIcon* but it was something American – voices in a foreign language. From the big old squashy sofa, two blond heads looked round, a boy and girl about my age.

'Hello,' the girl said. She had a snub nose and round glasses, and wore combat trousers, Birkenstocks and a fleece. Her boyfriend – they were holding hands – was dressed almost identically. They both looked pink and smiley and scrubbed.

I sat down on the spare sofa and balanced my plate on my knee.

'Are you staying here also?' the boy asked.

'Yeah.' I wasn't in the mood for chatting with strangers, but they were like puppies wanting to play.

'And you are Irish?' the girl asked as if this was something really exotic.

I sighed. 'Yeah.'

'We're from Germany. We're so excited to be in Belfast! This is our first evening.'

Then why are you wasting it sitting in a dingy hostel lounge watching shite TV? I stuck my fork into my pasta and shovelled it into my mouth.

But Florian and Julia didn't seem to notice that I wasn't up for chatting. They were travelling round Ireland, starting in the north, and they loved folk music and Irish culture, and they'd driven over from Germany, yes, all the way, up through England and over from Liverpool on the ferry in their little Polo. Had I not seen it parked outside? And they were so tired! And the crossing had been rough, so they were having a rest this evening. They would have an early night. *Good luck with that,* I thought, imagining what Paula's Hen Party would sound like six hours from now. And they thought the Crossroads was very – what was the word – *basic,* and it had looked much nicer on the Internet, but they liked places with character.

'We want to see the real Ireland and the real people,' Florian explained.

'But this—' Julia waved at the TV. 'We have this in Germany also. It's very popular.'

On screen an overweight girl with obvious hair extensions and no obvious musical talent wailed through 'I Will Always Love You' in front of orange-tanned judges. 'You made that your own!' said Orange 1. Orange 2 looked at her in disbelief. 'Well, that's one way of putting it,' he said, and the studio audience booed.

I turned away and concentrated on my pasta.

'Are you on holiday too?' Julia asked.

'Not really. I've been here a while. It's cheap and cheerful.' I don't know why I said *cheerful*; it wasn't, especially not in here, with its brown velvet curtains and mismatched beige sofas. You wouldn't think shades of beige could clash, but they really can.

'So where should we go?' Julia asked. 'We want to see the Titanic Centre, of course, and the famous murals—'

'And hear some real Irish music. I have been teaching myself the Irish drum – the *bodhrán*,' Florian said, only he pronounced it bod-ran so it took me a second to work out what he meant. I didn't think walking through the streets round the Crossroads with a *bodhrán*, however mispronounced, was the smartest move, so I told them that. I also had a pile of leaflets in my room, from the days when Toni had appointed herself my virtual tour guide, and I said they could have them. Most of the things Toni had suggested cost money, and the Belfast I'd discovered was mostly of streets and cheap cafés.

'Ah, you are so kind!' Julia said. 'We're so lucky to have met you.'

Over the next few days, she said this several more times: when I told them there was a traditional session in the Amsterdam on a Monday (and that they shouldn't *assume* their *bodhrán* would be welcomed); when I advised them that the street outside the Crossroads wasn't the safest place to park their car – there'd been three cars stolen in the weeks I'd been there – but that the street next to it was better; when I showed them how the radiator worked – theirs had the same eccentric ways as mine.

They were grateful and I liked feeling I wasn't the rookie outsider any more. Beany was pleased too, because they took to hanging round his counter when he was checking his online bets and asking him involved questions about Northern Irish politics, so the more I took them off his hands the happier he was. Not that I knew the first thing about Northern Irish politics, but I didn't mind letting them waffle on while I zoned out.

It wasn't like having friends. It wasn't like Toni and Marysia, but it was better than nothing. And when Toni phoned me, uncharacteristically squeaky with excitement, to say her mum was away for two days at a marking conference, and that there was nothing to stop us going to the open mic at the Bluebell, it seemed only fair to mention it to them.

The crowd at the Bluebell was similar to the one that had been there the time I'd gone on my own, though I couldn't help being relieved that The Maloners weren't there, which meant no Olivia.

There were several earnest songwriters with neck

beards and whining songs. Marysia and I got the giggles over one, whose three songs were all about a girl called Imelda. Apart from the fact that in the first one he fancied her, in the second one he shagged her (though he didn't put it like that), and in the third one she dumped him, they seemed identical. Certainly the chord sequences were. His rhymes were so predictable that we started guessing the end of every line. And if you think nothing rhymes with Imelda, you're wrong. It became a game – you had to take a drink if you got it wrong. Toni, who was driving her mum's car and kept looking out the window to check it hadn't been nicked, got more and more disapproving. 'The writer of "Jenny" is hardly in a position to comment on other people's songwriting,' she said. Her lips were tight; they didn't look at all like the lips that I'd kissed. I tried not to think about how much I wanted to kiss them again.

Marysia raised her eyebrows at me. 'PMT,' she mouthed.

'TMI,' I mouthed back.

Toni frowned. 'Have you tuned up?' she asked. 'We're on next. At least *he'll* be an easy act to follow.'

I saluted. 'Yes, ma'am.'

Florian and Julia looked from one to the other of us in bemusement.

'Did you get new strings?' Toni went on. 'They sounded really dead on Friday.'

'Not yet.' I would have to make a trip to Frets for the first time since I met Shania in there. Playing for hours every day meant I went through strings pretty quickly, and all I had left were the six on the guitar. This week it had been a choice between the coat and new strings and the coat had won. But who knew, maybe I'd make a fortune tomorrow.

'Don't let her boss you so much,' Marysia said, wrinkling her nose at Toni.

'She knows I love it really,' I said.

I didn't love it. I'd never liked bossy girls and I'd had years of being controlled by Ricky. But two things made it all bearable: the fact that, even though she could be an uptight cow who talked to me like I was five, Toni was also the sparkiest girl I'd ever met and when she smiled at me something gave way inside me. And – probably more importantly – the moment we played the first chord onstage, and our voices and guitars blended – all three of us – I was happy in a way I'd never been.

A few people in the audience recognised us now, because of Backlash, though thank God we weren't as well known as Toni had hoped. Despite her best efforts, Matt's article hadn't gone viral. We need our music out there online, she kept saying, but she was too busy with her schoolwork to do anything about it, which suited me fine. Busking was OK; playing in a low-key local competition was OK. Being all over the Internet – no way.

We ended with our upbeat new song, 'Northern Streets'. The crowd got really into it, singing along with the chorus:

Northern Streets got that northern beat
Feel the dancing beneath your feet

It was our last song, and I really let rip. Marysia's thumping bass sounded almost like a drum. As we got to the last line, Toni turned and smiled at me, and circled her finger to say, *Play it again,* so I kept strumming, and the audience kept singing. Florian and Julia were lapping it up, clapping their hands and beaming round as if to say, *We know the band*.

We'd felt in rehearsal that this song was lively and catchy, but I don't think we were prepared for the audience to like it so much. I crashed down the final chord and then leapt back as the bottom E-string broke and sprang up in my face. We ended the song laughing.

Toni hugged me with one arm and Marysia with the other as we got down off the tiny stage. 'You'll have to get those new strings now,' she said, and the lovely feeling of her arm round my waist made up for her bossy tone.

I walked home with Julia and Florian – 'I'm sorry, but I'd be *far* too scared to drive round those streets,' Toni said, not quite so rock and roll offstage. I didn't mind. To be honest, it was pretty nice to bathe in their admiration, even though it segued into a long description of the music scene in their town in Germany, including a countdown of their top ten gigs.

As we passed the old warehouse which always gave me the creeps, Florian looked round and, even though the street was empty, lowered his voice. 'You're kind of a cool guy, aren't you?' he asked.

I shrugged modestly.

'We're looking for – you know. Someone to buy some stuff from.'

'No,' I said quickly. 'I wouldn't know. I don't—'

'We only want a little weed,' he said.

I shook my head. A cat jumped out from a broken plank in the warehouse door, making us all jump. Julia nuzzled into Florian. 'I wouldn't have a clue,' I said honestly. 'And whatever you do, *don't* ask Mervyn. He's totally against drugs. Like ... pathologically. And if you get what you want, don't smoke it in there or you'll be thrown out.'

Florian looked amused. 'That wouldn't be such a hardship. Anyway, we leave on Saturday evening. We go to Dublin.'

'Well, then, you'll get whatever you want there.' I mentioned a few bars where he'd probably find what he wanted, and we walked back to the hostel.

28

It had to come. Deepest Fear Friday. Why was I even bothering to try to play? My cramped, cold hands slithered on wet strings, and the streets were deserted. Anyone with the choice was at home or in a nice warm café, or just dashing from shop to shop, umbrellas up and heads down. But I was skint. Quite literally not-a-single-penny skint. And soaked. I gave up busking and went into shops where at least it was warm and dry, but walking round shops with a heavy guitar case and no money, with your wet jeans sticking to you, and people eyeing you suspiciously, is about as much fun as it sounds.

The only thing getting me through the day was the thought of rehearsal that evening. The last one for a week because it was half-term and Marysia was going to Poland to see her granny. I wished it was at Toni's, instead of Marysia's, but at least there'd be people and something to do, and Marysia's hot strong coffee. I could have gone back to the Crossroads and had some food, but I couldn't be arsed to walk all the way there and then on out to Marysia's. They were in opposite directions.

By the time I turned into Marysia's street, the rain was easing off. A blue car slowed beside me, swishing through the puddles at the kerb, and the passenger window slid down.

'Get in,' Toni said. 'It's only a couple of minutes but it'll be better than nothing.'

I tossed my guitar into the back seat, and folded myself into the passenger seat. There was a large brown envelope on it.

'Don't drip on that,' Toni said. 'It's our contracts for the Backlash final.'

'Contracts?' My stomach flipped over.

'Just boring stuff mostly. About procedures on the night; not being signed to a record company; not making a full-time living from music. As if!' She laughed. 'There wasn't all that fuss about the first round, but I suppose it's getting more serious now. Remind me to get you to sign tonight.'

I blew my wet hair away from my face. Her hands on the steering wheel were confident, the nails turquoise like the first time we met. We hadn't been alone together since the morning after the kiss. At least panicking about the contract stopped me thinking about the awkwardness of that.

'You should have got the bus,' Toni said. 'You look like you've been out in that all day.'

'Most of it.'

'Why didn't you stay in? You *could* be taking that free-spirited troubadour vibe a bit far.'

'They don't let you. There's a lockout until five.'

'That sounds a bit grim.'

'Nah, it's grand.' I shivered. 'I'll be glad to get somewhere warm and dry though.'

Marysia's shed wasn't exactly warm, and it was only dry in the sense that it had a roof and walls. Damp clung to the air.

'We can't keep practising in here in winter,' Toni said, hauling her guitar strap over her huge blue woolly jumper. 'We'll all get pneumonia.' She touched my anorak. 'Wow, that's soaking. You shouldn't sit around in it.'

'It's only the outside. I'll freeze to death if I take it off. When is Queen Jane going to let us practise at yours again?' I asked hopefully.

Toni shrugged. 'She's just not that keen on music,' she said. 'I suppose it reminds her of the bad old days.'

'What do you mean?'

'When my dad filled the house with layabout musicians and hopeless dreams.' She bit her lip. I knew she didn't like talking about her dad. Was he a *free-spirited troubadour* too?

'I know what'll warm us up.' Marysia reached past some tins of paint and gardening stuff on the shelf on the wall and brought out a bottle of dodgy-looking Polish vodka. After the slightest hesitation, I took a slug from it. It burnt a path down my gullet, and made me gasp.

'Let's get started,' Marysia said. She seemed jittery, not her usual mellow self at all. Maybe she wasn't looking forward to a week away with her family.

'Northern Streets' made us jig around a lot, and after we'd gone through it twice we were all shedding layers. But I couldn't concentrate. I fluffed a couple of chords, forgot to come in on backing vocals.

After the fourth mistake Marysia lost her temper. 'Look, Cal, you need to take this seriously! You can't play like that in the final. And your D string is way out of tune. I can't believe you can't hear it.'

'I do bloody take it seriously.' I clenched my jaw and twisted a tuning peg.

'That's not even the right string! You're not *on* something, are you?' Oh great, so Toni had clearly blabbed to her about me being in there.

I slammed my guitar down on a chair, making Marysia wince as it resounded twangily. I immediately felt awful: my guitar was the most precious thing I had. Its busking career had made it look slightly scruffy but not abused. I ran my hand down the neck as if in apology. 'For fuck's sake, no.'

'OK! Don't have a hissy fit.'

'Marysia.' Toni sounded annoyed. 'Lighten up!' She put her guitar down and came up to me. 'Are you OK?' she asked. She put her hand on my arm. 'It's not like you to make mistakes.'

And it wasn't like Toni to sound so sweet, and I didn't know if I could take it right now. But I didn't brush her hand off. 'Bad day,' I said. 'I haven't eaten. I'm sorry.'

'You shouldn't skip meals,' Marysia said. 'Or drink on an empty stomach.'

'He had about two sips.'

Their voices seemed to be far away even though the shed wasn't very big.

I breathed out a small dry laugh, and sat down in the chair with my guitar on my lap. I rubbed my hands over my face. 'Look, I – it wasn't deliberate. I just didn't make any money today. You know – because of the weather.'

'You mean you couldn't *afford* to buy anything?'

I ran my finger along a string. 'I suppose.'

'Oh God, Cal, I'm so sorry,' Toni said. 'Bit of empathy failure on our parts there.'

I looked at her face and saw, in the softness of her hazel eyes, that she felt sorry for me, and it was *horrible*. I'd much rather have had her pissed off.

'Marysia, could you go and scrounge something from your kitchen?' she said. 'Something hot?'

'Of course. We had mushroom soup for dinner. I think there's some left over. Why don't we all go up to the kitchen?'

I'd never been in Marysia's house before. The kitchen was warm – hot, after the shed, and once we all piled in, crowded. There were kids' pictures fastened to the fridge door, a pile of ironing on a chair. A pot sat on the hob. Marysia lifted the lid and nodded. 'Plenty left,' she said. 'I'll get you some bread, too. Toni – do you want to put the kettle on?'

Marysia's mum, Halina, came in to see what we were doing, and there were stilted introductions.

When Marysia said she was heating soup for me, a little crease came between Halina's eyebrows and she said something quickly to Marysia in Polish, which made Marysia frown. I didn't even try to mother-charm her. All I could think about was the smell of the soup filling the space. My stomach let out a loud, embarrassing gurgle.

I couldn't understand Polish but it was obvious what Halina was saying: *Don't use too much of that soup. I hope that's not the fresh loaf?*

'Cal,' Marysia said when Halina had gone. 'Have you actually got *no* money? Like at all?'

I spooned soup into my mouth. God, it was the best thing I'd ever tasted. 'Tomorrow'll be grand. Saturdays usually are.'

'I said this would happen if you relied on busking,' Toni said.

'What about paying for the hostel?' Marysia asked. She sipped her coffee.

'No, that's sorted.' I smiled to show that it was all cool. 'Paid up until the final anyway. Three weeks. And after that – well, who knows.'

'Look, you're only here because of Polly's Tree,' Toni said. 'We can't let you *starve*. I can give you—'

'No.' I put my spoon down.

'Lend, then. A few quid. Come on, Cal. It's an investment in the band. We need you fit for purpose.'

'You could get a job?' Marysia suggested. 'That's what people normally do.'

Yeah, I thought, and people normally have IDs and references and addresses.

'We should *all* go busking tomorrow,' Toni said. 'For the craic. We could go to Bangor. Let Cal see the Northern Irish seaside. I can probably get Mum's car again.'

'I'll be on my way to Poland,' Marysia reminded her.

'Well, you and I could go, Cal, couldn't we?' Toni grinned at me. 'A day out? Busking by the sea, fish and chips? It'll be like a holiday. Before I get down to a lovely half-term of studying. Oh,' she went on, 'that reminds me, Marysia – we need to get that contract signed and sent off, with you going away.'

I didn't let myself think about spending a whole day on my own with Toni at the seaside.

Just like I didn't let myself read the Backlash contract. What was the point? There were three copies. I just flicked through to the back page of each one and signed the lie: *Cal Ryan*.

29

The novelty of busking wore off pretty quickly for Toni. She huddled in her purple duffle coat.

'It must be time for a break,' she said. 'There's a lovely café over the road – see? With gingham curtains. We can look out at the sea.'

I bent over and peered into the guitar case. 'About three quid,' I said. 'That won't get two cups of tea.'

'I have loads of money.' Toni tapped the pocket of her coat. 'Come on. This was meant to be a bit of fun.'

I turned to her, puzzled. 'This was *your* idea. You know I need the money.'

'But you can keep whatever we make. I mean, I'm only here to help out. I don't want your money.'

'There won't be any money if we keep stopping for cups of tea! Come on – another hour and see how we go.'

An old man stood and listened for ages, eyes intent

on my flying fingers. After three songs he walked away.

'Mean old bastard,' Toni said. 'Does he think the music's free?'

'The music *is* free,' I said. 'We didn't ask permission to be here. He didn't ask us to play. He doesn't have to pay us.'

'Yeah, but he took all that music for nothing.'

I shrugged. 'Maybe he had nothing.'

'Well, it's lunchtime. And you know how grumpy you are when you don't eat. Come on – fish and chips. My treat.'

The sun was shining, so we went down to the seafront and sat on a wall looking at the boats, blowing on our chips to cool them. I hadn't realised how much I'd missed the sea until I smelt the salt in the air and saw the pewter sheen of the water. I inhaled the salty vinegary smell and felt the tension in my shoulders from too many hours with a guitar round my neck slacken. We tried to decide which boat we'd take if we were going round the world.

'You could just go and busk in every port,' I said. 'Stay until you got fed up or your money ran out. You'd never need to pay for a bed because you'd always have your boat to go back to. It'd be amazing.' But I didn't mean it. I was just saying what a free-spirited troubadour was expected to say.

'To be honest,' Toni said, 'I get seasick.' She packed up her fish-and-chip paper.

'Me too,' I said. 'Come on – we've got songs to sing.'

* * *

'You in a rush?' Toni asked, as we walked back to the car park later. She'd been quiet all afternoon, apart from singing.

I shrugged. 'Not really.' I don't think she realised how empty my life was apart from Polly's Tree.

'We could go down to the beach at Ballyholme? Mum wants the car back for this evening but we're OK for a couple of hours.'

We stashed the guitars in the boot and Toni drove a short distance. The beach was long, curving round beneath an old wall, overlooked by tall pastel-coloured houses. It reminded me so much of Dublin Bay. We parked the car and walked down crumbling stone steps. The tide was far enough out that we could walk on the sand. It was strange to be walking without the familiar heft of my guitar pulling at my shoulder, and on waving ridges of sand instead of hard pavement. Though – beach, pretty girl, sun going down – it was very hard not to take Toni's hand. The last time I'd been on a beach had been in summer with Kelly's friends. I rolled my shoulders inside my sad anorak and leaned my head back to feel the salty air on my face. A black dog ran into the sea and stood there, barking.

'It's harder work than I imagined,' Toni said. 'Busking. I don't know how you do it all day every day.'

'Ah, it's not all bad,' I said automatically. 'Days like today are easy.'

Neither of us mentioned the days like yesterday, and the possibility, as autumn tipped over into winter, of there being more of them.

'You work hard too,' I said. 'Are you really spending most of half-term studying?'

She sighed. 'Have to.'

'Is it worth it?'

She shrugged. 'It keeps my mum happy.'

'Does it make *you* happy?'

'It's a lot of pressure. But yeah, it'll be worth it in the end. This time next year I'll be at uni somewhere. That's kind of exciting.'

'Oxford?'

'Maybe. Or Durham. Or Manchester. Or Bristol.' All these English cities I didn't know much about.

'Where's Marysia going?'

'Queen's. They can't afford for her to leave Belfast.'

She didn't say she would miss her, or that the band would have to break up. For the hundredth time, I wanted to ask about their relationship, but I didn't want to hear Toni's voice actually telling me she was gay. Especially not now, on the beach, with streaks of red and purple slashing through the grey evening sky, like the first time we'd met. And Toni wasn't grumpy with me, or sorry for me, or any of the things I hated seeing in her face, just happily walking along beside me with her hands deep in the pockets of her purple coat, humming when we weren't actually talking. As days go, it had been pretty perfect.

The desire to take her hand was so strong I had to force myself to do something more than walk and talk, so I started looking on the sand for interesting stones and shells to distract me. And that's how I saw the perfect shell – small, worn smooth, and the most delicate shades of pink and purple. It was as though the entire evening sky was inside that one shell. I didn't know what kind of shell it was, but it winked in the fading sunlight and I picked it up.

'What is it?' Toni asked.

I wiped it on my jeans. Even dry, it still shone. I held it out to her. 'A present from Bangor,' I said. I kept my voice light. I knew it was a bit corny, giving her a shell. I thought she'd look at it and put it in her pocket and forget it, or even just throw it back where it had come from, but she held it in her hand, and said, 'Thanks Cal. I'll keep it for a good luck charm.'

'For Oxford? Or Backlash?'

'Both. Everything.' She smiled, and took my arm, just in a friendly way. Her body leaned into mine. 'I'll drill a hole in it,' she said, 'make it into a necklace.'

'You might break it.'

'I'll be very careful.'

If I'd known what was about to happen I wouldn't have given my luck away, not even to Toni. Then again, it would have taken more than a pretty seashell to make any difference.

30

I got Toni to drop me on the edge of the city centre.

On the way past Cash Converters I hesitated and fingered my watch strap. It might be worth knowing what they'd give me for it, just in case things got desperate. I went in. It was like a normal shop except it sold a weird mixture of stuff – from lawnmowers to cameras. There were even some guitars hanging on the back wall – a couple of cheapies like the old Westfield I had lying around in Ricky's house, probably discarded by beginners who hadn't been able to get past the throbbing fingertips stage, but also a really nice black Fender Stratocaster. I flipped over the price tag – not that I needed an electric guitar – and it was £299.

'That's a bargain.' A guy about my age, a uniform polo shirt straining at his belly, materialised beside me. He nodded at my guitar case. 'You looking to sell one?'

'No.' My hand tightened on the handle. 'No way.' I had this stupid moment of hoping my guitar hadn't heard him. 'But – d'you buy watches? It's a good one.' I held out my wrist.

His plump cheeks swallowed his eyes as he squinted at it. I smelt his deodorant. 'Probably do you a good enough wee price,' he said. 'You just need two forms of ID and—'

I snatched my wrist back. 'I was only enquiring. I'm probably not going to sell it.'

Fuck's sake, I thought, glooming my way down the darkening street. Did you need ID for everything? All I wanted was to make a few honest quid. It's not like the watch was nicked. I shoved my hand deep in my jeans pocket.

It was in there, where it always was, a bit rubbed and flaky but safe in its plastic bag. It had become a bit of a talisman. I can't say I'd never been tempted. But I'd never given in. It was one of the things that made me feel good about myself. I rolled it over in my fingers.

Florian and Julia were leaving tonight. And if they didn't get it off me, they'd end up in some Dublin dive getting into bother in that naïve way they had. Really, I'd be doing them a favour.

I knocked on their door, hoping they hadn't already gone, but Florian called out, 'Come in!' Two rucksacks spilled clothes all over the floor and the shower roared from next door.

'Cal! You have come to say goodbye.' His round face lit up.

I set my guitar case down carefully and closed the

door. 'D'you still want ...?' I lowered my voice. 'You know.'

'Huh?'

I whispered it: 'You asked me if I knew where you could get some stuff?'

'Ah! Yes.'

'I can probably help you. How much do you want?'

'How much do you have?'

I took the bag out of my pocket. Florian picked it up and peered at it. His eyes glinted behind the round glasses. He opened it and emptied the crumbling lump onto his palm. Its sweet smell brought back a million memories.

'There's at least an ounce,' I said. 'You can have it for 250.'

Florian wiped his dusty hands on his jeans.

My heart was pounding. I didn't know why. I'd never sold before, but I'd bought plenty of times. And this wasn't some street corner, or dodgy bar.

Florian turned the lump round in his hand, like he was ready to change his mind.

'Hurry up.' Now the deal was done I wanted the stuff gone and the money in my pocket in its place.

He pulled out a bulging wallet from his pack pocket and counted off tenners and fivers, one by one. 'I can give you 200,' he said.

'Whatever.' I held out my hand for the notes.

When the door opened I thought it was Julia coming back from the shower. Until I heard Beany's voice.

'Just inspecting for damage before yous head off.' His voice changed. 'What the—?'

He came further into the room. He gave me a squinty look that made his face mean. 'This better not be what I think it is.' His voice was conversational but with an underlying edge. 'See if I'm right, son …'

But he must have known he was right. There was no way to pretend it was anything but what it was.

31

There was no point even trying to argue or lie.

'You've had your chance. More chances than I've ever given anybody.' Beany's face was nearly purple. 'Dealing! In my hostel. The one thing, Cal. The one fucking thing!'

'I'm sorry.' It was all I could think of to say. I wanted to tell him it was a one-off, but what was the point.

He threw us all out. There and then. It was no odds to Florian and Julia. Just one of those adventures they would laugh about when they were middle-aged: *Remember when we were thrown out of that funny little hostel for buying drugs? Was that in Cork or Derry? Oh yes, it was Belfast. God, wasn't it a dump?*

We stood in the street. Julia packed their little Polo in silence, her hair wet and ruffled from the shower. My guitar case was at my feet; my backpack on my back; the drug money in my pocket.

'We feel bad,' Florian said. 'Why don't you come to Dublin with us?'

I shook my head. 'Have to stay here. Got the band.'

'But we feel so *guilty*. If I hadn't—'

I didn't need to hear how guilty he felt. From the front doorway, Beany's voice called out. 'Yous have one minute to get the fuck away from my hostel.'

'At least let us give you a lift somewhere,' Julia said. 'Another hostel or a B&B or ...'

She made it sound so easy. We all got in the car, but as soon as the door closed and Florian pulled off down the street and round the corner, I wanted away from them.

'Just drop me at the pub,' I said. 'Any pub.' But drinking on my own in an anonymous pub always ended in disaster. I wanted to be somewhere with someone who might be glad to see me. Someone who knew my name. Well, my assumed name. 'Take me to' – what was that pub Joe had mentioned? – 'McGroarty's.'

Julia looked it up on her phone, and called out directions to Florian. I hunched myself down in the backseat while we drove through dingy, half-demolished streets and then up a main road lined with boarded-up shops. We were west of the city, or maybe north – I wasn't really sure.

'There it is,' Julia said. She turned to me and frowned. 'It doesn't look very—'

'Didn't you want to see the real Belfast?'

'Are you sure?' Florian squinted through his glasses at the barred windows and reinforced door.

'It doesn't look very nice. I don't mind taking you into town.'

I gritted my teeth. 'It's fine. Have a good time in Dublin.' I flung the door open, dragged my stuff out and watched the car drive away.

McGroarty's was a shithole, and there was no sign of Joe. I felt stupid. He wouldn't remember me. I hadn't even liked him, I'd just liked the admiration in his face. But it was a bar, and right now the main thing was to be drunk as fast as possible. To sluice away the horrible feeling of stupidity, and the memory of Beany's angry, disappointed face.

I drank fast, drank up all my Bangor busking money and started into Florian's two hundred, but didn't feel drunk. I waited in vain for the edges of the room to soften, for people's faces to brighten and look more attractive and for me to think, ah, fuck it, it'll be grand.

There was a darts match on. Nobody took any notice of me. They just threw their darts and yelled across at their mates and downed their pints. I went for a piss and realised, fumbling with my flies, and trying to stop the STD poster on the wall from shimmering and floating, that I was drunker than I thought. I just wasn't getting the happy vibes.

I looked down at the arc of my piss and hated myself. Who was I trying to kid, with my new life? It had all been made from paper and now it had been crumpled up and tossed into the bin. I couldn't make an honest living busking and I couldn't manage to sell a few drugs without messing up. And my first instinct when things got tough? To go and get off my head. Two hours ago, when I was sober, I could have phoned Toni and told her – well, not the truth, but *something*. I could have pretended the hostel had shut down because of a gas leak or something and I could have stayed at hers for a night or two while I got myself sorted. Or gone to a nice B&B and got settled for the night. I could be lying on a bed now watching TV, or in a lovely hot bubble bath. Instead of pissing out beer in a smelly toilet in a backstreet bar in some dodgy part of town I didn't even know.

I'd left my guitar and backpack under my seat. I rushed back, but it was OK. More than OK actually: Joe was standing at the bar, talking quietly to a blond fattish guy.

I felt stupidly nervous that he wouldn't remember me, but when I said, 'Uh – Joe, isn't it?' he turned round, gave me a clap on the shoulder and said, 'Och, hiya kid! What's the craic? What're you drinking?' as if he wasn't surprised to see me at all. 'Kevin, this is – ah, sorry kid, what's your name again?'

'Cal,' I muttered.

'Cal! That's right. How's the music?'

'Fine,' I said. At least he remembered who I was, even if he'd forgotten my name. He started telling Kevin about the band. It was ages since I'd been in male company. Easy enough to talk shite and not say anything at all.

'I play the guitar,' Joe said.

'Ah yeah, Shania told me.'

'He can play three chords,' Kevin said.
'Four,' Joe said.
'Aye, right.'
I laughed and said it was my round. Fumbling in my pocket I realised that I was making quite a dent in the drug money. Beany had weeks of rent from me and now he'd get to keep the money *and* rent the room out to somebody else. Over a hundred quid he owed me. Surely he couldn't do that. I shouldn't have let him. I'd gone far too quietly. But I knew I wouldn't go back and argue.
'Party at mine tonight,' Joe said, lifting his glass. 'It's only up the street. You wanna come, sing a few songs maybe?'
I shrugged. 'Might as well.'
'Will we go after this?' Kevin said. 'Or should I get another one in?'
'Yous go on,' Joe said. He lowered his voice. 'I'm waiting on Mark. I'll see yous up there.'
'I thought Mark was off it?' Kevin said.
'Shut up, will you?' Joe said. He tapped the side of his nose, then turned it into a scratch. 'Wee bit of business to sort out. Know what I mean?'
I knew what he meant. I wasn't stupid. Well, I was. If I'd had more sense, I could have made money out of that lump of weed weeks ago, safely away from the Crossroads. And then I wouldn't be sitting here in this dump with nowhere to sleep tonight. Then again, selling on someone else's patch in a strange city was likely to have got me into a hell of a lot more bother than that.

I guessed what Joe's party would be like. These guys were exactly the kind of crowd I'd drifted around with in Dublin. The kind of people I'd avoided in Belfast so far. But I didn't care any more. The party would solve the problem of where to go for the night. And tomorrow—

Well. Tomorrow was tomorrow.

32

Joe's house was a tall scruffy red-brick terrace a couple of streets from the bar. It looked like a really bad student house, all the doors open, the halls and landings full of people sitting, talking, smoking, snogging. Rap blasted out of an iPod on the living room windowsill.

The smell of dope was everywhere, drifting down the stairs, fighting the smell of frying from the kitchen. That night I thought someone was actually cooking; later I discovered that the stink of old grease was more or less permanent.

The first person I saw was Shania, who looked like she'd already been partying hard. She didn't seem surprised to see me, which I suppose was proof that she was pretty out of it, in that realm where nothing seems incongruous, except normality.

'Where's Joe?' she demanded.

'On his way,' Kevin said.

Shania pouted. 'Aw, I miss him,' she said. She looked at me, her dozy eyes suddenly focused. '*You* wanna hook up?'

'No!' I was pissed but not so pissed that I wanted to get off with a kid. Anyway, wasn't she Joe's girlfriend?

And what *about* Joe? I thought. Joe's years older than I am. What's he doing with her? And what am I doing here?

'Whatever.' She shuggled her way through the crowd, skinny shoulders wriggling up and down.

It was skanky and crazy, like a lot of parties I'd been to in Dublin except I'd never been on my own. Booze was sitting around for the taking, discarded bottles of this and that; nobody seemed to mind. Everybody was pretty out of it. It must have been late; things had reached a mellow stage. People mostly ignored me. I thought of getting my guitar out but when I tried to spring open the catches of the case my fingers wouldn't work.

I leaned against a doorway, welcoming the stab of the doorjamb into my back as a reminder that I actually existed. I had been at the party two minutes, or two hours. I was holding a bottle of cider, or beer. I knew no one. Joe came back but I didn't see Shania. He was with a girl who looked vaguely familiar and I realised it was the girl I'd seen with Shania that first day on the street. Her sister, I'd assumed. She looked older than Shania. At least sixteen.

What was I doing with these people?

I took out my phone. I found Toni's number. I

wanted to text her. I wanted to be back on the beach with her. But my fingers just slid uselessly over the keys.

The doorjamb stopped holding me up suddenly and I slid down it into a hunkering position. 'Ow,' I said, as the wood bashed my spine.

Shania was beside me, sitting on the floor, her sleepy eyes level with mine. I didn't know if she had really dark eye shadow on or if her actual eyelids were that colour. 'Wanna hook up now?' she said, as if the night had nothing much left to offer but she thought I'd do.

I tried to say something but my tongue was numb.

She leaned her head on my shoulder. Her hair tickled my neck. It smelt like the fat on a lamb chop. My stomach turned. I hoped I wasn't going to puke all over her.

'You gonna play your guitar?'

I shook my head. 'Too pissed.'

'I'm stoned.' She mouthed it silently, or maybe I just stopped hearing her properly.

'Yeah.'

'My sister's a slag,' she said into my ear. Her boozy breath warmed my neck. For the first time in ages I thought about Kelly. '*I* love Joe. Georgia's a bitch.'

'Does Joe love you?'

She stared at me, her eyes huge in her thin face. 'Does Joe love *me*?' she repeated. 'Does Joe love me?' She kept saying it, over and over until I wanted to scream.

'Is this party going to go on all night?' I asked. The

more I tried to speak the better my tongue worked.

Shania shrugged. 'There's always a party here. One kind of merges into another. Joe likes parties.' She narrowed her dark eyes. 'Have I seen you on the TV? You look dead familiar. Even the first time I saw you … Were you on—?'

I gulped. 'No,' I said. 'Definitely not.'

'OK.' She slid further down into a slump beside me, and took out a tin. She started rolling a joint, looking at me sideways. 'Wanna share?'

I wanted not to be in that room, at that party, with that girl, in that life. I wanted not to have been thrown out of Crossroads and not to have nowhere to go. I knew that dope could take me out of there for a bit – it had always done it for me, not as good as the pills I'd been chucked in there to get off, but easier and sweeter than booze, which always made me sick when I overdid it. Even though Shania was so out of it, her fingers, skinning up, knew what they were doing. She laid a neat line of tobacco along the bottom of the paper, and started adding a generous amount of dope. Already I could smell it, or maybe the smell was just in my nostrils already.

I wanted to take the joint from her and take a long drag. It was only a bit of dope. But I'd carried an ounce or so around with me for weeks and never given in. If I took it now – it's not that I thought I'd wake up tomorrow as a junkie, I knew it wasn't that easy, whatever they tried to tell you in drugs education – but I'd have failed. I'd be Ryan again. And however messy things were right at this minute, there was a tiny bit of sense inside me that told me not to take it.

So I said, 'Nah. You're OK. You go ahead, though.'

Shania looked at me like I was an idiot and said, 'I wasn't asking for your permission,' and stuck it into her mouth. The smell was so strong I gagged. I dragged myself up, pushed through the crowd – mostly they were getting off with each other, or just lying around in heaps – and forced my way outside into a messy yard with a high brick wall and an old sofa with broken springs. The cold air hit me and I stood for a minute, looking up at the sky that was never totally black in the city, sweat cooling on my neck. I gulped in the night air. My legs buckled and I flumped onto the sofa, wincing as the broken spring scraped my back. I shut my eyes against the whirling lines made by the broken paving stones and the bricks of the wall.

'All right, kid?'

I didn't risk opening my eyes or replying. I wasn't too drunk to know I was pretty close to puking and I'd rather not have an audience.

'It's Joe. You having a good time?'

'Great.' I concentrated on breathing. I felt his weight on the sofa beside me. So much for being left alone.

'Did you and Shania ...?'

'Nah. I don't think we're each other's type.'

'Everybody's her type.' His tone changed. 'D'you want anything? You know – anything?'

'I've had enough.'

'Sensible.'

'Never been called that before.' I sat up, and the paving stones and bricks tipped alarmingly. So did the cocktail of booze inside me. I pitched forward and started retching.

Joe gave me an encouraging slap on the back. 'Aye, get it up there, kid.' I was vaguely aware, as I puked again and again, of his hand on my back and his voice, over the disgusting noises I was making, saying, 'You're OK, kid.' And even though I'd been wishing he'd go away, I was sort of glad he hadn't.

I leaned back and closed my eyes, letting the rain wash over my burning face. Was it only a few hours ago I was on a beach with Toni? Thank God she hadn't seen me in this state. I heard the hiss of a tap and the splash of water.

'Here.' Joe offered me a pint glass full of cold water. 'OK?' he asked.

'Yeah. Sorry.' I rinsed my mouth out.

'Och, you're OK. Least you made it outside. And the rain'll wash it away.'

I looked at the mess I'd made and shuddered. 'This is your house, isn't it?' I remembered.

'It was my granny's. She's in a home. I'm looking after it for her.' He did air quotes round 'looking after'. 'It got me away from home. My da's a bastard. Here I can do what I like. Have my mates round. We have the best parties in Belfast. Seriously. Mental. People stay all weekend. You can if you like. Play your guitar. It's not always this crazy. But there's always something going on.'

I sipped the rest of the water slowly. For the first time since Beany walked in and found the dope, things were staying still.

'You're not from round here, are you?' Joe asked.
'Dublin.'
'Where are you staying?'
'I'm – between places.' I looked sideways at him. Behind the beard he had a roundish face with very pale blue eyes. Very ordinary. Kind, even. Who was I to judge him for having an underage girlfriend when he wasn't judging me for puking all over his yard? 'I was in a hostel but I kind of – well, had a bit of a fall-out.' I grinned to show it wasn't a big deal.
'Homeless hostel?'
'Christ, no.' What sort of person did he think I was? 'Just a backpackers' hostel. Need to find another one. Or a B&B.'
'Ah, you don't wanna do that. Wasting your money. Stay here.' He waved his hand at the house behind us. 'There's a couple of free rooms. Seriously.'
'Ah no, you're grand. Thanks.'
'Well, if you ever need a place. Give us your phone.'
I scrabbled it out of my pocket. He looked at it in disbelief. 'My granny had that exact phone,' he said. He keyed something in. 'Right, you have my number now, kid. Just in case.'
'Cheers.'
Joe looked up at the sky and shrugged his shoulders against the cold. 'Frigging baltic out here,' he said. 'I'm going in. You wanna—?'
'I'm grand here.'
'Soon be morning.'
Not soon enough. After a damp shivery hour in the yard, sobering up, listening to the party at a

remove and wondering why the neighbours weren't complaining, I decided the house was the lesser of two evils. I was shivering so badly the boozy, druggy fug wrapped round me like a blanket when I headed in through the back door. Shania was asleep in the living room doorway where I'd left her, a thin trickle of saliva congealed on her chin.

I'd find somewhere to crash for a couple of hours, and then I was out of this crazy dump and never coming back.

33

'Cal?' Toni took a step back, her eyes widening in surprise at seeing me on her doorstep. 'We don't have a rehearsal today. Marysia's away, remember?'

'I just thought – I don't know, you might want to hang out or something.'

'I'm working.'

'So, maybe I could just come in watch TV or something? I won't be in your way.'

'You smell like a brewery.'

'Oh.' I clamped my mouth tight but then had to open it to talk. 'Sorry. Bit of a party last night.'

'Whose party?'

'Joe? Remember he came to see Backlash?'

'Oh.' She wrinkled her nose; I didn't know if it was at the memory of Joe, or the smell of my breath. 'You can't just turn up here when you feel like it, Cal. I have stuff to do.'

'Sorry. I just – well, I didn't feel like busking.'

And I thought, after yesterday at the beach, we were back to being proper friends? Who could call in on each other? Not that I exactly had anywhere that Toni could call in on.

She pulled the door open wide. 'You're in luck,' she said. 'Mum's taken my granny to some National Trust house. She won't be back until teatime. I'll put the kettle on.'

I grinned. 'You're an angel.'

'You look like shit. Are you hungry?'

'I don't know. Pretty hungover. You know how—'

'No,' she said. 'I don't. Look, go and have a bath. You know where it is. There's clean towels in the cupboard.'

'Cheers.' I lumbered upstairs, my guitar case bashing the wall.

'Leave that here before you wreck the place!'

I lay for ages in the hot scented water, imagining it sluicing away all the alcohol from my pores and all the stupidity and embarrassment of last night. I imagined Toni coming into the bathroom. A fantasy that went the way you'd expect it to. That left me feeling worse in a way. Because it wasn't going to happen, and even though she'd let me in, and been nice to me in an exasperated way, she hadn't been *pleased* to see me. She was only putting up with me. And I was mainly here not because I was in love with her but because I had nowhere else to go.

When I went into the kitchen, in clean rumpled clothes, my hair drying in waves on my neck, she was sitting at the table, frowning at a book, holding her hair out of her face with one hand.

'I don't want to distract you,' I said. 'I know you have work to do.'

She gave *Hamlet* a dirty look. 'Ever read this?'

I shook my head. 'We did *Macbeth*.'

'Yeah, well, at least Macbeth got on with it, even if he was a psychopath. Hamlet just *talks* about it, and pretends to be mad, and faffs about – I mean, he's very poetic and tortured and everything, but he does my head in. Such a loser.'

'You going to say that in your interview?'

'Oh God – if I even get an interview.' She said it like it meant something to her – I wasn't so sure she was doing this Oxford thing only to please her mum.

'I need a break,' she said. 'Do you want some lunch? I could make scrambled eggs.'

Lunch, as I'd hoped it might, segued into lolling on the sofa, chatting about Backlash, and what the standard would be like in the final, and what Marysia would be doing in Poland. Then Toni picked up *Hamlet* again, said, 'Stay if you want,' and I lifted the *Observer* from the coffee table, and started reading the music reviews. I didn't care what I did; I just wanted to stay here. It all reminded me of the week I'd spent with Toni back when this all started. The gas fire was lit, and I had to struggle to stay awake. Billy came in, sniffed at my backpack and jumped up between us.

'Cal?' Toni asked suddenly. 'Why do you have all your stuff with you?'

'Oh,' I said. 'I've kind of – I'm moving on. From the

hostel, I mean. Had a bit of a – well, a row I suppose, with Beany – Mervyn – the guy who runs it. I did a favour for the Germans and it went a bit wrong ... It doesn't matter. I'll find somewhere else. I've actually booked into a B&B for the next few nights. Near the university. Only I can't check in until later.' I hoped it wasn't too obvious that I was kind of using her as a place to hang out until then.

'What kind of favour?' She frowned. 'No, don't tell me. I don't think I want to know.'

And how could you be so broke on Friday that you couldn't buy anything to eat, and flush enough on Sunday to be booking into a B&B? She didn't ask that, but I could see her wanting to/not wanting to.

'Don't look so worried,' I said, because I couldn't bear her to know how worried *I* was, and how close I'd been to accepting Joe's offer to stay in that horrible house. 'It's grand. I'll get back to busking tomorrow. Or maybe I'll get a job. I'm going to start asking around in bars and that.'

'Cal – you're not just going to disappear? I mean – you are committed to Polly's Tree?' Her eyes were dark with worry.

'I'm not going anywhere.' I put my hand on her wrist. 'You know I'm committed to the band. It's why I'm here.'

'I know,' she said. She pulled away. 'I'm being daft. I'm sick of that whingeing Hamlet. Fancy working on a couple of songs?'

34

I stood at the corner of two grey streets with a gale blowing up the back of my anorak. My fingers were too frozen to play, and anyway, nobody was stopping. I'd paid for a third and last night at Greenacres B&B, which was like the Ritz compared to the Crossroads, so I might as well head back there now. After that – I didn't know.

There was less than a pound in my guitar case. And weeks to go before the Backlash final. *You won't disappear?* Toni had said, as if she couldn't quite trust me. And I had promised. Right now that promise felt like the only thing I had. But I wasn't sure how to keep it.

35

Joe and I stood in the doorway of the attic. 'Em, there's kind of no bed,' I said. I didn't want to sound ungrateful. He hardly knew me, and he was happy to let me doss in his house for free. I couldn't start making demands. And the room wasn't bad – a back attic, overlooking the yard, though you could only see it if you stood on tiptoes and pushed open the skylight. There was a huge mahogany wardrobe, obviously his granny's, and what looked like a table but was actually an old sewing machine. That was it.

Joe looked thoughtful. 'All the beds are taken. Kevin's fell out with his girlfriend so he's moved in downstairs. Anyway, sure whatever you like. I've to head off here and do a bit of business. Here' – he pulled a key off a ring – '*Mi casa es tu casa.*' He grinned.

He left me looking at the room. On the minus side, there was no useful furniture and the house was stinking. I couldn't believe the first time I'd seen the Crossroads I'd thought it was a dive. It was a palace compared to this.

But on the plus side, Joe was friendly. The house clearly wasn't full of drugs and parties 24/7, and this room was tucked away at the very top and back. Its lack of amenities probably meant it wasn't used much – in fact, though it was dusty enough to be tickling my nose and making me sneeze, it was probably the cleanest room in the house.

And best of all, bottom line, if I stayed here, I could afford to have a bad day's busking and not worry that I wasn't going to have a roof over my head that night. I would even be able to stay here during the day and just chill. Maybe some of Joe's friends would be nice. Maybe there'd even be a girl who'd help me forget about trying to impress Toni. Which was never going to happen.

Yeah, some jailbait kid, Toni's voice in my head whispered. *Shut up,* I told her. I didn't let myself think about Shania. It wasn't any of my business.

* * *

I went out exploring the neighbourhood, feeling light without my guitar and backpack weighing me down. I'd been here before, of course, but it had been dark, even when I'd left the morning after.

It wasn't a middle-class area like Toni's but it wasn't a wasteland like the streets round the Crossroads either. You could see the mountains beyond it. I liked that. That day in Bangor – the sea air, the bigger sky – had reminded me of how hemmed in I felt by city streets. Maybe after Backlash, wherever I went and whatever I did, it would take me back to the sea.

Joe's house was on the main road, on a terrace of other identical houses. The one beside it looked empty, the windows bricked up, and the one on the other side had the same down-at-heel look as Joe's, with grey net curtains hanging raggedy in the windows and weeds choking the front garden. It wasn't derelict, though: two bikes leaned against each other on the front path, and a TV blared from an open upstairs window.

Two blocks down the road was a pound shop. It was full of cheap Halloween costumes and plastic pumpkin lanterns, but there was normal stuff near the back and I bought some cleaning stuff and a few cheap packets of pasta. I didn't really want to cook in that kitchen, but I knew how fast money went when you had to eat out. And I definitely needed to clean my room; I'd been sneezing my head off ever since I'd been in there. It was the kind of area where most of the shops were charity shops, pound shops, carryouts and pubs. And it was in a charity shop that I found the sleeping bag. The idea of sleeping in someone else's sleeping bag did gross me out a bit, but I unzipped it and made myself smell it, and fair play to whoever had donated it, it was a bit worn but it smelt of fabric conditioner and there were no stains. I could roll up my clothes for a pillow. That's what I used to do on camping trips with Louise when I was a kid. She'd hated camping, but I loved it, so every summer she'd take me into the Wicklow mountains in an orange-and-blue tent. I wondered where the tent was now.

I tried not to think about Louise as I cleaned up my room. There was an ancient hoover in the cupboard under the stairs and I dragged it up to the attic and hoovered up the worst of the dust. I wiped the surfaces with a damp cloth and wedged open the skylight. The stairs and landing carpet looked disgusting compared to the clean swept lines in my room so I gave them a bit of a hoover too, much to the shock of Kevin, who came out of one of the first-floor rooms rubbing his eyes.

'Fuck's sake,' he said. 'I came here to get away from all that.'

'Cheers,' I said. 'You're welcome.' And went on hoovering. Maybe I should have apologised for waking him – after all, we were going to be house-mates, but I wasn't going to turn into some kind of wuss just because Joe was letting me stay here. Partly to annoy Kevin, I hoovered the bathroom, living room and kitchen as well. The house was a funny mixture of granny and dosser chic. The living room was dominated by a huge three-piece leather suite that looked brand new, and the biggest TV I'd ever seen, even bigger than Ricky's. A few dog-eared posters – *Keep Calm and Skin Up*, and the Mona Lisa smoking a joint – clashed with the pink-swirled granny-wallpaper. There were no books, but loads of DVD box sets of American series stacked up beside the TV. I emptied ashtrays and filled a bin bag with takeaway cartons and empty cans. The kitchen, clogged in grease and piled with unwashed dishes, was worse, but I wanted to be able to cook in it without getting salmonella so I cleaned it as well as I could. There was a radio on the windowsill and I turned it on while I washed two sink-loads of dishes.

Louise would have fainted if she'd seen me. She could never even get me to take the mugs out of my room and put them in the dishwasher.

I didn't know why I kept thinking about her.

Joe came in as I was wiping down the cupboard doors, and I suddenly worried that I'd offend him.

'Oh my God,' he said. 'You got OCD or something?' He set down a plastic supermarket bag on the table.

'I hope you don't mind?' I ran the cloth through my fingers. 'I – um, I just wanted to thank you for letting me stay, and I – well, I haven't really much money so ...'

'Work away, kid. I don't mind. It looks like it did when my old granny was here, God love her.'

Unless his granny had had pretty low standards – I hadn't even tried to do anything about the fag burns and teabag stains over most of the worktops – I doubted this was true, but at least he wasn't annoyed.

'Only thing is, kid, it's going to get messed up again pretty quick. Halloween party tonight. This place is going to get wrecked.' He smiled in anticipation.

My first thought was I'd go out. But where? It was Halloween. The city would be crazy, and I didn't want to be in a bar full of drunk strangers. Might as well stay here with drunk strangers. And it would look a bit standoffish not to join in with the craic on my first night.

Only I wasn't going to take anything. I wouldn't even drink much. Not after last time.

'You can play your guitar,' Joe said. He grinned. 'It'll be mental.'

* * *

I wasn't sure if it was more or less mental than last Saturday. I was sober, which made me more aware of everything. The house seemed smaller now, and some of the faces were familiar – Shania sitting on Joe's knee, rubbing her head against his cheek; Kevin, drinking vodka in the corner and moaning about his girlfriend, and of course Joe himself. All the rest might have been the same as last week, or different. Some stuck around all night, others came for an hour or two. I sat on the broad arm of one of the leather armchairs and played my guitar. Some people ignored me, which didn't bother me at all. It was just like busking except without the money, though Joe kept bringing me cans of lager. After the third one I refused any more. I didn't want him thinking I was a freeloader and a pisshead, though I didn't think he minded about either of those things. He watched my fingers attentively.

'I wish I could do that,' he said. 'Could you teach me?'

'Sure,' I said. Maybe that would be my new job: travelling the world teaching people guitar in return for a free room. The teaching troubadour.

'Then you can play me those love songs I bought you,' Shania said, her face all shiny. Her eyes looked at him adoringly and I was reminded, with a squirm of unease, of Louise looking at Ricky. He didn't answer, but ran his hand down her thigh, and she rested back against his shoulder.

A girl said, 'Have I seen you somewhere before?'

Why did people ask that? But she was pretty in a plump, soft way, with dark hair and eyes, and she was at least as old as me, so I smiled – not a RyLee smile, just in case – and said, 'I busk a good bit round the city centre. You might have seen me there.'

'Nah. I'm never in the town these days.' She took a drag on her cigarette. 'You look dead familiar. I'm Lola.'

I looked down at the guitar. 'Maybe you saw me here last week?'

'I wasn't here last week. Couldn't get a babysitter.' She wrinkled her nose. 'You're class. You should go on TV.'

'Maybe. Hey – I'm tired. Going to head up to bed.' Lola looked at me suggestively. 'Um. See you,' I said and scarpered.

The first-floor landing was crammed with people smoking and talking, and the bathroom was in the kind of shape you'd expect after four hours of partying, but when I went up into the attic and closed the door, and wedged the sewing machine against it just in case someone was looking for somewhere to shag, it wasn't too bad. I'd made up a bed on the floor with the sleeping bag; my guitar was leaning against the wall, my clothes were in the wardrobe and fresh air came through the skylight with the occasional distant squeal of a banger. The party sounds were only a dull bass roar and the odd raised voice, not enough to disturb someone who'd stayed at the Crossroads Hostel for weeks.

Best of all, I'd been to a party and had managed not only not to be tempted by drugs but hardly even to drink. I hadn't got off with anyone. *See, Toni?* I said to her in my mind.

But I was glad Toni couldn't see me here.

36

There were good things about Joe's. Not having to hang round the streets all day was the best. If I felt like staying in, I could. There was Sky TV and there was usually somebody to hang out with: Joe, Kevin, and a sort of shifting population of Joe's friends and hangers-on. It could get chaotic – like the time Kevin's girlfriend, Nicole, came round and screamed in the street at three in the morning. Joe shouted out that he'd get the police if she didn't go away, but she must have known it was an empty threat – there was no way Joe would be inviting the police in.

One day I came in early from a crap day's busking to find Shania watching TV in school uniform.

'Joe's not in,' I said.

She shrugged. 'So? He doesn't mind. D'you want to make me some toast?' She stretched out her thin legs and leaned back, flicking through the channels. Her school blouse was unbuttoned far enough to show a pink lacy bra. She let the hand holding the remote rest between her small breasts, all the time watching me to see if I was watching her. I wondered if Joe liked her in her school uniform. She could be seventeen or so, I supposed. *So ask her,* I thought. *Ask her how old she is.*

'Jam?' I asked, escaping to the kitchen.

She came round a lot, sometimes with her sister Georgia but often on her own.

'She gets a hard time at home,' Joe said one night when she turned up late, eyes glassy, crying that she wanted him; she loved him; he was the only one for her. He left her to sleep it off on the sofa and came into the kitchen to carry on with his guitar lesson. 'Don't want to disturb her,' he said, with reason. Joe, for all his enthusiasm, and a decent Yamaha – he'd been given it, or maybe taken it, to pay off a debt – was as musical as a tin of beans. 'At least when she's here she's safe.'

It depended on your definition of safe.

Joe seemed to sense my misgivings. 'Look,' he said, 'the wee girl doesn't get on with her family. I know what that's like.'

'Me too,' I said without thinking.

'Yeah, kid, I guessed that. I can always tell when people are adrift. That's why I said you could stay here.'

'I'm not adrift.'

'OK. Cool.' He frowned in concentration as he tried to make his stubby fingers contort into an attempt at a C chord.

'Now, listen,' I said. 'Do you hear the buzz? That's because you're touching the E string. Try to only touch the strings you're meant to.'

When we went back into the living room Shania was awake. 'Joe!' she said, lifting her head up. 'You *left* me.' She pouted. Her head lolled; she was still pretty out of it. 'Joe,' she murmured, 'you're so good to me.'

'See?' Joe said. 'Lucky she's got me to take care of her.' He stroked Shania's long straggly hair, his big hand nearly as wide as her back, and she preened like a cat and flopped against him.

I shuddered.

Not my problem, though.

37

Tonight it was Toni making mistakes, not me. She had a cold, her nose a scabby blob in her pale face. The harsh uncovered light bulb in Marysia's shed made her look all white and red. I wanted to feel sympathetic but it was hard when she was being such a bitch.

'We need to rehearse more,' I said.

She banged her guitar down. 'It's all right for you. You've no idea of the kind of pressure I'm under. What do *you* have to do all day – hang round busking and living in that doss house?'

'It's not a doss house,' I said. 'And you shouldn't treat your guitar like that. Or will Mummy buy you a new one if you throw your toys out of the pram?'

'Are you saying I'm spoilt?' She sniffed, and then sneezed four times.

'You're acting like it tonight, *Princess*.'

'I'm not well,' she said pathetically. 'And don't call me Princess.'

Marysia said, 'You should have stayed at home, babe. You can't sing with a cold. And you must be really infectious, sneezing all over the place.'

'Thanks. Spoilt *and* disgusting.' She sounded like she was going to cry.

'Look, we should call it a night,' Marysia said. 'It's too cold in here anyway.'

'We can't,' Toni said, blowing her nose. 'We have to sort out this interview film thing.'

'What?' I said.

'I texted you about it.'

'My phone's been out of credit so I haven't checked it.'

'Well, get some fucking credit!' she snapped. Then she took a deep breath. 'How are we supposed to keep in contact? I know you don't have a lot of cash, but what if something important comes up? If you want to borrow a tenner for phone credit—'

'No, thank you.'

'Well, it's good news. It's just that it'll take a bit of organisation.'

I listened with rising horror as she explained: the Backlash organisers wanted to make a film about Polly's Tree to put on their website and maybe use in other places. Possibly even on local TV. 'They aren't doing all the finalists – but they saw that piece Matt wrote on *LiveScene BT* and they like our story. Marysia being Polish, me meeting you in the park like that – it is kind of a good story. We just have to sort out when and where they're going to do it. They want to see us all at home and then in rehearsal. It'll only be a couple of minutes of film.'

'No,' I said. 'No way.' I bent over my guitar and played the riff from the start of 'Plastic Girls' to hide how disturbed I was. 'You two do it. You're the ones they're interested in.'

'We're a band,' Marysia said. 'We should do it together. And it'll be fun.'

'You don't have a choice, Cal,' Toni said.

'I think you'll find I do.'

'I think you'll find you don't. You signed the contract, same as we did.'

I stopped playing. 'What contract?'

She gave a theatrical sigh, went to her guitar case and took out a sheaf of paper. She shoved it under my face. 'The one you signed?'

Heart pounding, I made myself look:

We agree to take part in any publicity organised by Backlash, including but not limited to print interviews, photographs, online video clips and television. And then: *Signed – Cal Ryan.*

It went on to declare that we were amateur musicians, had never been signed to a record company, hadn't performed on TV. And there again was my signature – or rather, *a* signature.

'So you have to do it,' Toni said. 'They're going to all our houses and then they want footage of you busking and some of us in school. It'll be really good fun. And don't pretend you're shy. You *love* performing. What are you so scared of?'

38

Toni's voice on the phone was somewhere between disgusted and disappointed. I didn't have to see her face to know what it would look like.

'Cal! You're not doing it because you have a *cold*?'

'I must have got it off you.'

'You don't even sound hoarse.'

I couldn't dispute that. 'They won't care; you two are the stars.'

'But will you have recovered for the real thing?'

Silence. Then, 'Course I will. It's not for a week.'

39

It wasn't a complete lie. I had a slightly scratchy throat and stuffy nose. But I probably didn't get it off Toni – Joe had been lying all over the sofa sneezing and coughing for a couple of days. OK, it wasn't bad enough to stop me doing anything I really wanted. But it was a good excuse to get out of something I didn't want to do.

Not didn't want to. *Couldn't.* Being filmed, being all over the Internet as Cal Ryan, being found out – the thought was enough to make me feel like I really was ill. As for the rest of what I'd signed – I couldn't think about it now.

I lay around the house with Joe most of the day, watching a box set.

'I got this bug off Lola,' he said, blowing his nose. 'She got it off her Lacey-Mae. Dirty wee bastards, kids.' He tossed another used tissue onto the pile on the floor.

After a bit his snuffling, and the hot air in the room, got to me and I decided fresh air would do me more good than resting in the fug of Joe's germs. 'Get us some Lemsip,' he said thickly. 'The strongest kind. Oh, and a couple of six packs of Bacardi Breezers.'

It was nearly December now and the air was sharp. There were no painted kerbstones round here and there were some street names in Irish, just like in Dublin, so I was a lot more relaxed about my southern accent. But when you walked as far as the roundabout, it was all red-white-and-blue kerbstones and loyalist flags. The tribalism was so in your face it was scary. I'd tried to write a song about it, but I'd torn up all my efforts. The last thing Belfast needed was some naïve southerner writing about it. And I didn't even want to imagine Toni's reaction.

I went to the park. Most of it overlooked rows and rows of red-brick terraces, but you could always look up and see the hills beyond the grey estates. Not gentle suburban hills: the streets just bled into wild bare mountain. No wonder Belfast felt so edgy when its actual edges were like this. I sat on a bench and looked down over the city. The lough was pewter-coloured, lots of ships in. I had one of those kicks of homesickness for Dublin Bay, and pushed it away. I concentrated on more immediate problems.

The Backlash final was in a week. What was I going to do? I couldn't bear not to be there; it was what all of this – these weeks of trying to make some kind of life here – had been about. Backlash had been the focus. If I lost it, I'd lose myself. I couldn't just not do it. And Toni and Marysia were relying on me. OK, Ryan Callaghan – RyLee, whatever you called him – had been a fuck-up, but Cal Ryan, despite a few blunders, wasn't. And it was Cal Ryan who'd signed that contract. What were the chances of being found out? I tried to work it out. If we won, there'd be publicity; the competition was obviously bigger than I'd realised. And then there'd be another fuck-up to add to RyLee's glittering career – what would it count as? Fraud? I could imagine Ricky's disdain. Louise's disappointment. And Toni and Marysia – especially Toni? How would she take being lied to?

If we just came nowhere, nobody would be interested in us. So – should I go and make sure we *didn't* win? By not doing my best?

But how could I get up on stage and deliberately not play my heart out? I remembered what Toni had said after our first gig – that her dad was a cheater and a liar. That would be cheating, all right. And anyway, I knew the moment I hit that first chord, and looked out into the dark expectation of the audience, and saw Toni's red hair glinting under the spotlight, I'd be carried away by the music.

All the thinking and the raw mountainy air were making my head ache. I walked back to Joe's, stopping at the corner shop and the off-licence for what he'd asked for, and a few bits of food. Now I had a proper kitchen, which wasn't always that clean but at least had most of the stuff that kitchens are meant to have, I'd learned how to do vegetable soup and a thing with tuna and tomatoes. I tried to make Joe take a few quid from time to time, for bills, but he always shrugged it off, so at least cooking was a contribution. I knew Joe had plenty of money, and I knew why; it was just never mentioned.

Until now.

When I got home, Joe was shivering and sweaty, and coughing like an old hag. 'I'm away to my bed,' he said, dragging himself off the sofa. He bent over and coughed. He didn't cover his mouth. 'Trouble is, it's Friday.'

'So?'

'Few wee regulars call. You know.'

'Ah.' I was never normally here on a Friday evening; we usually rehearsed.

'I've the stuff all ready for them.' He waved towards the cupboard above the TV. 'All in bags. I call them their lucky bags.' He smiled at his own wit. 'Anyway, kid, would you mind just giving them their stuff and taking the money? The big bags are thirty quid; the wee ones are fifteen.' He spluttered and hacked. 'Bring them in, don't do it on the doorstep.'

I didn't like it. But I was happy enough to sleep in Joe's house, drink his beer. It would be pretty hypocritical to say I wouldn't hand out a few bags of dope or pills or whatever was in the bags. And in a way it would be another good test for me. There was always someone smoking a joint at Joe's, or getting pissed, and I'd been proud of how I'd been able to hold back; but this – leaving me alone, on a day I was already finding pretty stressful, with bags of drugs –

this would be more of a test. In a twisted way, it was good to know he trusted me.

Who was I kidding? What did he think I was going to do? Run off and sell it for myself? Joe knew I relied on him for the roof over my head. He wasn't stupid: nobody asked to come and stay in the house of someone they'd met twice if they had many alternatives.

There were seven bags in the cupboard, all labelled with people's names. Some I recognised – Aoife came round to the house pretty regularly; Ciaran was Kevin's brother. Others meant nothing to me. I set the bags out on the coffee table to make life easier and then I thought, don't be daft, what if the police call at the door? My drug dealing history hadn't been impressive so far.

Aoife came first, handed over her thirty quid and said, 'Quiet tonight. Where's the big lad?'

'In bed with flu.'

'Aye, it's going round.'

A couple of guys my age came next, looked suspicious at Joe not being there, but paid up and left quickly. I started to feel less jittery. I turned the TV on.

The door rang again. It was two kids. And I mean kids. Maybe not even at secondary school. I looked at them in disbelief. Had they come to ask for their ball back or something?

'Joe's got something for us,' said the shorter, fatter one. He had a buzz cut and an earring. He pushed in past me and sat down on the sofa.

'Names?' I asked.

'Dean and Tyler.'

I found the bags easily enough. Then hesitated. Dean and Tyler were watching TV, mouths open. Dean was so short his feet hardly reached the floor when he sat back. Tyler was wearing a Simpsons T-shirt. I wanted to say, *Look, lads, save your money for sweets. You should be out kicking a ball around, not taking drugs in alleyways*. But I didn't. I took their money, handed over the bags and away they went, not a bother on them, jostling each other.

'Thanks, mister,' said Tyler.

I felt sick as I closed the door behind them. And it was nothing to do with my cold. I was relieved when the seventh bag had gone, even though the girl who came for it was about Shania's age. For the first time I got why Beany had thrown me out so fast. I put Joe's money into the cupboard. £150. About ten good days' busking.

And then, just when I was settling down to watch TV, Shania came with two of her friends. She looked disappointed to see only me. 'Is Joe not in?' she asked.

'He's in bed with the flu.'

'Aww.' Her thin face drooped. 'This is Madison and Caitlin,' she said. 'I've been telling them how cool it is here.'

She flopped down on the sofa. Her friends stood behind it, looking round the room and at me. They were in track bottoms and tight tops, with big doughnuts of hair high on their heads and painted-on eyebrows. Caitlin was really fat. 'So where's the party?' Madison asked. 'Shania says there's always a party here.'

'Not tonight,' I said.

Shania pouted. 'Joe said he'd get us Bacardi Breezers.'

'Shania said we could hang out here,' Caitlin said.

'Yous can,' Shania said. 'Take no notice of him. He's *nobody*.' She glared at me and went out to the kitchen. I heard the fridge door open and a shout of triumph from Shania. Five minutes later all three girls were watching TV and drinking Bacardi Breezers. 'Tell Joe we're here,' Shania said. 'It'll make him feel better.'

'*You* go up and make him feel better, Shania.' Madison stuck her tongue out and waggled it and they all shrieked with laughter.

My phone rang. I looked at the display: Toni. I frowned at the girls to shut up.

Toni sounded tired, but no longer grumpy. 'Cal? I'm sorry if I was a bit harsh. I've been – well, I suppose I got a bit stressed out, just trying to juggle everything. School and – anyway. Are you OK?'

I moved into the kitchen so she wouldn't hear the girls shrieking.

'Yeah,' I said. 'I'll be grand in a couple of days.' I forced out a cough that I didn't really have, which had the useful effect of hurting my throat and making my next words genuinely hoarse. 'How did the filming go?'

She sighed. 'Stressful! We're both exhausted.'

I started to say I was sorry, but she cut me off, suddenly business-like again. 'Will you be OK to rehearse during the week?' she asked. 'It will be our last chance.'

'Yes. Say – Thursday?'

'All right. Take care.'

I didn't want to end the call. I didn't know how I could bear to wait until Thursday to see her. I stood in the kitchen for ages, looking out at the backyard through the grimy window. I heard the front door slam and Kevin's voice in the living room with the girls. I didn't want to go in there with them. I really didn't know what I was doing here. And this time in eight days it would be Backlash and after that, whatever happened, I would have to sort myself out.

40

I was stupidly nervous of seeing Toni on Thursday night. And, Sod's law, I was starting to feel like I actually *was* coming down with a proper cold now, shivery and stuffy. But it was a good rehearsal, in her dining room. We all fizzed with energy. Maybe the break had done us good.

Toni had typed out the set list for Saturday – 'Plastic Girls' to open; 'You Think You Know Me', 'Northern Streets' to get them all dancing and singing along and then slow it right down to end with 'Secret Self'.

'I'm not sure.' I sucked on the end of the pen I'd dug out of my guitar case. 'Wouldn't it be better to end with "Street Song"?'

'It's not called "Street Song". You always get that wrong.'

'Whatever. It's better to leave them on a high.'

'It might be,' Marysia said.

Toni glared at her. 'Marysia, we discussed this on Friday.'

'We weren't all here on Friday.'

'Exactly.'

I shrugged. 'Look, I don't mind what order we do them in,' I said. 'Why don't we ask Queen Jane what she thinks?'

'She's not into music,' Toni said.

'She's into giving her opinion, though,' I said. 'Like you.'

She gave me the tiniest smile, and Marysia laughed.

Queen Jane agreed with me. Amazingly.

'Now I'll have to retype the set lists,' Toni said, 'Like I haven't enough to do with exams starting on Monday and—'

'You don't need a set list for four songs,' I said.

'Yes, you do. You have to hand it in to the judges, actually,' she retorted.

In two days' time.

41

I climbed the long slow hill out of the city centre, my guitar dragging at my shoulder. If I timed it right I'd miss the Friday regulars coming for their lucky bags.

I couldn't feel the same about Joe since Dean and Tyler had come round. After the rehearsal last night, I'd tried to say something to him.

'I was surprised how young some of them were,' I said.

Joe shrugged. 'They're old enough to know what they want,' he said. 'If they weren't getting it off me, it'd be somebody else. And at least what they get off me's good stuff.'

'It's not *good stuff*. Christ, Joe, I was in rehab for three months last year. I dropped out of school …' I shook my head. 'I've seen the damage they do.'

And was Shania old enough to know what she wanted? But I didn't mention her name.

'Look, kid, if you don't like it, you can move on.' He didn't sound threatening, or angry, or even annoyed. He was just reminding me how things were. In what was, after all, his house.

By the time I arrived back, Shania, Caitlin and Madison were in the living room, with Joe and Kevin and a couple of older guys I didn't remember seeing before. Shania had her head on Joe's lap. They were all smoking, and the air was thick with the smell of dope.

I hesitated in the doorway. It should have been a happy enough scene. A few girls, a few guys. No one was out of control. It was far mellower than some of the crazy nights here. Kevin was even drinking a cup of tea.

But Joe and his friends were all older than me, and not one of those girls looked over fifteen. And they weren't tough, confident girls like Toni and Marysia. Madison's arms were criss-crossed with scars, Caitlin was fat and nervous, and Shania – Shania was as brittle as that shell I'd picked up on the beach. She was gazing up at Joe like he was some kind of god, her eyes never leaving his face. Like Louise and Ricky. Only worse because Louise was an adult.

Joe held out a spliff, careful not to hit Shania with it. 'Want to join in, kid? Play us a song?'

'Sorry,' I said. 'I'm all played out.'

Kevin threw me a can of Carlsberg. 'Ach, get your gob round that,' he said.

Madison giggled. 'D'you say that to all the girls, Kevin?'

'I'm tired,' I said. 'I'll see you.' I threw the can back.

42

I jerked awake in the dark with my head pounding and the unmistakeable realisation that the vague cold I'd been fighting had finally burst out as something nastier. I swallowed down nails. Shit. Backlash started in – I checked my watch – thirteen hours.

I hated the thought of crawling out of my sleeping bag but I was desperate for water. And there'd be plenty of drugs in the kitchen – not the lucky bag kind, but the stuff Joe had maxed out on when he'd had this bug last week. If I dosed up now and rested all day I'd be grand by tonight. I had to be. I was never ill, apart from hangovers.

The house was quiet, though snores stuttered from behind Kevin's door and the fourth stair creaked as usual. The kitchen light was on and the room looked worse than usual, grease shining on the worktop, the floor crunchy with crumbs under my bare feet. I ran the tap until it was cold, and then had to unearth a pint glass from the mound in the sink. I opened a cupboard and riffled among the pot noodles and boxes of teabags. I found some kind of flu-max thing with night-time tablets for zonking you out. Perfect. I took one and washed it down with the water, and pressed out a couple to take back to bed with me for later.

'What are you doing?'

I swung round.

'Shania.' I was suddenly aware of being only in boxers and T-shirt, which was more than she was wearing. She had on a T-shirt of Joe's and I couldn't help seeing, no matter how hard I tried not to look, nothing else. 'What are you doing still here?'

She wrapped her arms round her thin childish body. 'Couldn't sleep,' she said. 'Took some uppers.' She giggled. 'Need some downers. But a hot chocolate will do. Want one?' She reached across me and switched on the kettle.

The last thing I wanted was to shiver in the kitchen drinking hot chocolate with a half-naked Shania, but then I thought, well, maybe it'll be a chance to talk to her, so I said I'd have tea and sat down at the table, stifling a yawn.

'Here.' She plonked two mugs down, sat opposite me and lit a cigarette from the packet on the table. She looked at me with her bushbaby eyes, and stretched out a bare foot towards my leg. I jerked away.

'Oh my God, what is your *problem* with me?' she asked. 'You used to be dead nice and since you moved in here you're like – not.'

'I don't like seeing you – well, off your head, or …' I was maybe not up for this conversation at four in the morning, after all.

'Oh – so *you've* never been off your head? Yeah right.' She waved her cigarette at me. 'That first night you came here you were so pissed you could hardly stand.'

I coughed. 'I know,' I said. 'And I used to do a lot worse. And I see you doing the same kind of stuff and I suppose it makes me scared for you.'

'I just like having a good time.'

I looked down at the steam coming off my mug. 'Or is it more that you let other people have a good time with you?' I held my breath. Was this going too far?

She was quiet for ages, just smoked and looked at me. 'What's that meant to mean?' she said after a while, her voice brittle.

'Joe's a lot older than you.'

'So?'

'And Kevin and – I don't know, maybe those guys tonight? They treat you like – like you're a piece of meat.'

'Don't be stupid.' She scratched her neck with the hand that wasn't holding the cigarette. She had false nails, bright pink with some kind of glitter on them. 'They're lovely. Specially Joe. They treat me really well. They're always buying me stuff and—'

'They're grooming you,' I said. 'They give you the drugs and the drink so they can—'

'That's rubbish. That's like paedophiles and shit.

Oh my God. You watch too much TV.' She shook her head like I was some kind of idiot.

I wanted to ask if she'd slept with any of them, but couldn't think of any way of asking that didn't make me sound dodgy myself. So instead I said, 'Well look, if you're not happy about anything you should – you know – tell somebody. Your mum or – or someone. Georgia.'

She looked scornful. 'My mum's a cow. And Georgia hates me because Joe doesn't fancy *her*. Look – I'm fine. I love staying round here. And tomorrow – well, today, I suppose – Joe's taking me out, just me, not Caitlin or Madison or nobody. And he's buying me loads of stuff. So butt out.'

The way she talked about Joe. The way her eyes shone. I knew who she reminded me of: it wasn't just Louise. It was Ryan Lee Callaghan, aged 16, when Ricky first paid attention to him at *PopIcon*. I'd wanted some of Ricky's shining confidence. Most of all I'd wanted him to notice me. He'd been the judge I'd wanted to impress. I'd stood there week after week doing exactly what he told me, being who he wanted me to be, singing the vapid songs he'd picked for me in the way he'd told me to sing. I'd even secretly worried that I'd some kind of gay crush on him. When he'd got together with Louise it had seemed like the perfect happy ever after. For about five minutes.

He'd told me he could make me into somebody and I'd let him make me into nobody.

My throat closed against the tea. I poured it down the sink.

'And you know what,' Shania said, as I was lifting my glass of water to take back upstairs. 'You've been sponging off Joe for weeks. So don't start bad-mouthing him now.'

I nodded as I walked past her. 'Yeah,' I said. 'I know.'

43

'Toni? Hey. Just wanted to check the time for the soundcheck.'

'Six o'clock. We're meeting outside the Ulster Hall.'

'Oh yeah.'

I hadn't forgotten. I'd got her two reminder text messages yesterday. I just needed to hear her voice.

'You OK, Cal? You sound hoarse.'

'I'm grand.' *Please don't go away.* 'Uh – you all set for tonight?'

'Of course I'm all set. You know me.'

I don't know if I do. Not really.

'Oh,' she said, as if she'd forgotten something. 'I got my Oxford interview date. Mum's just booked my flight.'

'Wow, congratulations.' *Stay on the phone.*

'Yeah – just after my mocks end, so you know, big week. So – I'd better go and do some revision.'

'OK. See you later.'

'You sure you're OK? You sound weird.'

'I'm fine. See you at six.'

44

The knocking got louder. It wasn't a dream; it was someone at the attic door.

'Come in,' I said, my throat scraping. I'd slept on and off all day, aching and sweating, and the little rectangle of sky in the skylight was darkening again.

Shania burst through the door. I had a confused moment when I thought that only a few minutes had passed since I'd seen her in the kitchen. Then I realised that she was fully dressed, in a short black dress I'd never seen before, and that she was crying her eyes out.

I wriggled out of my sleeping bag and pulled on jeans and a hoody over my sweaty T-shirt. 'What's wrong?' I asked.

She stood inside the doorway, shaking. I drew her in and sat her down on the sleeping bag, since there was nothing else to sit on. She reeked of sweat and alcohol and men. Her nose was running and she kept dashing her arm across it. Her arms were bare, skin reddening to bruises. She hugged herself and shook. One of her pink glittery nails had come off and the real nail underneath was bitten and ragged. I dug out my other hoody from Granny's wardrobe and wrapped it round her, trying not to touch her.

'What happened, Shania?' I asked gently. But I knew.

She looked down at herself, at the skimpy black dress, and gave a huge sniff. She shook her head, her wispy blonde hair swinging round her. 'You were ri-i-ight,' she said. She started sobbing really hard, catching her breath like a child. I knew I should comfort her but I was scared to touch her.

'Someone hurt you?'

She nodded silently. 'Joe took me out and bought me this dress. Like he promised. And he was dead nice to me.' She sobbed harder. I dug out a wad of tissues from under my guitar case and handed them to her. 'He took me to this big house. He said it was his friend's. He said we'd go and have a drink there. He wanted to – to show me off.' She was quiet for ages. I could hear both our breathing.

'What did he give you?' I asked gently. 'Something you're not used to?'

She nodded. 'Pills. And whiskey. He said I looked so grown up I should have a grown-up drink and that's what they were all drinking.'

'All?'

'His friends. Three of them.'

'Did they—?' I didn't want to put words in her mouth. And, oh God, I did *not* want to be here on my own dealing with this. I checked my watch. It was nearly four. Two hours before I was due at the Ulster Hall.

I reached out and pushed the hair off her face. 'Will I take you home?' I suggested. 'To your mum?'

'Don't be stupid!' She pulled at her hair. 'My mum'll kill me.' She bent over, and started rocking herself. 'They took turns,' she whispered. She clamped her hands over her mouth. 'Gonna boke,' she muttered. There was no time to get her to the bathroom, so I yanked over the bin and held her hair for her. I remembered Joe's hand on my back that horrible night in the yard, how kind he'd seemed. When she'd finished she curled up on my sleeping bag, crying. The room reeked of alcohol and sick. 'Shania,' I said, stroking her hair but still afraid to touch her body. 'Tell me where you want to go and I'll take you, I promise. Will I call Georgia?' But Georgia was only a kid herself. 'Shania, please let me take you to the police.' I thought of Toni's words the one time she'd met Shania: *She's jailbait*.

'No!' She sobbed until she was retching again.

'Shania, these men – Joe and his friends – they've committed a *crime*. If you report them now, they won't be able to do it to any more girls. Like Caitlin or Madison or—'

'They didn't *force* me,' she sobbed. 'Not really. And I didn't mind Joe – just – not the others.'

'You're underage,' I said. 'You have bruises.' I was pretty sure there'd be more evidence when they examined her, but I didn't want to say that in case it terrified her even more. 'How did you get away?' I asked her. 'Where does Joe think you are now?'

'Oh, he knows I'm here,' she said. 'He dropped me off. He's away to do a message and then he's bringing us back a Chinese. To celebrate. He doesn't know I'm upset. He – he said he was proud of me. He's getting me an iPad.' She blinked back her tears and tried to smile.

My skin turned to ice.

'Shania. *Please* tell the police. They'll look after you, be really nice to you, I promise. They won't blame you.'

'No! I'll get took into care.'

'Is this going to be your life? Being *used* by men? They took advantage of you!'

'Joe *loves* me!'

'Is that why he hurt you?'

She chewed her lip for a long time. Then, in a tiny voice, she asked, 'Will *you* take me to the police?'

What could I say?

'Yes,' I said. 'Course I will.'

I threw all my stuff into my backpack. The sleeping bag, rolled up small, just about fitted. 'What are you doing?' Shania whispered.

'Well, I'm not coming back here.'

'So where will you go?'

'Don't you worry about me. I'll be grand.'

45

Where the hell are you? It's ten past.

Really sorry, something's come up.
Emergency.
Will be there asap promise.

Tell me you're joking.

I wish. At police station.
I'm not in trouble.

You ARE.

I don't know why I thought I'd get away with just texting. I'd had my phone on silent since I got to the police station – I wasn't meant to have it on at all, but I couldn't ignore the flashing *TONI CALLING*.

'What the hell—?' she demanded. 'We've had to go ahead and soundcheck without you.'

'I'll be there. Soon as I can. Can you maybe – I don't know – get us a late slot?'

'Where are you? What's so important you had to do it *now*?'

'I'm at a police station. I have to give a statement.'

'What have you done?'

'Nothing. I can't really talk, but – remember Shania? She—'

My phone went dead.

'Hello?' The policewoman smiled. 'They're ready for your statement now.'

'Is Shania OK?' I slipped my phone into my back pocket.

She sighed. 'Well, we're looking after her, but it's not the same thing, is it?'

They'd been really gentle with Shania, and fetched her mum, who cried and said she couldn't cope and didn't want her kids taken away. And there'd been a social worker and a nurse and it had taken *hours,* in a succession of musty hot rooms, and I kept trying to leave but they wouldn't let me. They'd brought me tea and sandwiches but I couldn't eat. I'd thought I was doing my bit by taking her there and helping her to explain, but they wanted way more than that. At one stage I even wondered if they thought I'd been at her myself, and I nearly wished I hadn't got involved, but I remembered her voice saying, *They took turns,* and I knew I hadn't had a choice.

Making the statement took ages. When it came to signing it, I hesitated. But I was in a police station. 'Just your normal signature,' said the policeman. And

I signed the name I hadn't written for months: *Ryan Callaghan*.

They let me go. I stood on the street outside the police station, backpack over one shoulder, and guitar case in my hand. I checked my watch. It was twenty to nine.

46

From behind the closed doors into the Ulster Hall auditorium I could hear the thump of a bass. But it wasn't Polly's Tree.

'The event started at eight,' the woman behind the box office desk said. 'You've missed most of it.'

'But I'm with one of the bands!' I gestured towards my guitar case.

'We can't let anyone in after the competition's started,' the woman behind the desk said. 'And bands had to register by six o'clock.'

'I got held up. It wasn't my fault.' I tried a RyLee smile but it was a pretty small, exhausted one, and all it got me was a grudging, 'Well, let's see your ID.'

'I – must have forgotten it. Look . . .' I tried to think. 'Where's Gillian? With the blue hair? She'll know me.'

She looked at me as if I was crazy and I knew I wasn't going to be allowed in.

Well, nobody could say I hadn't done my best. I turned to go. God knows where.

And then I heard my name.

'Cal?'

I didn't know the man coming out of the toilets. He was short with shaggy ginger hair.

'Cal? From Polly's Tree?'

'Yeah?' Was he one of the promoters? I didn't remember him. Had Toni sent him out here to wait for me? And then I saw his hazel eyes and the shape of his nose and I knew who he was.

'You're Toni's dad? How did you know—?'

'Ah, she sent me pictures of the three of you.' He said to the woman at the counter, who was watching us with great interest, 'This lad's with my daughter's band. And they're on next. Now you wouldn't stop him going in, would you? Wasn't it the luck of God I went out to answer a call of nature in time to rescue him?' He gave a lopsided smile, and you could see the woman melt. I began to see why Queen Jane had issues with me, if she didn't like being reminded of her ex. 'She doesn't know I'm here,' Anto told me as he steered me towards the auditorium. 'I thought I'd surprise her.'

He pushed open the heavy wooden doors and a wave of heat and noise hit me, as the audience clapped.

'I'm too late,' I said.

'No, you'll be grand. They changed the programme round so they'd be last. Now I know why. That'll be the band before them coming off.'

But he was wrong.

That roar of applause was to welcome Polly's Tree onstage.

The stage looked miles away, and huge, and in the middle of it stood two girls looking tiny, dwarfed by all the sound equipment. Toni's face was pale in the spotlight, her hair a flame. She and Marysia looked at each other, and Marysia counted in the way I normally did. Toni grabbed her mic and smiled out at the audience, and if you didn't know her you wouldn't have thought there was anything wrong at all.

'We're Polly's Tree,' she said. 'And this is "Plastic Girls".'

She struck a G chord, smiled at Marysia, and started to sing.

And all I could do was set my guitar case down and watch from the back of the hall.

'Ah, son,' whispered Anto. 'It's too late, isn't it? What happened that you let them down?'

What about all the times you've let her down? I wanted to say, but I couldn't say anything. All I could do was watch numbly as two-thirds of the band I'd been so proud of limped their way through their set without me.

In a film, they'd have started off rubbish, and the audience would have booed, and Toni would have been singing bravely through her tears, looking helplessly down into the audience. Then I'd have burst through the doors, carrying my guitar, which would be magically in tune. I'd have joined in as I made my way through the crowd, and then I'd have leapt on to the stage, never missing a note, and joined Toni at the mic. There'd have been this amazing roar from the audience and suddenly she'd have been singing like a diva, smiling through her tears at Cal, the boy who'd saved the day. It would have ended with us all grouped round one mic, arms round each other, singing together, and the audience swaying or maybe clapping along. And naturally Polly's Tree would win. And then Toni would kiss me and the credits would roll.

But it was real life. So none of that happened. They did their best. Toni sang her heart out, and her guitar wasn't bad at all. But bass and rhythm guitar just wasn't enough of a sound in a venue like this, especially in what were meant to be the instrumental bits. I knew every note of every song, so I knew how it should have sounded.

And so, of course, did Toni and Marysia. Toni was overcompensating for the thinness of the sound so, by the time they got to "Northern Streets", her voice was faltering on the high notes. I'd seen Toni in all kinds of moods, but, up on the stage of the Ulster Hall, I'd never seen her so vulnerable. Or so magnificent.

When it was over, they hugged for ages, and ran off stage, clasping hands.

The applause was polite but not enthusiastic, except from me and Anto, and I suppose, somewhere in the crowd, Queen Jane and all the Nowalczyks.

Anto turned to me. 'Weren't they great? he said. 'But,' he went on, more musician than parent, 'they missed you, didn't they?'

'Yeah.'

I couldn't bear to hear the adjudication, so I pushed my way back out of the hall and out into Bedford Street. Lights shone from the restaurants and bars. Cars, mostly taxis, drove up and down. I wished I could go away. Just away. But I crossed the road and waited in the shade of an empty building, guitar and backpack at my feet, folding my arms against the cold of the night.

At last people started to throng out of the Ulster Hall, laughing and chatting. But not Toni or Marysia. I saw Jess in a crowd of girls, but she didn't see me. More than once I was tempted to leave, and if I'd had somewhere to go to, I might have done. The pavement sent chills through the thin soles of my Converse.

But at last they came out. Toni and Marysia, with Queen Jane and Marysia's family behind them. I looked for Anto but there was no sign of him. Maybe he'd talked to her inside and that was why they were so late.

Toni looked small and defeated, swamped by the guitar case on her back.

'Toni!' I moved out of the shadow of the building and started to cross the road, dodging a beeping taxi. For a moment I thought she hadn't heard, or was going to ignore me. But she stopped and looked at me. She didn't come towards me and I realised she wasn't going to make it easy.

Well, I hadn't made it easy for her.

I stood in front of them. I could hear my own breathing, loud and fast. She was wearing a necklace I hadn't seen before. It was the shell, on a thin leather thong. She saw me looking at it. 'So much for luck,' she said. She yanked it off and threw it down on the pavement. It lay, delicate and perfect against the grey, still showing the hazy purple sky from our perfect day. I thought she was going to stamp on it.

'Let me explain—'

'No,' she said. 'Whatever it is, I don't care. You're a—'

'Toni,' Marysia said. 'We should let him try—' She bent down and picked up the shell and after a small hesitation, slipped it into her pocket.

'No!' Toni shook her head. Her eyes were full of tears. She dashed her hand across them and said, 'I never want to see you again. You're *nothing*.'

In a film she'd have slapped my face and then we'd both have cried and fallen into each other's arms and made up.

But it was real life. So she turned and walked away.

47

I sat in McDonald's and tried to look like I had some tea left in my cardboard cup. This was the second time they'd come round and brushed the floor. The other punters were loud and drunk and young, apart from an old guy on his own like me. I wondered why he was sitting here after midnight. He wasn't scruffy and he didn't have any bags. Maybe he just couldn't sleep.

So. I was down to my last three pounds with seven pence phone credit – not even enough to send a text. The battery was dying anyway and I'd left my charger plugged in at Joe's. There wasn't a single place in Belfast where I'd be welcome. Joe's was out, obviously. If I'd any sense I wouldn't go near that part of town again.

Maybe it was time to go home now. I'd run out of options.

Facing Ricky – not just his anger that I'd assaulted him, but his scorn at me creeping back with my tail between my legs, with nothing to show for my months away except broken friendships and a bad cold – would be horrible. But at least I wouldn't be sitting in a late-night café with nowhere to go and all my possessions in a backpack. And God, I felt like shit. I wiped my nose with the scratchy paper napkin, and shivered. I couldn't stop myself fantasising about arriving home, letting Louise look after me, the coolness of clean sheets, the light warmth of my duvet, all my music and clean clothes and the sparkling kitchen and Sky TV. Maybe Ricky would be away. And I wouldn't have to *stay*. I could pick up my ID, get some stuff together, organise a new life somewhere else. Only better this time.

There was nothing to stay in Belfast for.

I went to the toilets and saw myself in the mirror: I hadn't shaved for a few days and I hadn't washed or combed my hair today; my face was red and sweaty. I looked like a wino. No wonder the police had been suspicious. No wonder Toni had recoiled.

I never want to see you again. You're nothing.

And though the memory was enough to flay the skin off my face, I knew I couldn't leave Belfast without trying to apologise. Even if it was the last time I ever saw her, I wasn't just going to disappear.

Somehow I'd keep myself safe and dry tonight – at least it wasn't raining – and in the morning I'd find somewhere to wash and shave and make myself look less like a tramp, and I'd go and explain to her. Then I'd busk until I had the fare for Dublin, and then I was out of here.

I was no stranger to being up all night, but it was usually to party. Staying awake because you'd nowhere to sleep was a whole different thing. The city was alien. When I left McDonald's at closing time I thought I'd just walk and see what happened. After all, I'd been asleep half the day, though that felt like weeks ago. And as long as I was walking I could tell myself I was a normal person with somewhere to go.

But my guitar and backpack felt twice as heavy as usual and every step sent waves of pain through my back and legs. Even my skin hurt. Bloody Joe and his germs. Every street was endless. People piled out of clubs, laughing. Lines of taxis crept up to street corners, their headlights stabbing my eyeballs. Everyone had somewhere to go.

The club crowds dwindled; the streets emptied. A fox dashed across my path, its tail a bright plume under the streetlights. Like Toni's hair. I wandered vaguely in the direction of Toni's house, so I wouldn't have so far to go in the morning. I passed the park, and thought of trying to get in – because that seemed in keeping with being a free-spirited troubadour. It could be a story – *Did I ever tell you about the night I slept in a park in Belfast?* But the fence was far too high and spiky to climb, especially with a guitar. In the end I found a deep sheltered doorway, the porch of a big old house that had been made into a solicitor's. I felt self-conscious rolling my sleeping bag out, but that was daft, there wasn't a sinner about. And I'd slept on the beach a few times, and I liked camping. What was the difference?

I knew the difference. I was just trying to make it OK with myself. I might be kipping in a doorway with my guitar behind me to keep it safe and my backpack as a pillow – and thank God for my sleeping bag! If Joe's attic had had a bed and bedclothes I'd be really scuppered now – but only because I was a traveller – a free-spirited troubadour – who hadn't organised things very well.

At first it felt good to be lying down. But the doorstep cut into my hips every time I tried to move, and soon the coldness of the ground seeped through my sleeping bag, right into my bones. I couldn't make my mind switch off. I wondered if Shania was asleep in her own house, with that worried-looking mother crying downstairs. And what would happen to Joe, if he'd be arrested.

She's jailbait. Surely if Toni knew *why* …

I stuck my head inside my sleeping bag, and somehow, for minutes at a time, I slept, and the minutes joined up until a creeping grey dawn and the rumble of early-morning traffic told me the night was over.

48

This time, it was obvious she wasn't going to invite me in. She didn't even let me say hello.

'No way,' she said. 'You can't keep messing up and then turning up on my doorstep.'

'I wanted to expl—'

'No.' She looked me up and down, and the hurt I'd seen in her eyes last night had gone. I saw only anger and disgust and disappointment.

Mostly disappointment. I'd seen it in enough faces to recognise it.

I didn't have the energy any more to try to explain. I half-turned away, my guitar case bashing my leg. 'Oh,' I said, 'I'm leaving town.'

She shrugged. 'Nothing's stopping you.'

And she slammed the door.

49

Nothing's stopping you, Toni said.

But she was wrong.

I had less than a pound.

I thought of hitching to Dublin but even though I'd washed in a café toilet, dug out a comb and changed out of last night's clothes that reeked of stale sweat, I didn't look like someone you'd pick up at the side of the road. I wondered where Anto was. Had he seen Toni? Had she been pleased? Would him being there have made up in any way for me letting her down? If I'd had my wits about me, I could have scrounged a lift back to Dublin with him.

At least I had my guitar. And if I didn't earn enough for the bus fare home today, there was always tomorrow. I'd already survived one night. OK, it had been horrible, my hip bones still felt the ache from every time I'd turned over in the night, but nobody had hassled me, no dogs had pissed on me, and I was still here. Alive, if not exactly kicking. If I had to do it again, I could.

I walked into town. It was much colder today, and every time I stood still shivers nipped my back, so I found a spot in one of the malls, out of the wind. Christmas shopping had started properly. The shops belted out Christmas songs. I had to sing really loudly to try and be heard, but my throat was too raspy to make much noise.

Two kids in red anoraks stopped beside me. I smiled. They started walking backwards away from me. 'You're shite, mister,' one of them said.

I stopped smiling.

* * *

I nearly didn't see the paper. And if I hadn't, if I'd got on that bus and ended up in Dublin, I don't know what would have happened. Because in Dublin there were places I knew, people I knew, where I could have gone. I probably wouldn't have ended up sleeping in doorways, but I can guess what other kind of trouble I'd have ended up in.

Anyway, that's not what happened. This is.

50

Considering how rough my voice was, I didn't do that badly. Maybe people were full of early Christmas cheer. By mid-afternoon I had nearly ten quid. But my throat was on fire, and my head like a cement mixer, and standing busking all day after a night in a doorway was starting to get to me. Another few quid and I could get on the bus and sleep. What happened when I woke up in Busáras in Dublin, still miles from home, I didn't let myself think about. And what would happen when I came face-to-face with Ricky I definitely didn't think about. You can only take so much at a time.

I needed a break. I gathered up my money, hoisted my backpack onto my back, grabbed my guitar case and looked round the shopping centre. There was a food court upstairs but the thought of dragging everything up the stairs made me shudder, and anyway I didn't want food, I just wanted to sit down and maybe have a cup of tea. There was a little café opposite the newsagents. It was busy, the only seats left were outside, but I didn't care as long as I could sit.

I set my tea on the table, unloaded all my stuff and sank into the small upright wooden chair, trying not to think about the cosy beds all over Belfast that were barred to me through my own stupidity. Even the attic floor at Joe's – well, I hadn't lost that through stupidity. However grim things were right now, I knew that helping Shania had been the right thing to do. I wondered briefly if she was OK, but to be honest I was too wrapped up in my own problems.

I wasn't really reading the headlines on the papers outside the newsagents. I was sitting there, not focusing on anything, trying not to get too settled because I knew I'd have to get back up and try to earn the rest of the fare. My brain also wasn't working that well because I had a fever and hadn't eaten all day. So when I saw a familiar face and read *I WON'T TURN MY BACK ON LOVE RAT NOLAN SAYS LOYAL LOUISE* my brain just went *Ah, there's my mam,* until the message kicked in.

'Would you mind keeping an eye on my stuff while I run and get a paper?' I asked one of the women at the next table. She nodded without breaking her conversation with her friend, and I dashed over to get the *Irish Sunday Star.*

Most of the front page was about some rugby player who'd been caught with his pants down. The fuzzy picture of Louise, looking rabbity and tired, was quite small; I suppose it had only caught my eye because she was my mum. Under the headline it said, *Story on Page 6*. My fingers fumbled with the cheap paper, and there it was:

Louise Callaghan Nolan, wife of pop impresario Ricky Nolan, has spoken on social media of her heartbreak at recent revelations about the mogul's affair with model Tiffanie Tierney. Louise (39) told Twitter followers, 'Ricky and I are made for each other & we aren't gonna let some teenage tramp break us up!' Nolan (47) denies having an affair with Tierney (19) despite the model's assertion that she is pregnant with his baby. The couple deny splitting up, but Louise was seen yesterday boarding a flight to Palma de Mallorca, where Nolan has a luxury apartment. Nolan issued a statement saying, 'Louise and I have not split up.' However, he had 'no immediate plans' to join his wife.

Louise, who has been married to Nolan for under two years, is the mother of 'bad boy' PopIcon *winner Ryan 'Rehab' Lee, once managed by Nolan. Lee, who has battled addiction, is thought to be abroad but it is not known if Louise plans to join her troubled son.*

I stared at the paper. Why hadn't I known any of that?

Because I'd been living in my own world. My own wee world, as they'd say here in Belfast.

Well, there was no point in busting a gut trying to earn the rest of the bus fare. No point going back to Dublin if Ricky was in the house without Mum. I couldn't even imagine him letting me in to get my stuff.

I sat until my tea went cold and the waitress gave me the kind of unfriendly look I was getting used to. Then I picked up my bag and guitar and moved on.

51

'Hello? Sir? Can you hear me?'

I poked my head out of my sleeping bag.

It was a girl wearing a fluorescent tabard. Behind her was a guy about my age.

'We're from Homeless SOS,' she said. 'Sorry to disturb you. Would you like some hot soup?'

'Or a sandwich?' the guy asked, like I was in a restaurant.

I shook my head. 'It's the middle of the night.'

'Honestly, there's help available,' the guy said. 'Nobody has to be on the streets.'

'I'm not on the streets,' I said. 'I'm a travelling musician.' I tried to remember what Toni had called me. A trouba-something, but I couldn't. I stuttered out a few attempts at the word and abandoned it.

'There's a lot of danger associated with rough sleeping,' the guy went on. 'But there are services for homeless people. There aren't any hostel beds tonight, but tomorrow – you can get advice and help with any issues that might be contributing to your situation.'

'Alcohol,' suggested the girl. 'Or drug addiction.'

The guy handed me a card. 'Here's our contact details,' he said. 'There's an address on the back – there's a drop-in centre there.'

They left in a white van and when I woke in the morning there was no sign of the leaflet. Maybe I dreamed it. I was having trouble working out what was real and what wasn't.

The hours stopped joining up. I couldn't keep thoughts in my head for long. I tried to sing but it hurt to breathe. And I made hardly any money even at the best busking spots. It seemed like the more you needed it, the less likely people were to give it to you.

* * *

Shopping centre toilet. Stripped to the waist, washing my armpits. Cold. Looking forward to being clean. Hating the smell of myself. Hard squeezing out the soap from the dispenser. My fingers slid off the lever. A fat kid came in with his dad and screamed.

'This isn't a public washhouse,' the dad said. 'Come on, son.' He pulled the kid's arm.

'I'm wetting myself!' the kid wailed.

'We'll go in the disabled,' the dad said.

* * *

A girl sang 'Oh Holy Night' in the arcade. She had a backing track. She got loads of money.

* * *

There was a wall between me and normal people. I'd always been on the other side of it before.

You're nothing.

* * *

Dizzy. Enough money for a Burger King meal. I queued up in the one opposite the City Hall. I ordered my meal and sat in a corner where nobody would look at me. I unwrapped it. The smell of salt and fat made my stomach fizz. I chewed on a chip for ages. It wouldn't go down. I drank the Coke, all of it, even when the ice cubes melted into watery slush, but every time I tried to swallow the food I gagged. I wrapped it all up and shoved it into the bin and went back outside. Probably I'd regret it later, but that was nothing new.

* * *

I hit down on the strings hard and one of them twanged into my eye. I cradled my guitar. It was useless with five strings but if I put it down I didn't know what I would be.

I remembered the girl in the fluorescent tabard. Had I dreamed her? *There are services for homeless people*. But that'd be saying I actually *was homeless.* Which would be ridiculous. I just had to get through this rough patch.

My guitar was too heavy. I had to set it down. As I bent over to put it in its case a fit of coughing seized me so suddenly I crashed to my knees. My guitar broke my fall with a sickening crack and a jangle of strings.

Street level. Ugg boots and men's shoes. Jeans and woolly tights. Someone sidestepped. Tutted. I could just keel over now. Give up. Someone would have to do something. Take me to hospital. Take over.

But there'd be questions and forms. Maybe Ricky would come. Maybe Mum from Spain. To see how badly I'd messed up.

I fought hard to breathe. And after a bit the coughing stopped and I could sit up, leaning against the shop wall. The lights round the City Hall sparked in my eyes. I didn't try standing. I was scared to look closely at my guitar. I stuffed it into the case and clicked the clips shut.

Two girls in uniforms like Toni and Marysia's walked towards me. One of them was Jess, her mane of hair flowing down the back of her school blazer.

I opened my mouth to call to her, to tell her – I don't know what. Then closed it again. She hadn't recognised me.

Her friend pulled her arm. Jess rummaged in her bag and threw a couple of coins on top of the guitar case. As soon as they'd gone past I looked and it was two two-pound coins. I couldn't believe I'd got to the point of being pleased by earning four pounds.

Except I hadn't earned it. I hadn't been playing. Which meant I'd been begging. Not deliberately, but that's what it amounted to. Someone had given me money because I was down and out. Because I was nothing.

52

I stayed leaning against the shopfront and watched the two girls go down the street. The pavements were starting to glitter with frost. And I knew, with a clarity I hadn't felt in a while, that I had to do something. I couldn't face another night outside. Maybe I'd have gone to the drop-in centre if I'd known where to go. Maybe not.

Drop in. Drop out.

Ricky used to call me a drop-out.

You're nothing.

But if I could get through the next few days, surely things would get better? Things seemed worse because I was sick – it wasn't just a cold, it was some kind of flu thing, and being outside all the time wasn't helping it. But it wouldn't kill me. I could buy some paracetamol with my four quid. If I could just go and sit it out somewhere.

I knew where.

53

It took me a while to find the right garden, walking along the back entry beside the railway line – we'd always gone through the house before. I kept having to stop to cough, but at last I was pushing open the shed door. I'd expected it to be locked; I'd been prepared to break in, but the padlock hung open from the lock.

Inside it was warmer than the street. I fell over something and risked putting on the light. Maybe they'd see it from the house. Maybe I sort of wanted them to.

I set my stuff down in a corner. I didn't open my guitar case to see the damage. I felt like I could never open it again.

What I'd tripped over was Marysia's practice amp. What was it doing out here? Marysia was always so careful with her equipment. And on the windowsill was a pile of stuff that had never been there before

– a jumble of guitar strings and picks and a couple of leads. And the programme for the Backlash final. I picked it up and then set it down again without reading it. In the middle of the pile was the shell. Still perfect, cool in my hand, filmed with condensation from the damp air. I picked it up, rubbed it dry then set it back. I remembered Toni wrenching it off her neck; Marysia bending down to pick it up from the street outside the Ulster Hall.

It looked like Marysia had stashed all this stuff in here because she couldn't bear to look at it. I knew how she felt.

And beside it was the bottle of Polish vodka. I lifted it, wiped condensation from its red-and-white label. The cold smoothness of the bottle reminded me of the night I'd taken a nip of it in here. I remembered how the vodka had burnt its comforting way down through me. The night when things had seemed so hopeless after a miserable day. The night I'd had friends to help me out, and a clean room in the Crossroads to go back to, and the prospect of going to the seaside with Toni the next day.

The night before I'd messed it all up.

And every time I'd made a mess of things I'd always made it worse by getting off my head. I set the bottle carefully back on the windowsill.

I unfolded the garden lounger Marysia and Toni always sat in, and unrolled my sleeping bag. It felt dampish and it didn't smell great. There was a spare cushion on the old deckchair too, and a pile of dust sheets beside the paint pots on the shelf. It was pretty makeshift but it was a hundred times better than a doorway. I took out the bottle of water I'd bought on my way here, and the packet of paracetamol. I took two because that was what it said to take. They were hard to swallow.

And then the coughing started again, worse than before, wracking me, choking me.

For the first time I thought it probably wasn't going to be grand.

54

Someone was saying my name.

'Cal?'

It must be a dream. I was in Joe's and Shania was knocking at my door.

Someone was touching my shoulder. Gently at first then shaking me.

'Cal?'

Somewhere in the mix of damp and stale body odour, a scent of roses and something sharp. Toni.

Definitely a dream, then. I didn't move. Didn't want to wake up and lose her, like I had so many times. I breathed in her scent but next second the cough gripped me. I struggled to sit up because it was worse when I lay down, and through the horrible burst of coughing I could see that it was her, the real Toni, not a dream.

'Oh God, Cal, what are you doing here?' she said. 'What happened you? You're freezing. Here.' She pulled off her thick duffle coat and put it round me. She didn't take her arm away and I let myself relax into her when the coughing stopped, let myself enjoy the feeling that she was holding me even if it was just the way you'd comfort a sick child.

She touched my forehead with her cool fingertips. 'You're burning up.'

'It's just a bad cold.' I closed my eyes and breathed in her scent. 'What are you doing here? Is it – a rehearsal?'

She gave a brief unamused laugh. 'Nothing to rehearse for.' Then she said, 'Actually, I came for this.' And she reached up to the windowsill and lifted down the shell.

We both looked at it in her hand, small and perfect.

'It's – I'm being stupid,' she said. 'But I was getting ready to go to Oxford and – well, it didn't seem right not to take it. I remembered Marysia had it. She's away this weekend but I knew she'd left it here and so I decided to come and get it.'

'I hope – it brings you luck.'

'Have you been *staying* here?' Toni asked, as if she couldn't believe it. She looked round at the dusty, grubby space, my backpack, the bashed guitar case. I saw her eyes light on the vodka bottle.

'I didn't drink it,' I said. 'I'm stone-cold sober.' And I tried to laugh, but she didn't join in.

'*Sleeping* here?' she asked.

'I sort of ran out of options.'

'But you were at that guy's – Joe's?'

'No.' I started trying to explain why, but it brought

on the cough again, worse than ever, jackknifing my body, ripping me apart. I saw fear in Toni's eyes, and I remembered her once telling me she was squeamish. *Remind me not to get sick,* I'd said, and it had all been a joke. I tried to tell her it was OK, it was just a cough, I'd be OK in a minute, but the more I tried to speak the more it wracked me. Finally I coughed up a lot of green gunk that spattered over my sleeping bag.

And then I pretty much just wanted to die.

I didn't though. I started being able to breathe better and experience a few feelings. Mostly mortification.

'Sorry,' I rasped, trying not to look at the mess, trying not to look at Toni's face. She stroked my hair back from my forehead and I remembered doing exactly the same for Shania. Though Shania's hair had been clean. Where was she now? Was she OK?

'I've got Mum's car outside,' Toni said. 'I'm taking you to hospital.'

55

The doctor took us into a cubicle and pulled the curtains. I could see what she was thinking: that Toni and I looked wrong together. I looked and smelled like a down-and-out, and Toni was obviously a nice middle-class girl.

'Now, the nurse is concerned about your breathing,' she said. 'And your temperature's very high. Let's have a listen to that chest. Sit up on the bed for me. Take off your coat.' She was middle-aged, bossy and kind. She reminded me of Queen Jane.

She listened to my chest and lungs, her stethoscope cold on my skin. My breathing was harsh and loud in the small space. 'OK,' she said. 'You've a nasty infection there. A touch of pneumonia.'

'So much for a bad cold,' Toni said.

The doctor went on, 'Have you had a drink today, Cal?'

I shook my head. I don't know why she had to ask that

– but then again, it wasn't an unreasonable assumption.

'Have you been sleeping rough?' She said this as if it wasn't a big deal, as if she saw people in this state all the time – maybe she did.

'Few nights.'

'Where?' Toni asked, her voice a hoarse whisper.

I shrugged. 'Just – wherever. A doorway.'

She bit her lip. 'No! I can't believe—' She took my hand and I thought of how often I'd wanted to take hers. But this didn't *mean* anything; it was just pity, just like me looking after Shania. Even so, I couldn't help gripping hers quite hard.

'Well, you'll be in a nice warm hospital bed for the next few nights,' the doctor said. I could feel her looking at us, at our joined hands, mine grubby, Toni's clean, and wondering. 'You'll go up to the ward as soon as we can get a bed sorted out. For now, we're going to get some antibiotics into you, and some fluids. You're severely dehydrated. When's the last time you had something to eat?'

I shook my head.

'And is there anything else I should know about? Any HIV? Drug use?'

'No!' I bent over to cough. 'I haven't taken anything,' I said when I could talk again. 'Not for *months*. I promise.'

'Well, you rest now.' She looked at Toni. 'You can stay if you want. Get him to drink some water. A nurse will be in soon.'

When she had gone, pulling the curtains behind her, Toni filled a glass with water and held it out to me. It reminded me of Joe the first night I'd met him. 'Take it slowly,' she said. It felt wonderful. I lay back against the cool pillow, eyes shut. For now, it was enough to be here, with Toni holding my hand again as if, maybe, I wasn't *that* disgusting.

'Why didn't you come to us? Me or Marysia? You know we'd have helped! Christ, Cal, I can't bear to think you were on the streets.'

'I was too – ashamed.'

She didn't say anything for a long time. I kept my eyes shut and willed her just to stay there, not to let go of my hand. But something pushed at the edge of my memory. Something that had made me feel good, but was now starting to worry me. I sensed a restlessness in her, as if the Florence Nightingale act was starting to lose its novelty, and when I heard her mouth open I knew she was going to say she had to go.

But she didn't. She said, quietly, 'What was the worst thing?'

'The loneliness,' I said without even having to think about it. 'It was really fucking lonely.'

And then I remembered. I snapped my eyes open. 'Your interview!' I said. 'You said' – I tried to remember through the feverish fog – 'you were getting ready to go to Oxford. When?'

'It doesn't matter.'

'*When*?'

'Tonight. But it's OK,' she said. 'I don't think I even want to go. And maybe they'll let me reschedule or something. Or maybe I'll just forget about it. It was more Mum's dream than mine ...'

'You went to the shed to get the shell?'

'Well, yeah, but ...' She sounded embarrassed, like she'd been caught out in some great foolishness.

'You went to all that bother for something you say doesn't matter to you? Toni! Are you sure you're not only saying this in case you fail?'

'No!'

'I don't believe you.' I pulled myself up on the trolley, trying not to start coughing. 'What time's your flight?'

'Half eight, but I don't have to—'

'You do.'

'But I'd feel so guilty leaving—'

'I'm grand here.'

'You're not grand! What would have happened if I hadn't found you? You were on the streets, Cal. You could have *died*.'

I looked up at the clock. It was nearly half six. 'I'm not wrecking another dream on you,' I whispered.

It was the first time either of us had even hinted at Backlash. Toni looked at me with shock, and then puzzlement, and then something I couldn't read.

'Look,' I said. 'When I let you down last week I had a reason – a really good reason.' I wanted to explain but I was so tired, and I was coughing every couple of words. She had to lean in and I knew she'd be able to smell me. 'I can't tell you now because – oh God, it'd take too long – but part of me was glad of the excuse.'

'*Why?*' Her eyes were wide and puzzled. 'You were so into it. I thought it was the only reason you were staying in Belfast?'

'I was, but – it's complicated,' I said after a pause. 'But Toni – don't do the same thing. Don't use *me* as your excuse. Go to Oxford. Do your best.'

I pulled my hand away. 'Go on,' I said. She looked into my face then, and her eyes darkened with something I couldn't quite read, but it was something I hadn't seen in anyone's eyes for a long time.

I don't know how easy it was for her to walk away from me. I know how hard it was to let her go. But when she turned at the door and looked back at me, I knew what that look in her eyes was.

Respect.

56

I've always dreaded being in hospital, but compared to the streets and the shed, it was bliss. They kept coming in and apologising about how long it was taking to get me a bed, but it was warm, and dry, and there were people around. Voices and movement at the edge of my consciousness. I still felt lousy, the room coming and going round me, and my chest on fire, but they gave me something to help the cough and now that I wasn't alone I wasn't so scared of it. The worst thing about that time in the shed had been coughing and coughing and thinking I'd never get a breath again, and then lying in a pool of icy sweat.

I kept replaying Toni's arms round me, her cool hands on my burning face, her fingers in my hair. How it felt when she left.

I tried not to remember how disgusting I was – smelly and pathetic and coughing my lungs up all over her. Would she be in Oxford by now? The clock said it was after ten but my head ached so much when I opened my eyes that I squeezed them shut again. Outside the cubicle were voices and action. Someone kept yelling out, 'Don't tell Jack. Don't tell Jack.' Over and over again.

I'd get to stay here for a few days, I supposed, and then—

I closed my eyes.

* * *

Back in the street, fighting the cough. Cars zooming, lights attacking my eyes. No. Hospital. Movement. Bright lights overhead. A lift. Swoop of nausea as the lift plunged upwards. A foreign accent telling me it was OK. Cool hands on my head. *Lie still.*

* * *

Different noises, new voices. Someone pulling at my clothes.

'He'll need a bath.'

'One thing at a time.'

'Cal? Cal? Can you hear me? Are you with us?'

'Looks like he's been on the streets.'

I tried to open my eyes, but it was too hard.

* * *

Too hot. Shivering. Cool water. *There you go. That'll help.*

'Toni?'

'I'm Sarah. Who's Toni?'

* * *

The room stayed still and it didn't hurt so much to keep my eyes open. I was in a ward with other beds. I didn't look closely at the other people; the lights were low. I was hooked up to a drip. I'd vaguely known, last night, that they were doing all that. I still felt like shite, but not as spectacularly ill as last night. Two of the others were snoring.

I closed my eyes again.

* * *

'Marysia!'

'Is it OK to hug you?'

'You might not want to.'

'I could only catch pneumonia if my immune system was already compromised. Which it's not.'

'It's not that. It's – I keep asking them to let me have a shower. They gave me a bit of a wash but I still stink. I know I do.' I could never have said that to Toni, though with Toni I'd be even more aware of how revolting I was. And much as I ached to see her, I hoped I wouldn't be wearing this hospital gown when I did.

'I don't care.' She hugged me tight and I relaxed against her soft warm body. There was none of the fizz I felt when I hugged Toni. 'Don't you *dare,*' she said fiercely, 'do anything like that again.'

I didn't say anything.

'How could you let things get that bad? I mean – you have a family. Why didn't you go home?'

'It's complicated ...'

'I can't believe you were in our shed and we never

even knew. Why didn't you come to the house?'

I winced. 'I kept thinking things would get better. I knew I was sick, but I thought if I lay low for a few days it'd pass and then I could get back to busking and – I don't know. I wasn't thinking straight.' The more I looked back at those feverish shivering days the more nightmarish and unreal they seemed. 'Can we talk about something else?'

'Where will you go when you get out?'

'Don't know. Don't make me think about it. Tell me what you've been doing.'

'Just exams and stuff.' She grimaced. 'Like you said: talk about something else?'

In the end, we didn't say much, especially as I had a really messy coughing fit, but having her there was the next best thing to having Toni. Easier in some ways. I wasn't as embarrassed. Marysia held the cardboard dish and said, 'Well, you don't want that shit clogging up your lungs, do you?' as if it didn't bother her.

'You'll make a good doctor,' I said.

When it was time for her to go – they were really strict about visiting – I said, 'Can you come tomorrow?'

'I don't know. My mum and dad are both working late. I'm meant to be babysitting. I can probably leave Tomasz at his friend's house, but Kryssie doesn't *have* friends and Mum'll kill me if I leave her on her own. I might have to bring her with me. That would probably set your recovery back at least a week.'

'Well – that would put off having to find somewhere to go,' I said. 'Or I could cough up more of that delightful phlegm and scare her off.'

Marysia smiled. 'I thought you'd be – I don't know, different. Sorry for yourself,' she said, 'but you're just the same old Cal, aren't you?'

I couldn't answer that.

* * *

There was a TV thing attached to the bed, but you had to put money in. I'd no phone, nothing to read. I was trying to make myself eat, but, between feeling sick, and the hospital food being pretty disgusting, that wasn't going too well. The most interesting thing that happened was when they took out the drip. There was a small bruise where it had been.

I was forcing down a cup of greyish tea when an older nurse I hadn't seen before came up to me.

'Cal Ryan?'

'Yeah?'

She smiled, but I could see her taking in the general grossness of my half-washed state. *It's not my fault*, I wanted to say, *I keep asking for a bath!* 'We're having difficulty finding your records,' she said. 'I just want to check I have the correct details.'

I hesitated. I had some vague notion that I must be entitled to some kind of healthcare in the North, but not if I didn't exist.

'That's not my full name,' I said.

'Ah. That possibly explains it. So what's your full name?' She held her pen poised.

I chewed my lip. This woman wouldn't have heard

of RyLee. But now that the time had come, I was a bit reluctant to get rid of Cal Ryan. He hadn't been a bad guy, even if he'd messed up in the end. But he'd reached the end of the road.

'It's Ryan Callaghan,' I said.

She started to note this down on her clipboard. 'Any middle names?'

'Yeah,' I said, since there was no help for it. 'Ryan *Lee* Callaghan.'

57

Marysia came again, dragging the sulky-looking Krystyna with her. Krystyna flumped into the only chair, clutching *Heat* magazine and an asthma inhaler. She fiddled with her phone.

'She was meant to wait in the canteen but she won't go there on her own because she said men keep looking at her.' She raised her eyes to the ceiling, and I started to smile, but then remembered Shania. *They took turns.* I shivered. 'She watches too much TV,' Marysia went on. 'Kryssie, sit over there and don't earwig.'

Krystyna gave her the middle finger and then pointed at her earbuds. She shuffled backwards in her chair until she was as far away as possible.

'Sorry,' Marysia said. 'It was the only way I could get away.'

'Have you heard from Toni?'

Marysia nodded. 'She should be home anytime.

She thinks it went OK. I bet she was brilliant, though.'

'She was brilliant the other night,' I said. 'I mean – I know she's squeamish, and I was pretty gross, but – she was amazing. Really – well, caring.'

Krystyna sucked loudly on her inhaler.

'Well, you know *why*, don't you?' Marysia looked at me coolly with her wide-set grey eyes. 'She loves you.'

'Don't be daft.' I nearly said, *I wish.* 'That's insane! I drive her mad—'

'That doesn't matter. And you love her too, don't you?'

I opened my mouth to protest, but closed it again. Because all I had left was truth. I looked down at my hands.

'Yes,' I said.

Krystyna sucked on her inhaler again. Noise leaked from her earbuds, a tinny beat with a high vocal; it didn't sound like real music at all. I couldn't believe she was just sitting there like a cow chewing the cud, reading her celebrity gossip and not even looking at us.

'Well, that's good,' Marysia said. 'What's the problem?'

'The *problem*? Well – aren't you and Toni – you know?'

'What?'

'A couple?'

Marysia laughed. 'No! What made you think that?'

'Everything! You're always – hugging, and calling each other babe and – you know … all that.'

'That's what girls are like, Cal! Toni and I are best friends. But not lovers!'

Krystyna didn't even look up at the word *lovers*.

I tried to make sense of this new reality. 'So you're not gay?'

'Ah,' Marysia said. She stopped laughing and sucked in her lips. 'I didn't say that.'

'So …' This was too complicated for me.

When Marysia spoke again her voice was low and serious. 'I – I'm gay,' she said. 'Toni's not. But we've been best friends for years and for a long time she was the only one who knew, so …' She shrugged. 'She's protective of me.'

'But being gay's not a big deal,' I said. 'Not these days. Being gay's cool.'

Marysia raised her eyebrows. 'Maybe in your world, Cal.' She looked at her sister and continued, in little more than a whisper. 'My family are very traditional. Very Polish. Very Catholic. And even at school – you *say* it's cool to be gay, but you've never had to deal with the bigots and the haters.' She looked down at her hands. 'It's not all rainbows and Pride,' she said. 'I'm glad to be who I am. But that doesn't mean I'm ready to shout about it just yet. Does that make sense?'

'Yeah.' More than she realised. 'So your parents don't know?'

She shook her head. 'Not yet. Only Toni – and you now, and – well, I've been seeing someone. Katie. I met her at a group I've started going to.' She blushed.

'So Toni – she's not—?'

'Definitely not.' Marysia laughed. 'I think,' she went on, 'that she sometimes wishes she was – you know, part of her's a bit annoyed with herself for being heterosexual. It's so *ordinary*. But' – she sounded serious again – 'she might not admit it, but she's been in love with you for ages. That's why she was so hurt and angry when you let us down.'

'And' – I could hardly bear to ask – 'is she still?' I looked down at the blue bedspread.

'Am I still what?' asked Toni's voice.

'Ah,' Marysia said. 'Toni! He wants to know if you're still angry with him. Or still in love with him. I'm not sure which.'

Toni, in a smart black dress I'd never seen before – she must have come straight from the airport – looked at me. 'Both,' she said.

58

'So,' Marysia said. 'We'll give you a bit of space. Come on, Kryssie.'

The curtains hadn't parted behind them before Toni's lips fluttered against mine. It was much gentler than our first kiss, and it went on for much, much longer. Even when we had to stop – because I hadn't enough breath to keep going – she didn't move away.

She sat down beside me on the bed, holding my hand, rubbing her thumb over my calloused fingertips.

'I didn't think that would ever happen again,' I said.

'I was scared it would.'

'Scared? I'm not that bad, am I?'

'I mean – I didn't want to fall for you. You were too like ...' She looked down at our hands.

'Like Anto?' I suggested.

'Maybe. I was always so scornful of my mum – falling for such a loser.'

'Hey! I'm not a loser.' I snatched my hand away.

'I'm sorry.' She reached and took it again. 'I didn't mean that. I meant, you were another—'

Musician? Free-spirited troubadour? Actually, my loser credentials were pretty strong.

'I let you down,' I said, just to get in first.

'Yes. That really hurt. It was easier just to hate you.'

'Can I tell you what actually happened?' I explained about Shania. Already she seemed like someone from another life.

'I *told* you she was trouble,' Toni said. 'Well. *In* trouble.' Then her voice softened. 'Poor kid. So you were helping her? When you said her name I – I don't know, I assumed—'

'I couldn't just abandon her. And that's how I ended up with nowhere to stay.'

'But – I'd have understood that,' Toni said. 'If you'd explained.'

'In fairness, I did try.'

We looked at each other. Someone out in the ward rang a bell for a nurse. There were tiny flecks of green in her hazel eyes. I'd never noticed before.

'In fairness,' she said at last, 'you didn't have a brilliant track record. You said *Shania* and I – I didn't really listen to the rest. Because I can't deal with being messed around. I told you about my dad – I saw what it did to my mum. All the lies. Having a whole secret life. So – no secrets?'

'No secrets.'

I was just about to kiss her again when the curtains swished open.

'Have you two been snogging the whole time?' Marysia said. 'Sorry,' she went on. 'Kryssie thinks she dropped her inhaler. She wouldn't come on her own.'

Krystyna pouted in the gap between the curtains.

'Look for it,' Marysia snapped. Krystyna sighed and looked round the chair where she'd been sitting. 'It's not there.'

'Try under the bed.'

Krystyna bent over and looked under the bed, gave an exclamation, reached under it and came up again, clutching a blue inhaler. Then she stopped. She looked closely at the bottom of the bed where my notes were. Nosy little cow.

'That's so weird,' she said, sounding more animated than I'd ever heard her. 'You've got exactly the same name as …' She frowned, and came up right up beside me, her fishy eyes round in her pale face.

'Oh. My. God,' she said. 'You *are* him, aren't you? You're RyLee? Ahhhh! Selfie!' She pulled out her phone and before anyone could stop her, had placed her face beside mine and snapped a couple of pictures.

'What the—?'

'Nobody's going to believe this!' she said, beaming all over her stupid face. 'I can't wait to share this!'

'Don't.' My voice was hoarse. 'Don't you dare.' I grabbed her phone, and then flopped against the cold pillow, suddenly exhausted.

Toni looked from me to Krystyna to Marysia. 'Can someone tell me what's going on?' she asked. 'Who the hell is RyLee?'

59

'He's nobody,' I said. 'He doesn't exist any more.'

'You just disappeared!' Krystyna said, her eyes glittering in her round face. 'Some people said you were back in rehab; some people said you were in jail; some people said you were *dead*.'

I gave a short laugh. 'That suggests at least three people were even interested, which is a definite exaggeration.'

'*I* was. I loved *PopIcon*. Have you met anybody famous? Did you really crash that car? Did you have millions of girlfriends? Do you still do drugs? Marysia says you ended up on the street? Oh my God, this is *such* a good story.'

I closed my eyes. 'Can you make her go away?' I was still clutching her phone.

'This is the most exciting thing that's ever happened to me,' Krystyna shrieked. 'Though no harm to you, but you're not that hot any more. I suppose you're too old.'

'Will someone tell me what this is about?' Toni asked. She was staring at me as if she'd never seen me before.

Krystyna started burbling about *PopIcon* and its teen winner, and how his mentor on the show had ended up marrying his mum, and people had said it was all a fix, and then the show was cancelled and RyLee had crashed and burned and been dropped by his record company before even releasing an album, and now nobody ever heard anything about him. It was a pretty accurate account. I wanted to run away, but all I could do was lie there and listen.

'Cal? I take it this is all rubbish?' Toni asked, her eyes wide.

I blinked back sudden stupid tears. She would despise me enough without me actually *acting* like someone on one of those shows. I remembered my first televised audition. 'You're only sixteen; they love it if you're vulnerable,' one of the production team advised me. 'So think about your granny dying or your dog being put down or something. Have you ever been bullied? Because that always goes down well. But don't actually sob – a few attractive tears will be perfect.' I hadn't been able to think about anything sad, and I've never been a crier. But now I couldn't stop the tears running down my face. The only good thing was I still had Krystyna's phone. I bent over it, and deleted the two pictures.

Marysia grabbed the phone. 'Don't worry,' she said grimly. 'She's not getting it back.' She put it in her bag.

A nurse appeared and stared at us. 'What's going on? You're disturbing the whole ward.'

'Nothing,' Toni said. 'Kryssie was – she's leaving now.'

'I'll have to ask you *all* to leave if you don't—'

'No!' I wiped my face, and sniffed, which probably didn't count as attractive crying. 'Not Toni and Marysia. I need – I need to talk to them.'

'Go and wait in the canteen, Kryssie. Get yourself a Coke.' Marysia handed her a pound coin.

Krystyna stomped off. The nurse looked at me. 'Fifteen minutes,' she said. 'And keep it calm. You don't want to relapse, do you?' She went out and closed the curtains for us.

'So?' Toni asked. 'Is that true?'

I nodded. 'Pretty much.'

'So you're – some kind of reality show pop star?' Her words dripped with derision and disbelief. 'You were on TV and everything? And you didn't tell us? You lied about who you were?'

'Why?' Marysia asked.

'I knew you'd despise me. *I* despised me – him. When I met you that day, we had this instant, well, connection – and it was all about the music. I'd been a so-called professional and it had *never* been about the music. I knew what you thought about things like *PopIcon*, so I – I just didn't tell you. And then – it all went too far.'

'You gave us a false name. What are we meant to call you now?' Toni demanded, her hands on her hips.

'I don't know. I don't care.'

'So is that why you let us down? Because you didn't want to be spotted?' Marysia asked scornfully. 'Was it such a comedown, playing with Polly's Tree?'

'Don't be stupid,' I said. 'It was the best thing I've ever done.'

'I'm sorry,' Toni said, 'but this is too much. I have no idea who you even *are*.'

And for the second time in two days, she turned to walk away from me. Only this time it wasn't with my blessing.

And this time, I couldn't let her go.

I reached out and grabbed her wrist. 'Toni! I ...' She was the one who could always find the words. *No secrets!* 'All those things Kryssie said – they're true. I was stupid. I was so blinded by the promise of being a star. I got lost in that. I forgot who I really was – a boy who just wanted to play his guitar.' She half-turned, so at least I could see her face. Tears sparked in her eyes too, just like the first time I saw her in the park. 'And then I met you – both of you – and you helped me get back to myself. Yes, Cal Ryan was a made-up name. But everything about him was real – *is* real.' I took my hand away from her wrist. I couldn't hold her if she didn't want to stay. 'Being with you is the realest thing I've ever felt,' I said.

She was silent for longer than I'd ever seen Toni

silent. She sniffed back the tears, and spent a long time playing with a loose thread in her smart black dress. Then she reached out one hand to Marysia, and – so slowly – the other one to me. 'I know,' she said. 'Me too.'

60

It was Saturday. Toni had gone to Dublin to see Anto – 'I suppose he's not the absolute worst,' she admitted – and Marysia was going Christmas shopping with Katie, so I didn't expect any visitors. I certainly didn't expect Queen Jane. But here she was, bringing practical unromantic gifts like toothpaste and deodorant, and a pile of my clothes, freshly washed and ironed but definitely shabby, reminding me that I was being discharged in a day or so. I imagined her clean manicured hands going through my backpack, seeing what I had, the scruffiness and poverty of it all. I kept thinking I'd plumbed the depths of mortification but it seemed that every day there was something new.

'Here's something else,' she said, handing me a plastic bag. I looked inside to find a hard-backed black notebook and a couple of pens.

'I noticed you had a notebook with your stuff,' she said. 'Don't worry – I didn't read it. But it wasn't in great shape – must have got wet. So I thought you might like this.'

'Thanks.' I flipped through the clean creamy-white pages. I couldn't imagine filling them with words. I thought about my guitar and then pushed the thought away.

Jane sat herself down on the plastic visitor's chair. 'Toni's told me all about it.'

'All about ...?'

'Everything. Well, I hope it's everything. She says you won a TV talent show, made a mess of it all, got into drugs, changed your identity and ended up on the streets.'

'Well ...' It sounded so stupid, put like that. I looked down at my hands, picked a bit of hard skin off one fingertip.

'But what about what I've left out?' Queen Jane went on. God, she was harsher than I expected.

'*Please* don't say what else there might be. I know I messed up.'

'I didn't mean that,' she said more gently. 'You've left out that you managed to live off your talent and hard work for three months. You seem to have dealt with your substance issues, even when you were homeless. You made good friends. You made a big impression on my daughter, which let me tell you isn't easy. And you helped a girl out of what sounds like a terrible situation.'

I shrugged.

'So don't be too hard on yourself.' She patted my arm.

I looked down at the bedspread through a sudden blur of tears. God, I was turning into such a wuss these days. I'd been out on the streets for *days* and I hadn't cried. I sniffed, and she handed me a tissue. She was the sort of person who always had tissues.

'I think,' she said, 'it must have been very hard, having all that money and nonsense so young. Is your mother a sensible sort of person?'

'Well – no. Not like you.' Louise was the sort of person who never had tissues, or whose tissues were all smeared with lipstick.

'And where is she now? Is she likely to be any help?'

'Spain. And no. I – I think I'm on my own.' Which was fine. I was nearly nineteen. And Louise had only done the same as me – got as far away as she could.

'And what do you want to do?'

I'd never really asked myself that. For so long, life had all been about survival, getting through the days and not letting myself think about after Backlash. And before that, it had mostly been about what Ricky wanted.

I wanted Toni. But I couldn't say that to Toni's mother.

'I think – I want to stay in Belfast. Make some kind of life.'

'In music?'

I shuddered. For some reason, the very thought of music made me feel sick. I hadn't even asked about my guitar. I knew it was smashed up and useless. You could wash clothes, but you couldn't mend a wrecked guitar. Sometimes on the edge of sleep I heard again that jangling crash when it broke my fall.

'Toni thought,' Jane suggested, 'that you should sell your story. You know – *Teen Star Reveals Homeless Hell!*'

My mouth twisted. 'Honestly – who cares? Everybody's forgotten RyLee, and I'd like to forget him too.'

'Even if it made you a few quid to get on your feet?' she said. 'I know – it does sound a bit crass. But maybe if you used it as a platform to highlight homelessness?'

I bit my lip. 'I don't think so. I mean – what do I really know about being homeless? Nobody threw me out. OK, I slept rough for a few nights. I know what it's like to be walking the streets all day, waiting for the day to end, and dreading it. I know what it's like not to know where you're going to spend the night – but I don't *know* about homelessness. Not like someone who's been dealing with it for years. Though I suppose I'll learn a bit more, when I go to this hostel.' I tried to sound casual.

'Hostel?'

'Someone came to see me today. A social worker. He's got me a place in a hostel.' It was a place for homeless men, a temporary measure until I got myself sorted out. 'It's maybe not the *best* place for you,' he had admitted. 'Most of the men there have complex mental health needs. There are places for young people which might be nicer for you, but all our services are so stretched. And you're over eighteen.' To be fair to him, he didn't say, *Get yourself back down south where you belong, instead of coming up here, clogging up our services.* And I'd looked down at the grey floor tiles and thought, *How did I get here?* Relying on strangers and services. And I'd had to say, yes, thanks, that'd be great.

But it didn't sound great.

'Well, look,' said Jane. 'To be honest, I'm not happy with Toni hanging round some homeless hostel.'

'No.' I couldn't see Toni being happy with it either. It was all very well, a few kisses and all that intense *feeling* between us – when it came down to it, I hadn't much to offer her.

'I won't be there for long,' I said. 'I'll get a job. And some qualifications. I know you don't think I'm good enough for Toni but— '

'What sort of job?'

God, this was like the third degree. I might not know what to do with my entire life, but, actually, I'd thought about where I could start. One thing about lying here for days, waiting for this infection to piss off out of my lungs, was that I'd had plenty of time for thinking.

'I'd like to do some kind of youth work.' It sounded a bit daft. I wasn't even nineteen until next month. But I thought I might be able to work with kids like Shania. Maybe even kids like RyLee.

'OK,' she said as if it wasn't the stupidest thing she'd ever heard.

'The social worker was getting me information about what courses I could do.'

'Good,' she said. 'And you can pop down to my college, get some information there. Look – I have to go now.' She gathered up her bag. 'But don't be worrying about that hostel. When you're discharged you can come and stay with us.'

'With you?' My heart leapt. I thought about that comfortable room, being able to leave things down and knowing they'd be OK, being able to stay in during the day in bad weather and, best of all, Toni being around. Even, in a funny way, Queen Jane. I made a vow right there that I'd never have to go into the hostel. I'd get myself together, find a job, get a bedsit. Having Queen Jane on my side might mean I could get a reference, save up a deposit.

'Not for ever,' she warned. 'I don't want to live with two loved-up teenagers having what my daughter calls a blast. I can't think of anything more revolting. But nor do I want Toni hanging round some hostel. You can stay – well, certainly over Christmas. Say – until the end of January? By which time I'll expect you to have found a job and somewhere to live. You're able-bodied and reasonably intelligent. And, as you've proved, fairly resourceful. If you mess up, or hurt my daughter, you can look for somewhere else, but I'll give you reasonable notice. How does that sound?'

'It sounds brilliant. Is that what's called tough love?'

She gave a dry laugh. 'I think it probably is. You might as well get used to it.'

61

It wasn't a blast, staying at Toni's. A blast was the last thing I wanted. It was quiet and predictable and safe. And warm and clean. Things I'd never take for granted again.

I hibernated, watching box sets, even reading, which I'd never bothered with much before. The weather was mostly terrible – icy rain and sleety winds, and every afternoon, long before Toni or Jane got home, I'd pull the heavy curtains closed with a shiver of relief that I was in here, and not out on the street. Toni and I were gentle with each other, not pushing anything, affectionate rather than passionate. I'd never before been with a girl I'd got to know as a friend first. She wasn't as stressed now she'd got her interview out of the way, though she wouldn't hear the result for another couple of weeks.

Jane kept asking me when I was going to go down to Dublin and pick up some stuff, and I kept saying when I felt better.

The truth was, I felt fine. Just not fine enough to face Ricky.

Toni found Shania on Facebook and sent her a message. 'Nothing heavy,' she said, when she told me about it, sitting on her bed one evening. 'Just that we hoped she was OK and to keep in touch. And I thought she might like to go to the community centre where Katie and Marysia's LGBT group is.'

'But she's not gay.'

'They have all sorts of groups, and there's one for girls that I think would be really good for her. It's all about assertiveness and stuff.'

'*You* won't go on an assertiveness course, will you?'

'Don't be daft.' Then she saw I was joking, and gave me a quick kiss on the forehead. I went to kiss her properly, but her phone pinged and she checked the message and smiled before passing it over to me.

Im ok thnx for gettin in touch yeah wd luv to meet use & my mum wd wet hrslf at the thought of me goin to yuth group but mite b better than sitin round here fightn with my big sis lol. Giv my luv 2 cal xxx

'We'll keep an eye on her,' Toni said. 'Maybe she can pal up with Kryssie.'

'Toni, you can't just organise everybody like that!'

'I'm joking!' she said. She reached out and lifted her guitar from its stand beside her desk. The honey glow of the wood, the glint of the strings, gave me such a rush of pain that I had to look away.

'Feel like a jam?' she said. 'You can use my guitar. I don't mind just singing.'

I shook my head.

'But you …' I could see her wanting to push it, and changing her mind.

I hadn't played a single note since my last day on the streets. I didn't even ask Toni what she'd done with my guitar. I didn't want to know.

'You can play my guitar anytime you want,' she said.

'OK.' But I didn't want. I felt panicky when I thought about it.

Next day, Louise Skyped: she looked thin, and her hair was blonder. She was managing a bar and singing karaoke to encourage the punters to get up and do it. Juan, her boss, said she was his little Irish linnet. She gave a glassy tinkle of laughter. 'What do you think of that?'

I didn't think anything, very much. She said I should come and visit some time, and I said, maybe, but I was pretty busy here in Belfast, and then I said I'd speak to her at Christmas, and ended the call.

I sat on my bed in the small neat guest room and took down the notebook with my song in it. It had dried out, but the pages had all melded together in a lump. I managed to pick it open and read the words, in smudged and bleeding red ink:

We said goodbye today.
I couldn't let you stay.

Because you always wanted things
Your own destructive way.

I might as well write them out again in my new notebook. I'd never finished the song. I'd thought it had been about Kelly and then I'd thought it had been about Ricky. Over the months I'd added the odd line, messed around with the melody. Now I realised it was about me. It was about letting go of RyLee. Or maybe, of accepting him.

I tried to shut you up.
But you wouldn't let me be.
Don't know what you're about
But you're still inside of me.

I wanted to sing it. Now. I looked for my guitar. Maybe it wasn't that badly damaged. At least if I knew I could face up to it, find out if it was fixable, and try to save up for it. I looked into all the rooms. It wasn't a big house and a hard guitar case isn't an easy thing to conceal, but it was nowhere. I hesitated about taking Toni's – but she had said I could, and I felt a fizz of wanting to get the song right that I hadn't felt for ages.

I sat on the sofa, rested Toni's lovely Martin on my knees, and strummed a few chords, wincing at how out of tune it was. I tuned, the mechanical task easing me into playing. It was so long since I'd played that my fingertips smarted at first, like a beginner's. It was hard to believe I'd often played all day, in all weathers. My voice was rusty and breathless, but as I sang through the new version of the song it warmed up.

The room darkened round me but I was too engrossed to get up and turn on the lights. Outside the wind flapped sheets of rain against the window, but for once I didn't leap up to shut the curtains and shut it out. I was inside and it was OK.

I played around with some minor chords, noticing as I sang that I wasn't getting out of breath.

With a click, the room lit up. I spun round. 'Toni?'

But it was Jane. She stood in the doorway, looking a bit weird. I glanced round, remembering the first time she had come home unexpectedly. But the room was pristine. A capo sat on the coffee table, and the notebook with the scribbled chords and words, but even Queen Jane couldn't mind that.

She sat on the sofa opposite me. 'Don't let me put you off,' she said. 'That's a lovely melody.'

I smiled. 'Toni's better at words.' I carried on playing but no way was I going to let Jane hear my lyrics.

'It was like old times, coming in and seeing you like that,' Jane said. 'Anto used to play his guitar all day long. Actually,' she went on, 'it drove me mad – sometimes I'd come in and he'd be playing, and Toni would be crying, and he wouldn't even have heard her. And then he'd dash off to some gig or other, leaving me with the baby.'

'Doesn't sound like you were soulmates,' I said, embarrassed.

'Oh, we *were*. That was the easy bit. It was making normal life work together that drove us apart.' She looked sad. 'You remind me of him. Anyway, do you want a cup of tea?'

'I'll make it,' I offered. 'You've been working all day.'

She laughed. 'Suddenly you don't remind me of him any more.'

I put Toni's guitar back in the case but when she picked it up later that night, sitting in her bedroom, she knew I'd been at it, because it was in tune.

'You been playing my guitar?' She was careful not to make it sound like a big deal.

'Hmm.'

'New song?'

'What makes you think that?'

'You've been humming an unfamiliar melody all evening.'

I hadn't even realised.

'Play it to me?'

'You'll hate it. You know I can't do words. Remember "Jenny"?' I was going to say it before she did.

'Ah come on, Pop Icon.'

'Don't!' I threw a cushion at her. But I didn't mind, really. She said she was going to call me it ironically until it stopped annoying me. She said I had to own it, and that it had quite a ring. Other than that she still called me Cal. What else?

I didn't play the song, but I started playing the intro to 'Secret Self', and pretty soon she joined in. We were self-conscious at first, and then we relaxed into it, my fingers finding the familiar chords, Toni's voice high and clear. After 'Plastic Girls' and 'You Think You Know Me', I set Toni's guitar back in the case. When I turned back to Toni, she kissed me, softly at first, then more urgently, pulling me down beside her. And for the first time since the kiss in the hospital, we weren't hesitant.

Later she said, 'We have a gig next week: Katie's LGBT youth group Christmas party. We were going to do it as a duo because you didn't seem to want to but ...'

'I do want to.'

'We'll get paid in cheap wine and goodwill.'

'That's OK. Only' – I was going to have to face this – 'what am I going to do for a guitar? Mine was kind of wrecked, wasn't it?'

'Pretty wrecked,' she said. She looked as if she was about to say something else, but closed her mouth.

'Could someone lend me one?'

'I can't think of anyone.'

'Do you not have an old one you learnt on?'

She shook her head. 'Gave it to a charity shop.'

'You could just sing and let me play?'

'No way! Number one, the sound's too thin with one guitar – you heard us at the Ulster Hall. And number two' – she grinned – 'well, you spent a lot of time making me a better guitar player. I'm not going to go back to just singing.'

'So what do I do?'

It was staring me in the face, of course. In my

bedroom in Dublin was my old guitar, the cheap Westfield I'd had since I was about eleven. It was pretty shit – it would be a comedown after my lovely Taylor – but it would be better than nothing.

And I couldn't put off facing that room, and Ricky, for ever.

62

For a moment, when I saw the skip halfway along the road, I panicked. Was it too late? Had Ricky chucked all my stuff out just to make a point? Then I realised that it was actually outside the house next door, and was only full of old windows.

'Take your time,' Anto said, when he'd parked his rusty Primera outside. 'I have my paper here.' He looked up at Ricky's house, the white mansion shining against the dusky sky. 'That must've cost a few quid, eh?'

I swallowed. I was going to have to walk through those wrought-iron gates, up that driveway, ring the doorbell – he knew we were coming – and face Ricky.

'Three million,' I said in a strangled kind of voice.

'Jaysus! And you sleeping in a cardboard box.'

'Dad! He wasn't—'

'It's OK,' I said. I wondered if Toni realised that

she'd got her tactlessness from Anto, as well as red hair and music.

We didn't speak on the way up the drive. I could see Toni's mouth open to comment – on the top-of-the-range Merc on the driveway, the topiary in the shape of an electric guitar – but she didn't form any words. I couldn't have replied. With every step, my stomach shrank and my heart swelled.

Ricky opened the door so quickly that I knew he'd been clocking us walking up the drive. I couldn't help looking for a scar on his forehead but it was smooth. Botox smooth.

His eyes lingered over Toni as if assessing her for one of his girl bands. She stared back boldly.

'Well, well,' he said. 'Not your usual style, Ry.'

I tightened my grip on her hand, but she didn't need me to defend her. 'Yeah, he's gone upmarket,' she said, and Ricky's eyes bulged.

We went into the pale gleaming hall. It all looked the same. I remembered standing at the door watching Kelly leave. 'I hear you've been busking,' Ricky said, 'and playing in some kind of amateur set-up ... bit of a comedown, eh? How are the mighty fallen! But then, you were never going to make it without me.'

Ryan was inside me. Ryan cringed. *You're right,* Ryan thought. *I didn't make it.* And then Cal drew himself up. He was taller than Ryan. He was actually, he realised, taller than Ricky.

'The opposite,' I said. 'Playing proper music, with proper people. Being my own person. Having freedom.'

Ricky laughed. 'I hear that went well. The freedom of the streets. The romance of the roads. I suppose you can always write a song about it. Don't think you can come crawling back to me though.'

'Come on, Toni.' I pulled her after him, up the wide shallow staircase, and into my old room. I pushed the door shut and leaned against it, breathing hard.

'I can see why you hit him,' Toni said. She went to hug me but I couldn't let her.

'Hey,' I said. 'Let's just get the stuff.'

The room had been dusted and tidied since I left, and looked clean and impersonal. But still full of *stuff*. My MacBook on the desk, the shelves of old schoolbooks and some music magazines. I opened the built-in wardrobe and stood looking at the rows of clothes. It was funny to see all this designer stuff – shirts and jumpers and a couple of neat racks of boots and shoes – I'd got so used to wearing the same few pairs of jeans, over-washed T-shirts and hoodies, and the old Converses which were so badly trashed that Jane had bought me a new pair for an early Christmas present.

'I don't *need* all this.' I imagined pulling all the clothes off the rails and having them drown me. 'My new place is tiny.'

I was moving in the new year – not to a hostel, thankfully. One of Jane's colleagues let rooms to students and his current one had just dropped out of uni so he was happy to let the room to me. I even had a job, at the community centre where Marysia's LGBT group met, teaching guitar to beginners. It was only a few hours a week, minimum wage, but it'd be a start. And it would help me with my application for a youth work course in college.

'Take your favourite stuff,' Toni suggested. 'No, actually' – she became all practical – 'take everything, and sell what you don't want. This is all top gear. No point in leaving it for *him*.'

I gave a small laugh, which broke the tension. 'Good plan.'

We busied ourselves filling bags.

My old guitar looked worse than I remembered. And it was blue. I hadn't forgotten it was blue, but it looked bluer and crapper than I remembered. The strings were corroded and when I played a chord we both winced. But it was a guitar. It didn't have a case, so I wrapped it in a coat and set it by the door with the other stuff. When I turned round Toni was unhooking the RyLee photo from the wall.

'Ugh. Don't.' I turned away.

'No. Look.'

'I don't need to look.'

'You do,' she insisted.

And she shoved it in front of me. There was the stage with the *PopIcon* logo in the background. *RyLee* was printed across the bottom in a faux-handwriting font. It wasn't my writing. RyLee, with no guitar, grinned out at the camera, his hair gelled into a shape that must have been fashionable a couple of years ago.

'Just leave it,' I said, 'or smash it.'

'No way,' Toni said.

Still holding the photo, she put her arms round my waist, resting her chin on my shoulder. 'You were quite cute,' she said, 'in a generic sort of boyish way. I mean, I wouldn't have fancied you then.'

'Thanks.'

'Whereas now' – she cupped my face in her hands – 'you're kind of gorgeous. In a grown-up kind of way. And I love you.' She kissed me. 'Take it,' she said. 'He's still part of you.'

63

'We're just going to swing by my dad's,' Toni said. 'We've loads of time before the train.'

'I don't know how you'll get all that on the train,' Anto said. 'I'd be happy to drive you to Belfast.'

'Dad, this car'll do well to get back over the Liffey, let alone up the M1,' Toni said. 'No offence,' she added quickly.

Anto's house was just round the corner from the park where Toni and I had picked each other up in September. Its greying curtains and weed-filled path made me wonder how Jane and he could possibly have lived together.

'I take it Bernie's left you again,' Toni said, when Anto opened the door onto a small hall full of speakers, leads and junk mail. 'Dad, not having a woman around isn't an acceptable excuse for living in a pigsty.'

Anto shook his head at me. 'Is she this bossy with you?' he asked.

I looked at Toni and laughed. 'Sometimes.'

He reached over and ruffled Toni's hair. 'Come on, I'll put the kettle on. I'm not totally helpless. And no, Bernie hasn't left me. She's just helping her mother out. She had an operation, women's problems. Bernie's away out to Ballymun to look after her. It was either that or have her ma here.' He shuddered. 'And if you think *Toni's* bossy ...'

He went off into the kitchen and Toni and I went into the small living room that looked smaller because of the guitars on the walls and on stands – four of them, though two didn't have strings and looked like they were being worked on. One of the ones with strings was a beautiful old Gibson that made my fingers twitch with longing. The walls were full of pictures of Anto playing with various bands. Toni talked me through them. 'That's the band he was in when he met Mum. That's the Spancil Hillbillies. No, you won't have heard of them.'

'He's been on the scene a long time, then,' I said. In some of the photos – in the nineties – he looked as young as me.

'That's the pub-covers-band scene, he means,' Toni said as Anto came in with a tray of coffee. 'Just in case you imagine he thinks you're secretly Bono or something.'

'Ah, Toni, Toni, you get more like your mother every day,' Anto said.

'Would you like to hear some of our songs?' Toni asked.

'Course I would.' Anto shook his head. 'I was never

a great one for songwriting,' he admitted. 'Every idea I had, it seemed like somebody'd already had it and said it better. D'you know what I mean?'

'Yeah,' I said.

'And sure, there's so many brilliant songs out there already.'

'Not like ours,' Toni said. She took down a battered old Yamaha from the wall. 'This'll do me,' she said. 'I wish Marysia was here.'

Anto reached for the Gibson, and I thought for a moment he was going to hand it to me, but he started tuning up as if he was going to play himself. I sighed, thinking of the old blue Westfield out in the car. 'I suppose I should go and get my guitar.' Soon, I supposed I could sell some stuff and buy a decent guitar again. But it would never be the same.

'Yeah,' Toni said. 'You should. Actually,' she said, 'I'll go and get it for you.'

I heard her go upstairs, but didn't hear the front door. Maybe she'd gone to the loo first. I picked up the Yamaha while she was away, strummed a few chords, and then started picking out a tune – just messing around, really, but Anto watched what I was doing and then joined in. The sound of the two guitars – we were both showing off a bit – filled the small room.

'Hey.' Toni stood in the doorway. 'Put that down, I'm going to need it. You'll have to make do with this.'

And then I saw that she wasn't holding a cheap blue Westfield, wrapped in a coat. She was carrying a guitar case – *my* guitar case, battered and familiar. She handed it to me.

'Is this …?'

'Open it.'

I set the case down on the floor and knelt in front of it. Something fluttered in my chest and my fingers fumbled with the catches. Toni leant over and flipped them open for me.

Inside the case lay my guitar. Not bashed. Shining, clean, with all of its strings – new strings, I realised, as soon as I ran my fingertips across them. I looked at Toni's shining eyes and couldn't say anything.

Anto broke the silence. 'First time she's asked me to do anything for her in years,' he said. 'It's not perfect,' he added, as I pulled the guitar out of its case and cradled it. 'There were a few scratches I couldn't get out – but sure, they're part of it, aren't they? Part of its story.'

I played an Em, softly, and then a G. And then a D. The guitar sounded better than ever.

'Well,' Toni said. 'Will we let Dad hear what we can do?'

'OK. But first,' I said, 'let me play you my new song.'

Acknowledgements

Music has been so important in my life that I can't quite believe I haven't written about it until now.

Thanks to everyone who has cheered *Street Song* on its way – especially my first readers, Susanne Brownlie, Lee Weatherly and Caoimhe Browne. I owe a specially big thanks to my wonderful agent, Faith O'Grady, whose wise response to an earlier draft pushed me into writing a much better book, and who has been tireless in her support. Everyone at Black & White has been wonderful to work with, with a special thanks to my editor, Megan Duff. Thanks for falling for Cal and Toni and helping me bring their story to readers.

I'm very grateful to everyone at the Belfast Welcome Organisation, especially Sandra Moore, for letting me spend a morning there and being so generous and helpful.

Writing a book can be as lonely as busking in a

deserted street in the rain, so I'm super-grateful for all my writer friends who help to make it more like a pub session in front of a roaring fire. I'm not naming names, but if you're reading this and think I might mean you, then yes, I do.

As always, thanks to my family and friends for all their support and belief in me, especially Mummy and John.

And I know this is a bit weird, because they can't read, but I'm eternally thankful for Castlewellan Forest and my guitar, both of whom are always waiting at the end of a long day's writing to help make real life beautiful.